R.W.W. Greene

THE LIGHT YEARS

ANGRY
ROBOT

ANGRY ROBOT
An imprint of Watkins Media Ltd

Unit 11, Shepperton House
89 Shepperton Road
London N1 3DF
UK

angryrobotbooks.com
twitter.com/angryrobotbooks
Let there be light…

An Angry Robot paperback original, 2020

Commissioned by Etan Ilfeld
Edited by Kwaku Osei-Afrifa and Amanda Rutter
Cover by Francesca Corsini
Set in Adobe Garamond

ISBN 978 0 85766 836 3
Ebook ISBN 978 0 85766 839 4

Printed and bound in the United Kingdom by TJ International.

9 8 7 6 5 4 3 2 1

To Emma Lazarus

ADEM

Versailles City, Oct 14, 3235

Maybe God will make it better.

The thought escaped Adem's throat in barely remembered Arabic. Years before, his grandmother had given him the words as a talisman against specters like the one he faced now. A crusted sore sealed its right eye into a squint, protein starvation bloated its belly, and its arms were thin as sticks. The little boy smiled and presented the bowl again. The blessing might have worked better in French. The Almighty always had a soft spot for Europeans and their descendants, the EuroD.

Adem reached into the belly pocket of his utilisuit and sorted through his supply of coins by touch.

"That bowl is an antique," he said. The technology used to produce them had been lost to Gaul a century before. Sealed in its bottom, an animated 3D image of a once-popular cartoon character offered a cheerful thumbs up in recognition of cereal well eaten. "You should take it to an—"

Adem finished the sentence in his head. An antiquities dealer would most likely swindle the boy, and he would come away little better off and in need of a new bowl. There wasn't much justice available to people like him. There were work programs and shelters for state-approved orphans, so the boy had to be an *illicite*: an illegal birth. His parents had abandoned him in fear of punishment or lost him to the streets when they went to prison.

Adem covered the cartoon's grinning face with triangular coins, enough for a month's worth of food. He dug into his supply of New Portuguese, a simplified language adopted by Gaul's civil service and foisted on the planet's refugee population, hoping to be better understood. "Keep it for yourself. Don't give it to any–"

The boy dashed away, the bowl tight against his narrow chest. Adem cursed. The money would likely end up in the hands of whatever kidsman gave the child his daily meal and a corner to sleep in. Adem pulled up his hood and resumed his walk.

The russet afternoon light turned the roadway's cracked pavement the color of dried blood. The area had devolved since Adem's last visit, the people becoming poorer, more desperate. Rows of refugee shanties and hovels pressed up against the elevator depot. In a taxi he could have blocked them out completely by darkening the vehicle's windows and watching a news or entertainment vid. But when he was on-planet, Adem walked where he could, curious to see what had changed. Once, his simple clothing helped him blend in with the locals but now his sturdy utilisuit made him a target.

A woman beckoned him from the next corner. She was standing in front of a crumbling building that had been a thriving noodle shop half a standard century before. She ran her hands down her short dress and raised its hem to reveal her scrawny thighs. "You look lonely, spaceman!"

"Bad luck," Adem said. "I'm getting a wife today." Talking to another child might have broken his heart, but he had thicker skin where adults were concerned.

"I'll give you my bachelor discount." She stepped closer. The smell of her sweat allied with the chemical tang of whatever drug she favored and the cheap ginja on her breath. Her tight dress was grimy, hugging bone more than curve. Her hair was dry and limp.

"Last time I was here this was a nice place," Adem said.

The woman shifted position, her malnutrition not quite eliciting the desired response. "How long ago was that?"

"Two and a half years relative. About fifty years your time."

She rubbed her lower lip with the stump of her missing left thumb. "I have a friend across the street. Maybe you'd like him better. Maybe you want both of us."

"I'm all set." Adem reached in his pocket for more coins. "Take a couple of days off. My treat. Call it a wedding present."

She limped away with the money. Rationed, it might keep her off the streets for a couple of weeks, but more likely she'd head to a tea shop and spend it on Bliss or whatever people like her were inhaling these days. If she forgot to save a few of the coins for her pimp, she might lose the other thumb.

Adem pushed his hands into his pockets. Nearly three standard centuries ago, during his first visit to Gaul, Adem had offered a woman named Tamara his virginity and four coins from his pocket. She had relieved him of both with algorithmic efficiency, and he'd been back on the street in fifteen minutes. Tamara had long been dust, but once she had been beautiful enough to attract well-heeled customers. The one-thumbed woman might be dead the next time Adem came this way, and her daughter or son, or even a grandchild, might be working the corner where the noodle shop used to be.

Four grim-faced men in cheap armor manned a checkpoint on the next block, slowing the creep into midtown. There hadn't been a checkpoint fifty years before, and the line between the central city slums – La Merde, as locals called them – and everywhere else had not been so sharply drawn. Adem brushed at the front of his utilisuit. A block prior it had made him desirable; at the border it made the authorities wonder why he was afoot.

"What's your business?" The guard was a big man, and his ceramic armor strained to cover the vulnerable parts of his body.

Adem kept his hands in sight. "I'm just down the elevator. Got an appointment with a matchmaker." He offered the address.

The guard inserted Adem's ID stick into his reader. Adem held his breath. There had been a couple of dust-ups when he was a kid. No one alive had anything to complain about, but the law could get complicated when relativity was involved.

The guard grunted and handed back the stick. "You crew?"

Adem shook his head. "Family. Part owner."

"You paying for gene work, then? Give her a big smile and no brains?" The guard's face darkened. "A nice little splice to keep you happy up there in space?"

Adem forced himself not to take a step back. "Nothing like that. Just a standard contract."

The guard sneered. "Lost my little sister that way. She married a Trader, too. Standard contract. Won't see her again until I've got gray in my hair."

"What ship?" Adem said. "Maybe I can get a message to her."

"Doesn't matter. She's gone. I tell Ma that she's got to move on with it." The guard gestured with his stun club back down the street. "Still better than that. Her contract got us out, but the shit keeps coming. Next time you're here checkpoint's liable to be a mile further up and all these pretty offices turned to squats." He spat on the sidewalk. "She's better off up there. She might as well be dead to us, and she's better off." He waved Adem on. "Go meet your wife."

Past the checkpoint, the midtown business district assembled along well-groomed streets. There was a green park to Adem's left, complete with a statue of Audric Haussman, a long dead city planner who had claimed descendance from the First Baron Architect of Paris. Adem double-timed the next two blocks with his head down, hoping to avoid anyone else who might want to flag him down for the novelty of a conversation with a spaceman. Too many times it turned hostile. No matter how far *La Merde* spread, no matter how many ad-hoc refugee settlements sprang up around the elevator, Traders like him could stay above it all. Take the ship up to 99.999 percent of light speed, and decades of standard time might erase the stain by the time it came back into port.

Adem held his ID stick up to the door scanner of a nondescript office building and walked through the airlock into the climate-controlled lobby beyond. He nodded to the robot secretary. "Adem Sadiq. I have an appointment with the matchmaker."

The repurposed robot stared blankly at him as it accessed the information. It was a bulky thing, nearly immobile behind the desk and built for construction or mining, but it seemed comfortable with its reprogramming. It gestured toward the waiting room.

Adem paced up and down the small room until the matchmaker came to fetch him.

"Monsieur Sadiq?" The small woman held out her hand as she advanced on him. Adem accepted it clumsily, unsure whether to shake it or offer it a kiss. "I am Madam Toulouse. You look younger than I expected." She spoke Trader Esperanto clearly but with a thick accent.

Adem touched his cheeks. In his rush to make the elevator he'd forgotten to shave. "We don't get a lot of solar exposure on board. Gives us baby faces."

The matchmaker smiled. "Your bride is lucky to have you." She had vetted Adem's application and verified his mother's credit, but that was as far as her knowledge of him went.

Madam Toulouse's heels clicked like a half-interested radiation detector as she led Adem into the lift and down a long hallway. "Are you nervous?" she said.

Adem stuffed his hands in his pockets. "Some."

"You'll just answer a few questions and sign some documents." She fiddled with Adem's collar. "Are these the best clothes you have? No, never mind." She studied his face. Adem half-expected her to lick her thumb to scrub at some smudge or other he had missed. "What happened to your hair?"

Adem brushed his hand across the left side of his face and head. The skin graft had taken nicely – his father did good work – but his hair hadn't grown back out all the way. "Conduit fire."

The matchmaker sighed. "You're pretty enough. She might not notice." She pointed to an alcove. "Get in there, and smile when the computer tells you. We'll get a picture for your future wife."

Adem had never found it easy to smile on command but felt he may have managed a friendly grimace by the time the computer had taken half a dozen shots. Madam Toulouse frowned at the test strip the computer printed out for her. "These will do." She propelled Adem by the arm farther down the hallway. "Let me do most of the talking. I know what your family is looking for and how much they are willing to pay."

The lighting in the interview room was warm and subdued. The chairs were well-stuffed, and the table in the middle of it all was an antique made of honey-colored fauxwood. Adem took a seat, interlacing his fingers on the tabletop. The matchmaker frowned, shaking her head an inch in either direction. Adem got the hint, slid his hands off the table, and rested them on the reinforced knees of his utilisuit.

The door swished open. A pear-shaped man in an old-style suit walked in first, trailed by Adem's future in-laws: a man and a woman in their early twenties. They walked closely together, and their clothes fit like they had been purchased for larger people. Adem experimented with a charming smile, but it felt phony. He looked at the table instead.

The matchmaker stood and discreetly touched Adem's shoulder. Adem lurched to his feet and, again not sure what to do with them, put his hands in his pockets.

Madam Toulouse smiled at the newcomers. "This is Adem Sadiq, son of Captain Maneera Sadiq. He is part-owner of the *Hajj*." She put her hand on Adem's elbow. "Adem, this is Joao and Hadiya Sasaki."

The Sasakis offered Adem a formal bow. He returned it clumsily, hands still in his pockets. The pear-shaped man ignored him completely. "I am representing the Sasaki family," he said. "They do not understand the Trader's language."

"Of course," Madam Toulouse said. "Won't you sit down?" She gestured to the chairs on the other side of the table.

The Sasakis sat close together with their attorney taking up more than half the table to their left. He tented his fingers. The cuffs of his shirt were worn. "Captain Sadiq wants the bride to study United Americas physics and engineering," he said.

Madam Toulouse looked at Adem expectantly.

"Yeah," he said. "I mean, yes. That's what we want."

"Not much use on a Trader vessel."

Adem had wondered about that, too, but his mother hadn't seen fit to enlighten him. "I'm sure we'll find a way to put her to use."

The attorney's eyes widened. "I'm sure. Are there any other skills and interests you would like her to acquire? Cooking? Materials recycling, perhaps? BDSM?"

Adem rubbed the back of his neck. "Maybe she could learn to play an instrument."

"Will children be required?"

"If it happens, it happens, but I don't want anything like that in the contract."

The representative whispered with his clients and turned back to

Adem's matchmaker. "My clients have no objection," he said. "Does the Sadiq family want naming rights? It will cost extra."

"Her parents can pick a name. That's their business."

"We want a contingency fund for genetic alteration in case the fetus does not have the math and science traits. If it is not used, it will revert back to Captain Sadiq."

"We are prepared for that," Madam Toulouse said. "There will be enough in the fund to get the work done on Versailles Station."

"Fine." The representative rolled his shoulders and adjusted the cuffs of his shirt. "Let's get down to it."

Adem tuned out. Madam Toulouse had a reputation for being fair and having a soft spot for the families of the brides she was placing. Both families were in good hands. Besides, he had a lot to think about, not least of which was turning his bachelor quarters into something a woman might like.

The matchmaker stood abruptly and offered her hand to the Sasakis' representative. "We have a deal."

Adem scrambled to his feet in time to see his future in-laws headed for the door. Hadiya Sasaki was crying. Her husband put his arms around her and pressed his mouth to her ear. She wiped her eyes on her too-long sleeves. Before Adem could say goodbye, they were gone.

"Congratulations," Madam Toulouse said. "You have a bride."

Adem looked at the door the Sasakis had gone through. "Will they be alright?"

The matchmaker's mouth twisted. "Their representative kept as much as he could for himself, but they will be far better off than they were."

"Thank you for that." Adem forced a smile. Marriage was supposed to be a happy thing, but what he felt was more akin to shame or embarrassment. "I should get back to my ship."

Madam Toulouse showed Adem where to sign his name and press his thumb. "Your mother has already transferred the funds to my account. Everything, minus our commissions, will go to your bride's rearing and education."

Preparations for departure were underway when Adem came aboard the *Hajj* and climbed to the environmental-control deck. He winked at the engineer in charge, a slim AfriD man named Sarat. "Everything all set in here?"

"We are breathing, and we have hot water to spare." Sarat turned from his workstation. "And you're married."

"Betrothed. I'll be married in a year." Adem's eagerness to see Sarat faltered. Making environmental-control his first stop had been a mistake. "Let's not talk about this now. We're about to leave orbit, and you know how my mother gets."

"Your sister can handle it."

"She's the pilot. I'm the one who makes sure the ship moves when she tells it to."

They both knew he was dodging.

"Let's have dinner tonight," Adem said. "My cabin."

Sarat nodded and turned back to his work.

Adem skimmed through the cargo manifest as he rode the lift to the command-and-control section in the bow. They'd invested heavily in food stuffs and building materials, an odd choice considering their next scheduled stop was Freedom, where entertainment and luxury items were in demand. Adem put his reader away as the lift slowed. Mother knew best. The *Hajj* hadn't ended a trip in the red since she'd taken over the bridge.

Adem took the five steps between the lift door and the entrance to the bridge and crossed to the command chair to kiss the captain on the cheek. "*Marhabaan 'ami.*"

She nodded, not taking her eyes off her display screens. "How did it go?"

"You have a daughter-in-law full of useless knowledge on the way."

"Nice family?"

"They didn't say much, and they left right after we shook on it."

"Probably afraid they'd back out." The captain rotated her chair to face the helm, where Adem's sister Lucy reclined in the piloting chair. While linked, she saw through the ship's cameras and sensors.

Lucy spoke through the bridge intercom. "Hello, little brother. How is Sarat?"

Adem refused to take the bait. "Did you get enough shopping done on the station?"

Lucy's sigh was amplified and dehumanized by the intercom's processors. "Can I ever? And it will be out of style by the time we come back."

"The time after that it will all be vintage and in high demand," Adem said. "You can sell it back at a profit."

"True. Did you buy me a new little sister?"

"A future math and science genius. Most likely spliced. Her parents are smart enough, but they don't have the genes for it. You'll have a lot to talk about when we pick her up."

Lucy had spent her teens and early twenties on Versailles Station to get the modifications necessary for piloting the *Hajj*. She'd had a wonderful time and never let anyone forget it.

"How close are we to leaving?" the captain said.

"Ten minutes, Mother, dear. Right on schedule."

Adem yawned. "I'll go back to the engineering section to keep an eye on things."

"There's a leak in the plumbing you might want to sniff out," Lucy said. "Wouldn't want our profits to go toward replacing water volume."

"I don't suppose you'd tell me where it is." Linked to the *Hajj*, Lucy could probably feel the leak.

"That wouldn't be nearly as fun as making you crawl through all the conduits," she said.

"I'm on it." Adem nodded to his mother. "Captain."

His mother waved, her eyes fixed on her readouts. There was nothing she could see that her daughter could not, but she was protective of the old ship. Her own mother had been captain before her, and her grandmother before that. She had spent years as ship's pilot before upgrades made her obsolete. Adolescent brains adapted better to the modifications.

"Say hello to Sarat for me," Lucy called after him.

Adem stopped by his quarters to leave his bag. The bottle of bourbon he'd purchased with Sarat in mind clunked against his bed as he set the bag on the floor. The continuous vibration he felt in his feet shifted in frequency as his sister moved the big ship out of orbit.

The ship's mass-grav system made a million calculations every second as it struggled to cope with the velocity changes. The vibration increased until Adem felt it in his teeth and the roots of his hair.

Adem's great-grandmother declared her family had left God behind when they fled to the stars. What God, after all, would have allowed His creation to be so utterly destroyed? Even so, the old woman would mutter to herself in Arabic at the start of every trip: "In the name of Allah, the merciful, the compassionate…" Adem heard the words in his head now, and knew that, on the bridge, his mother was hearing them, too.

Adem swayed as natural physics warred with ancient Earth science. Science won once again, and the *Hajj* slipped away from Gaul back into space.

JOAO & HADIYA

Versailles City, Fév 21, 3236

"Did we do the right thing?" Hadiya Sasaki put her hand on the small of her back and got up to pace the apartment. Her belly preceded her like a small moon.

"We've had this conversation many times," Joao said. He took his wife by the hand.

"Let's have it again."

Joao exaggerated a sigh. "If we had not made her a bride, she would have been an *illicite*. If she had been *illicite*, she would be dead, or we would be in prison. The arrangement will give her a better life."

Hadiya nodded, biting her lip at a pain deeper than the contraction that had jolted her into motion. "It's just that she is so tiny."

"She will be twenty-four when it is time to leave us. That is not so small."

"And what will she think of us?"

Joao took Hadiya's other hand. They stood together in silence for a moment.

"She will see it as it is," Joao said. "A chance to get out of the shit her parents lived in."

"Don't say that word."

"It's just a word." Joao massaged the small of her back. "Are you feeling better?"

"It's not just a word," she said. "You are not shit. Our daughter is not shit."

"It takes shit to make flowers," Joao said, "and my life is a garden full of them." He gestured around the small living room. "I couldn't have dreamed of this when I was a boy. There were seven of us in a room this size, with a bathroom shared by eight families." He helped Hadiya back to her seat.

"And all it cost us was our daughter," Hadiya said. "The Trader never smiled. Do you remember that? I can't imagine our daughter loving such a cold man."

Joao kissed Hadiya on the cheek. "Rest today. I will clean the apartment when I return from work. I want to see you perched on pillows, eating sweets, and watching vids when I get home." He smiled. "After I clean and make dinner, I'll read to her."

"I don't understand why you are so interested in reading that old poetry to her. She doesn't understand Japanese."

"I don't know much of it myself. But I want my little girl to know her heritage."

"What about her Turkish side? She's more Turk than Japanese!"

"Have you ever heard Turkish poetry?" He raised his eyebrows. "Do you really want to expose her to that?"

"I've never heard Turkish poetry, and I bet you haven't, either."

He laughed. "We'll try some on Sunday." Joao knelt and nuzzled his wife's ear. "Remember, if she were not to be a bride, then neither could you be. I had to tie you to me in some way."

She slid her hand along his cheek. "You bound me the day we met. Such a grubby little boy, full of dreams and poetry."

"Your grubby little ronin. Ready to lay down his life for love and family." He lifted the hem of her shirt and kissed her belly. "We should get her a pet."

"Only the rich have pets."

"We have riches beyond money, my empress." He bowed to her. "Besides, it will be a little pet and not until she is older. I will save up." He put on his hat. "Until I see you again, my love."

She put her fingers to her lips and blew him a kiss. "Until I see you again, grubby boy."

Joao took the stairs to save money. The ten flights down were not so bad, but coming up after a long day, he sometimes made a different choice.

Versailles City had been built in a crater, the first structures dug into the walls and rim and protected by an overhang made from ejecta. It had grown upward and inward from there, its atmosphere held in place by an artificial inversion. The original families, the rich families, still lived on the city's edge in a district they called *La Mur*. Joao waited at the shuttle stop at the end of his block and looked for familiar constellations in the early morning sky. *La Mur* and midtown had the wealth, but the view of the stars was far better from the center.

He sipped at the water in his distiller and tried not to sweat. Hadiya was sad now, but that would change when the baby was born. They would read to the little girl and teach her the family stories. In time, as all children did, she would leave. But she would leave home with the future at her feet instead of crushing her shoulders.

The ground shuttle approached, belching from its meal of waste hydrocarbons and garbage. The driver triggered the door as it pulled to a stop. "Hello, rich man," he said. "Are you ready to work with the peasants today?"

"*Jakkasu.*" Joao slapped the man on the shoulder and climbed into the passenger compartment. Compared to the other workers, he did live in luxury now, but that was only because of the money the Sadiqs provided. The Trader couldn't have his bride living in the heart of *La Merde*; what would all the other spacemen think?

The shuttle was full of bleary-eyed workers, most of them sleeping off their nightly inebriation. Some of them, from the smell, had only crawled out of the bar to meet the shuttle. Joao walked past four rows of seats before sliding in next to his friend, Davet.

Davet blinked his eyes open. "Do you have a bottle?"

Joao shook his head. "I, unlike you, my friend, have something to live for."

"Then what good are you?" Davet grunted and tried to find a more comfortable slouch in the hard plastic seats. He rarely had a good word to say, but Joao liked him anyway. Davet was an educated man; he had been a teacher in *La Mur* before he got too involved with a student and was driven away. Joao had asked him once if she had been worth it, and Davet hadn't talked to him for six days. He had not risked it again, because he loved to talk to the man about poetry and history.

Davet blew his nose on his sleeve. "What are you reading to your daughter tonight?"

"Ryuichi."

Davet nodded. "Not as much of a hack as some."

The older man looked weary. As a teacher, he had probably carried his middle-class heaviness well. Now, in exile, the skin hung in folds from his face. The other workers called him Hound Dog.

"Where did you sleep last night?" Joao said.

"Under a table. Under a bridge. It doesn't matter. No rain fell on my head."

It hadn't rained for a month, and the next scheduled shower was more than twenty days away.

"Did you eat?"

"I am not hungry."

Joao pulled his sandwich out of his pocket. "Amuse me. I made a bet with my wife that you lived only on words. If I am wrong, I sleep on the couch tonight."

Davet unwrapped the sandwich. His hands were shaking. "I can't have you living happy in such times." He chewed the sandwich with a mouthful of broken teeth. "Thank your wife for me."

Joao pulled a packet of protein shake out of another pocket. "She will be even crueler to me if you wash it down with this."

Davet finished the sandwich and sucked on the shake's built-in straw. "You may have saved my life today." He grunted. "I am not sure whether to thank or curse you."

Joao grinned. "Why should you escape when the rest of us are stuck in this misery?"

The shuttle took them through *La Merde* to the oxygen works. The works had been designed to be automated, but refugees had turned out to be cheaper and easier to replace than robots. The machines that still functioned had been pulled into service elsewhere.

The shuttle came to a stop outside the factory gates and the workers filed off, running the barcodes tattooed on their palms over the reader so the company could dock their paychecks for the daily ride. Only a few workers lived near enough to the oxygen works to walk. The din from its twenty-four hour operations kept all but the poorest and deafest from settling nearby.

A ragged man with a sign sprawled against the wall to the left of the gate. Joao squinted, his reading skills warring with the man's poor spelling. "Spare a coin for a comrade," the sign read. The man was missing both legs below the knee. Blood still blossomed among the bandages layered over the man's stumps.

Joao knew the machine that had taken the man's limbs. After all, he stood over it most of the day and lived in fear of a similar injury. He tossed a coin into the man's bowl for luck.

"Paying the reaper?" Davet said. Joao had not realized his friend had come alongside him. "He doesn't have use for such. What would he spend it on?"

"A good lunch," Joao said. "And a pet for his daughter."

Joao used his barcode to clock in and walked to his machine. He pulled two dirty wads of cloth out of his breast pocket and jammed them into his ears. It was a poor substitute for real hearing protection, but half-deaf was better than all. His eyes would have to fend for themselves until he saved up enough for goggles.

The job was mind-numbingly difficult. All day, Joao watched the conveyor belt and used a long hook to move rocks around so they would feed evenly into the machine. If too many large rocks went through at once, the crusher would jam, and he would be out of work. Rocks that were too big a mouthful for the crusher had to be pulled off and sent back up the line to be broken up. Joao had started out there, but his attention to detail won him a promotion. He'd saved his back at the expense of his ears and had enough money that he could take the lift in his building occasionally.

The men took lunch in staggered shifts, and by the time Joao's break came around, his stomach was growling. He studied the vending machines along the wall before opting for a biscuit and a cup of water, the cheapest things he could buy, and a seat near the wall. The water turned the dust in his mouth to mud, and he fought the urge to spit it out. The dense biscuit settled in his stomach like cement. Joao sipped at his water and read poetry off his cheap reader.

When his break was over, Joao returned to shift more rocks, the poetry only half-understood in his mind. Sometime later an alarm nearly caused him to drop the jagged stone he had just pulled off the belt onto his foot. The machinery around him rumbled into silence, leaving only dust and startled cries in the air.

Joao grabbed at the sleeve of a man who ran past. "What happened?"

The man pulled free and continued running. "Accident!" he said over his shoulder. "Crusher Twelve."

Joao followed the man and pushed past the rubberneckers to the machine's side. Davet had made a mistake, or maybe one of the large rocks had been too heavy for him. Either way, he had stumbled onto the belt and been pulled part-way under before the emergency stop cut in. Joao knelt next to his friend.

Davet's eyes were wide and sober as the blood rushed out of his ruined body. He smiled when he saw Joao. "You wasted your lunch."

His voice was barely more than a whisper. Joao leaned closer to grip his friend's undamaged shoulder. "Rest," he said. "We will get you to the hospital."

Davet coughed, but it might have been a laugh. Blood exploded from his mouth. When the spasm passed, he took in a ragged breath, and his eyes found Joao again. "She was worth it. I wish I could have done more for her." He coughed more blood and this time did not inhale. His body relaxed.

The supervisor stepped into the circle of workers. "Back to work." She spoke into the microphone clipped to her shoulder, and her voice echoed off the silent machines. "I need a cleanup and repair crew on Crusher Twelve." She addressed the assembled workers again. "Back to work or I'll dock your time. Come payday you'll wish you'd minded your machines."

The workers departed slowly, some of them swearing. Most were too beaten down to make a complaint. Heads slumped, they returned to their stations to wait the reactivation of the machines.

Joao stayed where he was. "I said, get back to your station," the supervisor said.

He closed Davet's eyes. "He was a bitter old man, but he was my friend."

"Be friends on your own time." She tapped her reader. "I just docked you thirty minutes. Go now, or it will be a full hour."

Joao climbed to his feet and returned to his workstation. It was just like the one that had crushed the life out of Davet and took the legs off the crying man outside. He thought of his wife waiting at home and the daughter inside her and picked up his hook; the machines started up again.

The shift-change bell rang five hours later. Aching and sore, Joao headed to the exit. The supervisor stopped him.

"They want to see you in the office," she said.

Panic cleared the fatigue from Joao's body. "I'm sorry for leaving my station. It won't happen again."

"It's not my problem." She raised her hand, cutting off further protest. "I don't know what they want, but I doubt it's to give you a medal."

Joao felt like his machine was squeezing his windpipe into a narrow straw. He was dizzy. It might take years to get a new job. If the company gave him a bad review, he might never work again.

Joao let the guard search him and vacuum his clothes at the office door. It was clean and well-lit inside, the heartbeat of the machines outside dimmed to a grumble like a stomach growling. A stern woman behind the desk frowned as he approached.

"I am Joao Sasaki. I was told to come here."

The woman peered at him through her glasses, flicking her eyes upward to summon his personnel file to the lenses. "Show me your hand and give me your registration number."

Joao went through the security routine even as his mind screamed at him to beg for mercy or club the woman to death before she could make his firing official and hand him his last chit.

The woman pointed to a cardboard box on her desk. "These are the effects of Davet Noiseux. He listed you as his sole beneficiary."

Joao blinked. Relief warred with gratitude and disbelief in his head, but he was sure his face, which felt wooden and numb, showed none of it.

"Do you have any questions?" the woman said.

He shook his head.

"His death benefit will appear in your next paycheck. You may keep the box to carry his effects in." She tapped the cardboard container with one painted fingernail. "That will be all, worker."

Joao picked up the box. He was searched again on the way out and had to jog back to the gate to catch the shuttle.

"Hey, rich man," the driver said. "You think we got all day to wait for you?"

Joao found an empty seat and opened the box. It was mostly empty. There were a handful of coins in Davet's purse, along with his ID, and a picture of a teenage girl. The girl's smile was wide and fresh, and someone had written on the back of the photo in English, a language Joao did not know.

Davet's safety glasses were folded into one corner of the box, and his earplugs, real ones, rolled around the bottom. The only other thing in the box was a hand-bound book. Joao thumbed through it, trying not to leave smudges on the pale pages. About half the book was filled with handwritten English, the other half was blank. Joao put it all in his pockets and left the empty box on the seat beside him. He leaned his head back and made himself as comfortable as he could.

"Are you going to keep that?" the man in the seat behind him said.

Joao turned his head to see the man pointing at the empty box.

"You can have it," Joao said.

The man took the box. "You were the Hound Dog's friend. Get off with me. It is only two stops after yours. We will get a drink."

"Did you know him?" Joao said.

"Not well." The man looked familiar, but, under the dust and grime, everyone who worked at the factory looked the same. "But I need a drink, and we should remember him."

"All right." Joao wasn't much of a drinker. He'd never gotten a taste for the syrupy sweet liquor sold on the streets or the grog sold in the bars where the workers went after work. The shuttle passed by his apartment building. Hadiya would be upstairs waiting to hear about his day. They went about a kilometer farther down the road and stopped in front of a dingy storefront.

"We are here," the man said. He slung his lunch satchel over his shoulder and stomped off the bus. Joao followed close, afraid of being left behind in an unfamiliar neighborhood. Even the air smelled different. Refuse perfumed with the herbs and spices of a different culture. Saffron, maybe.

"Who are you?" Joao said.

"A man who has ridden the same shuttle as you for many months." He smiled and held out his hand to shake. "Alfonse."

"Joao." His hand felt tiny in the man's massive fist.

Alfonse pointed west, away from the main road. "I live about a kilometer down there. Deep in *La Merde*."

"I lived there when we first arrived."

"And now you are rich. I have seen your home, Joao."

"It's for my daughter. She's in a contracted marriage. We couldn't afford it otherwise."

Alfonse tapped the side of his nose. "The daughter pays her way before she is even born. You are a wise man." He stopped in front of a low doorway and held the curtain aside, ushering Joao to enter in front of him.

It took a moment for Joao's eyes to adjust to the dim light inside. The bar was low, and the patrons were all sitting on floor cushions. Complicated water pipes were set up on low tables in every corner.

"Do you smoke?"

Joao pulled his eyes away from a colorful mural showing two barely clad prostitutes servicing a client on a street corner.

"A drink then." Alfonse clapped his hands. "Two whiskeys to honor our friend."

The whiskey burned all the way down Joao's throat. He had never had a drink so strong and, after the first sip found its way to his stomach, wasn't sure he wanted more.

Alfonse slapped him on the back. "Good whiskey?"

"It's fine." Joao emptied the tiny glass and put it on the bar. "I should be going. My wife will be–"

Alfonse got the bartender's attention. "Do you think so little of the old man? Is he already gone from your head?"

"Of course not, but–"

"Beer, then, to wash the whiskey down."

"Then I have to go."

"Of course," the big man said. "But eat first. They have a wonderful acarajé here. So good with chili sauce."

"I'll take some to go," Joao said. It would be a treat for Hadiya. She loved acarajé but rarely got it. With Davet's death bonus in his wallet, maybe she could eat it more often.

The bartender turned to the small grill behind the bar and began slicing onions.

Alfonse slapped Joao on the back again. "Drink up, bride father. The work day will begin all too soon."

Joao picked up the beer and sipped it carefully. It was cool where the whiskey was hot. It tasted like the citrus fruit his father had given him once. Joao took a bigger swallow of the beer and held up the glass. "To Davet!"

"To Davet," Alfonse said, holding up his own pint glass. The big man raised his voice. "We drink to Davet who died in the works today. He gave his blood so that we can breathe easier."

"To Davet," the small crowd thundered in response.

Joao looked at his beer and wondered how it had emptied so quickly. He signaled for the bartender. "Is the acarajé ready?"

The bartender shook his head.

"I'll have one more beer while I am waiting."

Joao made it home only minutes before curfew. The walk from the bar had been short on distance but long on paranoia. His imagination had made a mugger out of every shadow and put an assailant in every door he passed. His head felt thick, and he imagined that he weaved as he walked. He put his hand on the lift-call button and tried not to think about the cost.

Hadiya was still sitting in her chair, dark circles of worry on the skin beneath her eyes. "So late!"

"A friend died in the crusher today."

Hadiya's breath hissed through her teeth as she struggled to get up. "Are you alright?"

Joao knelt beside her. "I wasn't touched. Only him. I had a drink to remember him."

"And to help you forget."

"He named me as his beneficiary. His death bonus will be in my next paycheck."

"Why you?"

"I talked to him. Listened. He said once I reminded him of his son. It's not much. Two months' pay. He left me this, too." He showed her the book of poetry.

"Is this English?" she said, scanning through it. "Can you read it?"

"Not yet," he said.

ADEM

Thirty-three days out of Gaul

Sarat's eyes flashed. "We need to talk about it."

Adem rolled over. He had plenty of room. The bed was twice the size of original issue, and he figured to add on another couple of decimeters before his bride came aboard. He had read somewhere that women liked large beds. "We have."

"No. Whenever I want to, you come at me with a bottle of that rotgut you distill down in the engine room. End of conversation."

"There's not much to say." Adem covered his eyes with the crook of his elbow. "When she comes aboard this has to stop. Maybe it should stop earlier."

It had started this time in the engine room. Near the end of the shift, Sarat had accidentally-on-purpose squirted Adem with coolant, forcing him to make a run for the safety shower. Sarat had followed to make sure every trace of the chemical had been cleaned off Adem's skin. Now it was morning or as close to morning as it could get on a cargo ship travelling at the speed of light, or c as Einstein liked to call it.

"What if I don't want it to stop?" Sarat played with the hair on Adem's chest.

"It's going to be hard to keep it going by yourself."

"You don't even want to get married."

"My family wants me to." Adem shifted position to face Sarat. "I never made you any promises. We agreed we'd keep this informal."

"If you're so married, why are you here?" Sarat slipped his hand under the sheet. "Wonder how your bride would feel about that."

"She's…" Adem squinted at the view screen on the far wall and did some mental math. "She's about two years old right now. She probably wouldn't feel much one way or another."

Sarat traced Adem's thigh with his fingernails. "She doesn't even know you. Marry me instead. I'll study up. I can be part of the family."

"United Americas physics isn't something you can learn from the nearsmart."

"Your toddler can marry someone else then. Your sister likes women."

"She likes men more. And she doesn't want to get married, either." Adem lifted his hand to the side of Sarat's face, cupping his cheek. "It's just not how it's done, *amante*. You know that. Marriages like these are meant to bring something to the family that it doesn't have. We need this girl."

Sarat's fingers clenched. "I have other talents."

Adem hissed between his teeth. "You have plenty of talent." He lifted Sarat's hand from his groin. "And, maybe, if my wife doesn't mind, we can do this again someday. It's not personal."

"You say that like you believe it." Sarat left the bed. "I'm going to take a shower. You want to join me?"

"You go ahead. I want to check my to-do list before I put foot to floor."

"Suit yourself." Sarat went into Adem's small bathroom.

Adem stared at the bathroom door. He hadn't expected Sarat to put up such a fight. Their relationship had been uncomplicated. It made the nights less lonely, the black space between ports pass by more quickly. Adem hadn't noticed that Sarat had developed real feelings and wanted them reciprocated.

Adem slid out of bed and into a clean utilisuit. He snagged his boots and tool belt and left the room quietly. If he grabbed breakfast before Sarat made it out the door, they might not see each other for the rest of the day.

He thumbed through his to-do list as he walked. There was nothing pressing, just the usual, endless requests for maintenance that showed up after every night shift. He'd have a busy day, but there was nothing on the list vital to the ship's operation. The engines and the complicated systems that controlled gravity and dealt with the acceleration of a ship chasing photons were working perfectly. If not, they would be dead before an alarm could sound.

Adem ducked into an unassigned crew suite to shower and shave. His hair had finally evened out, and he had a good face – or so he had been told. He'd never had a hard time getting attention. His bride might take some comfort from that when her parents showed her his picture and told her she'd be leaving home for a life in space.

Third shift was just sitting down to dinner when he made it to the cafeteria. Odessa Romanov, a tattooed computer tech, invited him to join her at an empty table, but he shook his head and pointed at his reader. Lots to do and little time. Adem stuck a packet of protein shake and a meal bar into a pocket. His reader buzzed angrily, and he keyed in a response without looking at Sarat's message: *sorry. busy day. worklist is never ending. see you later.*

The message might cool him down but probably not. Sarat's temper was quick to flare then settled at a steady burn for what could be weeks.

The third shift bridge crew had reported a bad smell in their bathroom. Adem scanned his list in the hope of finding something more important to do and thus leave the bathroom to second shift.

There was nothing obvious, and the bathroom request had been signed by his mother. Bad smell it would be.

He headed to the spine that connected the ship's bow to its stern. The *Hajj* wore its cargo like a girdle, hundreds of pods bound around the ship's slender middle. The lift ran through the spine's center. During the ride to the command section, Adem successfully avoided thinking about Sarat by moving the search for Lucy's plumbing leak higher up his to-do list. If he could dedicate a couple of hours, he might actually find it. At the least, he could spend a good chunk of the day in the ship's crawlspaces where Sarat and anyone else would have a hard time finding him. There was a harmonica in his tool belt, and suddenly he wanted nothing more than to hole up in some forgotten corner of the ship and practice his riffs.

The lighting in the lift flashed to red, and a klaxon began hooting for attention. Adem fumbled his reader out of his pocket, absurdly grateful that something more important than the bridge toilets had come up. He pushed the feeling away. The last thing his mother needed was an unprofitable trip. They couldn't afford a delay or an emergency dock. A message floated on the reader's screen: *Pirates. Closing fast.*

Adem reversed the lift without stopping it. He'd pay for the action later in worn parts and hard work, but if it got him to his combat station five minutes earlier it might be worth it. The lift jarred to a stop, and Adem tumbled out. He tapped the comm unit clipped to his collar. "I'm in engineering. What's happening?"

"Hold that thought," the captain, his mother, said. "We're altering course. Lucy says they're going to miss us by a mile."

Lucy might mean a literal mile – the Earth measurement – or she might be feeling metaphorical again. Changing course quickly at near light speed was impossible. To fly the *Hajj* between the worlds, Lucy aimed where the nearsmart said something was going to be by the time the ship got there and accelerated. A course change could fuck up a whole host of things. Adem could get back to Gaul years late to find he was betrothed to an eighty year-old, and a contract was a contract.

Adem twinned the bridge's primary view screen to the monitors at his station. From that perspective, bright dots amid the field of gravity wells, the ships looked to be right on top of each other. "Keep me posted," he said.

The bridge didn't answer.

"Hello?"

The crew of the *Hajj* still practised for such things occasionally, but there hadn't been a real pirate attack since before Adem had been born. To hear his grandmother's stories, though, the trade routes had been snake-pits in the early days. Routes and departure times had been closely guarded secrets, but bribes could sometimes shake them loose. Pirates, running small, stripped-down ships, would race to intercept Trader vessels or leave before they did and decelerate to head them off.

He turned the comm unit on his collar off and on. "Engineering to bridge."

They'd miss by a mile, Lucy had said. Adem reached under his console to make sure the gun was still there. The low-speed rounds were safe for the hull but would make a mess of any flesh they hit. Fifteen rounds in the clip. Adem had plenty of practice with the thing but had never fired at a real person. He wiped sweat off his forehead.

The siren shut off abruptly, and the alert light stopped flashing. Adem waited for the all-clear announcement.

He tapped his comm. "Mom?"

If the pirates had gotten in at the front of the ship, they could have taken out the bridge crew and shut the alarm down. One armor-piercing round in the right spot, and pressure loss might open the bridge like a tin can.

Not even the nearsmart was answering. Adem pulled an emergency pressure-suit out of a locker, making sure to strap the gun on over the suit this time, and climbed back to the spine. The lift slowed into its place behind the bridge, and he exited cautiously. The lights were on in the outer hallway, but that was no guarantee the bridge would be the same. He drew his weapon and steeled himself for the sight of his family, most likely dead, strapped into their stations surrounded by a squad of well-armed pirates.

The bridge door hissed open, and Adem walked into light and warmth and air.

"What the hell are you doing in a pressure suit?" the captain said.

"I tried to call but—"

"The comm system is down. That's something you can fix before you start in with the bathroom."

"What happened to the pirates?"

The bridge speakers flattened any emotion out of Lucy's response. "They missed us by a mile and blew up. Engine overload, probably. They're all over the place."

HISAKO

Age three

Joao patted the arm of the overstuffed chair. "Come here, little muffin."

Hisako giggled. "Not a muffin. 'Sako."

"You look like a muffin to me." He held his arms out to the little girl. "Come here and let me eat you!"

Hisako pretended to be scared then ran across the room into Joao's arms. He swept her off the floor and buried his face in her stomach, making growling sounds. Hisako giggled and kicked to keep from being devoured.

"Riling her up like that is not going to help," Hadiya said.

"I know." Joao bent to his daughter's stomach and growled again. "But she is so delicious!"

"I hope you remember the taste when you fall asleep under the crusher tomorrow." Hadiya dried her hands on her pants. "Let me take her. I'll put her to bed."

"No!" Hisako said. "Read first! Read first!"

Joao spread his hands in mock surrender. "You heard her." He shifted his daughter to her favorite reading position, legs extended along his, her tiny back propped against his chest. Her feet did not yet reach to his knees. When they did, Joao feared, she would be far less interested in reading time. "I am helpless against her will."

Hadiya shook her head. "You spoil her."

"That will be true until her reach exceeds my grasp. For now, though…" Joao reached into a pocket on the side of the chair and pulled out a hand-bound book. "We read." He flipped open the book at random and read aloud in English.

I have dreams.
Wishes that I chant with every candle I blow out.
I want to fly free.
I want to be unchained. I want to let go. Let loose!
They pull the feathers from my wings.
One by one like snow.
Pluck, snip, cut, go my vehicles of swift escape.
I fall from the sun.
The beautiful sky I would fly through,
Crashing down like glass.

"What does that even mean?" Hadiya said. "You read to her from that old book every night, and I don't think you understand half of what you say."

"It's poetry," Joao said. "You aren't meant to understand all of it at once. Last time I read it, I thought it was sad. This time it seems full of hope." He jogged his knees up and down to make Hisako giggle. "Did you like it, muffin?"

She fidgeted. "Want a story!"

"That was a story! It's about a bird who wanted to be free."

"Real story." Hisako leaned over the arm of the chair and pulled Joao's reader from the charging pocket. "Fish-Peri!"

Joao complied and read Hisako the story of a magic fish who, caught by a lowly fisherman, revealed herself to be a woman so beautiful that even the sultan wanted to marry her. Hisako drew the time out with questions, but, finally, Joao put the reader back in the chair pocket.

"It's bedtime for muffins and magic fish." Joao lowered Hisako to the floor and stood to stretch. The chair had been the winnings of a Sunday spent cleaning out the flat of a dead woman in midtown. Her son, a supervisor at the oxygen works, had offered money for the work, but Joao negotiated for the chair and carried it home on his back. It was worn but easily the most comfortable thing in the apartment.

Hadiya came back in from the kitchen and took her daughter's hand. "Let's go to bed, *yavru*."

Hisako rubbed her eyes with her fists and followed her mother into the bedroom. Joao sat back in the chair and opened the hand-bound book again. He had enough English now to read the message on the back of the girl's photo: "Thank you for all you have done for me. I will never forget you." It was signed "Eleta."

"And what exactly did you do for her, Davet?" It was not the first time Joao had asked the question, and, like all the other times, it went unanswered. He tucked the photo back into the book and put it away in the chair pocket.

Hadiya came out of Hisako's bedroom. "She's asking about a pet again."

"Two more years. We decided."

"Just a small one, though. Nothing expensive. Maybe a rock crab or a dome slug."

Joao made a face. "She can't cuddle a rock crab."

"A slug wouldn't survive the experience. What's your point? The important thing is, she'll have a pet. It will teach her responsibility."

"We'll see."

"Did you want to read some more or watch a vid? I think we have some points left."

"Both. But I have to meet Alfonse tonight."

"It's late."

"Just a drink. I'll be home before you turn out the lights."

Hadiya narrowed her eyes. "You've said that before, and I've finished the night alone in the dark. What do you talk about with Alfonse and his friends?"

"They are my friends, too." Joao pulled his jacket off a wall hook. "We talk about politics. Things we would change if we had the power." He grinned. "We talk about our wives and how beautiful they are."

"You spend too much time with Alfonse. I don't trust him."

Joao kissed her on the cheek. "You don't know him."

"Change that." She put her hands on her hips. "Bring them here."

"You have a good job." Joao shrugged into the jacket and grabbed his makeshift club from behind the door. "If the EuroD knew you had been talking to Alfonse—"

"If it's a bad idea for me, how is it good for you?"

Hadiya's voice was growing louder, and Joao put a finger to his lips. "I crush rocks all day. You work for the Transit. No one cares what I do or whom I associate with. You? They would care." He turned to go. "I'll be home soon."

The door closed on her protests. Joao took the stairs two at a time and looked up and down the sidewalk before leaving the doorway of his apartment building. The neighborhood was safe enough in the daytime, but predators came out at night. He pulled the hood of his jacket up and got a better grip on his club.

The path to Alfonse's tavern was familiar to him now, and he wasted little time in getting there. The energy inside was tense in spite of the boisterous warmth of Alfonse's greeting. Joao had a heavy arm around his shoulders and a beer in his hand before his eyes could adjust to the light. "My friend," Alfonse said. "I am so glad you could come. Let me introduce you to someone."

Alfonse guided Joao to the back of the bar where a small group of men was waiting. At the group's center was a thin man with tired eyes. His skin was gray and unhealthy-looking.

"Joao, this is Teodoro, newly arrived from Imbeleko. He's not much to look at now, but he tells me he is directly descended from the Aztec warriors. He was on one of the last ships to leave Earth and has traveled far to be with us tonight."

Teodoro was sweating heavily. Joao had to resist wiping his fingers on his shirt after they shook hands. "Are you unwell?"

Teodoro pushed his limp hair off his forehead. "My wife–"

Alfonse put his hand on the gray man's back. "Fresh from the freezer. It takes a while to relearn how to regulate body heat." He pulled Teodoro close to him as if to share his warmth. "This meeting is for him. He is doing a job for us later tonight."

"What's the job?" Joao said.

Alphonse tapped the side of his nose. "The less you know the better, my friend." He winked at Teodoro. "Our friend here lives in a fine apartment. His wife works for the EuroD."

The man's face darkened.

"For the Transit," Joao said quickly. "She works on the schedules part time. Decides when and where the shuttles stop. Nothing more."

"Joao's daughter is promised to a Trader. It's sad. Our best and brightest go–" Alfonse snapped his thick fingers. "Like that."

Alfonse tucked Joao under his free arm and herded the two men to the bar. "Let's celebrate." He signaled the bartender. "Three whiskeys."

He released the men and picked up his glass. "To Teodoro." He held the glass high and raised his voice. "To Teodoro and to better days."

The apartment was dark by the time Joao stumbled home. He slid open the door to Hisako's room and studied her under the glow of her night light. She was perfect. Every part of her a miracle and a masterpiece. The best thing he had ever been part of.

"You can't save her." Hadiya stood in the doorway, her arms folded. She looked more weary than angry.

"I don't—"

"No matter what you and your little group of revolutionaries do, nothing will change. Babies will be made in *La Merde*. Your daughter will be sold to a Trader."

"We didn't sell her!" Hisako gasped in her sleep. Joao held his breath. The little girl was a beast when she was wakened unexpectedly. He dropped his voice to a whisper. "We gave her a chance."

"Be content with that." She uncrossed her arms and held up the reader she was holding. "Tell me you weren't part of this."

"I don't understand."

"A refugee just down from orbit. He ran to the gates of *La Mur* and blew himself up with a homemade bomb. The gates were barely scratched. Did you know about it? Was it Alfonse?"

"We were just at a party."

"The report said the refugee was crazy. His wife and child died in the freeze, and his brain was damaged."

"What was his name?" Joao rubbed his fingers on his shirtfront.

"It didn't say." Hadiya's arms fell to her sides. "I have to go into work. Everyone in Transit does. It's a state of emergency."

Joao was silent.

"Make sure she gets off to school. I'll be home when I can." Hadiya moved to leave the room. "You love her too much."

"She's my daughter!"

When she turned back to face him, there were tears in her eyes. "As soon as she was born, I knew she wasn't ours. She'll leave us. There's nothing we can do."

ADEM

Two months out of Gaul

Adem rested his chin in his hand and watched the show. Uncle
Rakin was in rare form.

"Imbeleko?" Rakin sputtered. "Why would we go there? They
don't have any money!"

"We were forced to make a course change out of harm's way." The
captain projected calm from her side of the conference table. "It put
us off the line for an efficient run to Freedom."

"The pirates? You're continuing with that nonsense?" Rakin
stabbed his finger at his sister. "There haven't been any pirates
since–"

"Since you stopped funding them, Uncle?" Lucy said. "Apparently
they found someone else to help them to their deaths."

Rakin's florid face flushed redder, and he put both hands on the
conference table as if his next action would be vaulting across it to
strangle his niece.

Adem forced himself not to overreact. Rakin's rage was partly a
fiction, probably. It was hard to be sure where the former racketeer
was concerned. In the past, Adem's uncle had worked with pirates
in exchange for a cut of whatever they brought back, and there was
a price on his head.

The captain cracked her gavel. "Enough! We keep personal

issues away from this table." She narrowed her eyes at her older brother. "The maneuver was necessary, Rakin. Imbeleko was the best option."

"Convenient that the comms failed and the sensor data on your pirates disappeared." Rakin's face twisted like he had eaten something sour. "I am part owner of this vessel, Maneera. I expect to be told about anything that might affect our bottom line."

The disgust and petulance were real. Rakin had left the *Hajj* after his mother declared his younger sister would be the better captain, and it remained a sore point.

"You are being told," the captain said. "I would have called an emergency meeting if I'd thought it would affect profits."

"Not all business goes through you, Maneera," Rakin said.

"By charter, I sign off on everything we haul. Is there something you want to tell me?"

Rakin leaned back in his chair. "There's nothing in the charter against selling a few personal items."

"So, I'm to assume that last-minute cargo pod that came up from Gaul is full of your personal items?" She turned to look at Lucy. "That pod wasn't on the manifest, correct? But someone made it a priority haul."

"We had to leave a freezer of cattle in orbit in order to pick it up."

"Looks like you cost us some money, brother." The captain considered Rakin. "I didn't know you liked Gaul's cuisine and crafts so much. Maybe I should take a look and see what's so wonderful."

Rakin pointed a stubby finger at his sister. "Stay out of that pod. It's private property."

"Lucy, make sure to bill your uncle for hauling his private property." The captain smiled. "It's only fair."

Rakin's financial troubles were an open secret at the table. He'd sold his stake in the ship when he left but came back on board in some desperation the last time they'd stopped at Nov Tero. His sister had made him buy his way back on, to the tune of three full shares.

The *Hajj* was a family business, but it was also a co-op. Ownership, a total of one hundred shares, was divided among the people around the table. The captain owned twenty-five percent of the *Hajj*, and her husband Dooley had worked his two-share marriage gift into an eleven percent stake. Lucy and Adem each held five shares. The remaining fifty-one shares were owned by the crew and a handful of investors.

"We'll load up with refugees at Imbeleko," the captain said. "The government will pay, and, provided Freedom will accept them, we can offload them there. Easy money."

"I'm sure we can all sleep better knowing we're providing refugee services." Rakin didn't share his sister's soft spot for refugees. He would vote in favor of leaving them in orbit around Freedom whether they were welcome or not. He'd done it before. "We're not going to stay solvent playing taxi. However," he stroked his chin, "I do have some contacts on Imbeleko who can put us in a position to make some real money."

"Is this one of your slaver pals, Uncle?" Lucy said. "Can he get us a good deal on genengineered women and children for the sex trade?"

"They're not children," Rakin snapped. "They're just small. We'd make three times what we would running refugees and raw materials back and forth."

"You're a sick bastard." Lucy colored.

"Another outburst like that, Lucy, and I will fine you," the captain said.

Kalinda Maynard, representing the investors' interests, cleared her throat. "I'd like to entertain Rakin's idea."

"Is that a second?" the captain said.

Kalinda inclined her head.

"We'll put it to a vote, then. Know, though, that should Rakin's plan be approved, I will be asking for a buyout today. The *Hajj* has never been a slaver, and she won't be with me as captain." She pushed a button to open the voting. "We have a motion to authorize Rakin to make us a deal to haul slaves."

"Slave is an ugly word," Rakin said.

"It's an ugly business." She folded her arms. "Ayes will be in support of Rakin's plan, nays against it. Cast your votes."

The ship's nearsmart made the tally: Twenty-two shares for Rakin's plan, seventy-eight against.

"Closer than I'd like," the captain said. "But your plan has been shut down."

Rakin smothered a yawn. "A few more lean trips and you might hear a different song playing. This ship can't run on principles."

"Any other business?" the captain said.

The crew's representative raised her hand. "We have a buyout request from Sarat Fawaz in engineering. He's from Duniya but says he's happy getting off anywhere."

"Did he say why?"

"Says he wants to try something new. He owns a quarter share and the value is up by thirteen percent."

"Let's buy him out at that rate and advertise for a new hand planetside." The captain leaned back.

"I second it," Dooley said.

"Any discussion?" The captain looked right at Adem, maybe daring him to say something. "All in favor?"

The motion passed. The captain looked around the table, taking in supporters and opponents alike. "Meeting adjourned."

Adem went back to his suite to get a guitar and his recording gear and carried them to the corridor where the spine of the ship widened to the hips of the engineering section. The space had excellent acoustics.

Adem set up his gear. He had been practicing an ancient blues tune about a train, a type of Earth vessel that carried cargo and people from place to place. The song's narrator was asking the train to take him from the world he knew to somewhere better. Adem recorded the song once, then a second time with different intonation. He listened to the playback. His voice was still better than his playing, but he thought he'd captured the right feeling.

He added his intro and outro to the first recording and ordered the *Hajj*'s nearsmart to broadcast it. The recording would travel for years or decades before finding a receiver, but for anyone tuned in, the Earth song would live again. Adem had been making such recordings for years. Learning the songs and then letting them go.

He checked the tuning on his guitar and tried a song called "Rocket Man" that he'd found the last time he'd had access to the Freedom worldnet. It didn't fit his voice as well. He dropped it an octave and tried again.

"You're getting better, little brother," Lucy said. She emerged from the doorway she'd been listening from. "Remember when you first started playing? It was horrible." She slid down the wall to sit next to Adem on the floor.

Adem flicked the top E string with his thumbnail. "Never stopped you from hanging around and listening."

"What were my options?" she said. "There's nothing else on this ship worth doing for a kid. I used to listen to you just to pass the time."

"Bullshit," Adem said. "You followed me around everywhere. You couldn't get enough."

Lucy used to have long black hair that flowed like a comet tail as she dashed around the ship after him. She had come back from

Gaul twelve years older while only eight months had passed for her brother.

"I listen to all the recordings you make," she said. "The ones I can find."

"I think I started making them with you in mind, but I never knew you heard them."

Adem played the first verse of a song Lucy had enjoyed as a kid. She'd made up stories about what she thought "crawdads" were. "Do you ever wish you hadn't come back aboard?"

"I had a boyfriend who said he'd pay Mom back if I stayed." She held her hands out for the guitar.

"Why didn't you?"

"I didn't love him, and it was too conservative planetside." She played the ghost of a G chord. "Maybe it's better now. But I didn't want to live through all the years I knew it would take to get there." She tried a C chord and winced at the sour sound that resulted. "So, I'm finally getting the little sister I always wanted."

Adem laughed. "You hated being younger than me. I think that's half the reason you wanted to be a pilot. You were sick of seeing me do everything first."

She grinned. "Maybe. When you started sniffing around Teresa, and Dooley said I was too young to have a girlfriend…"

"You were ten."

"Still wasn't fair."

"I think you've done all right. You might even have made up for lost time."

"You don't know the half of it. I could tell you stories that would straighten your hair."

He took the guitar back from her. "Shouldn't you be on duty?"

"I told Mom I was going to grab a nap." She hugged her knees to her chest. "She's worried about you."

"Can't have all that money she's spending on my wife go to waste."

"That's part of it. But she cares about you, too. This is marriage. It's supposed to make you happy." She listened to Adem noodle for a couple of minutes. "Do you love Sarat?"

Adem strummed a few more bars of the song, an Earth tune called "Heartbreak Hotel." "I care enough that it hurts me to see him in pain."

"That's just guilt."

"I was always honest with him."

"But you kept sleeping with him. If it had been just a week or two, then you moved on to the next pretty face..." She laughed. "But you're not like that. My brother: the romantic."

"I just don't like spending all that time getting to know someone new. It's exhausting."

"You don't have to know them all that well to have sex with them."

"I do."

"That's why you're doing this marriage thing, and I'm not." She stretched out her legs again. "You'll never leave this ship. You like being sad too much. You're like a message in a bottle just floating around out here." She pushed herself to her feet. "I'm going to get my nap."

"Were there really pirates?"

"No. Mother just wanted a course change."

"Why?"

"She'll tell us when she's ready."

HISAKO

Age six

I was already awake when Mom came into my room. "Get up, sleepy princess," she said.

I kicked my legs to make the covers jump. The lump of scales and bristles on my feet didn't move. "I'm a hostage!"

Mom covered her hand with her mouth and pretended to look surprised. "Oh, my!" she said. "How are you going to get to school if you can't get up?"

"I don't know!" I kicked my legs a little harder. Nibble raised his head and blinked at me. I lifted both my legs at the same time, raising him like a box on a fork truck. "I'm stuck!"

"Maybe I can help." Mom gathered the sandcat in her arms and held him against her chest. He whistled happily. "Can you move now?"

I lifted my legs straight up, kicking my covers off and making the cuffs of my pajama bottoms slide up my legs. "I'm free!"

Mom smiled. "Do you need anything else?"

"A kiss." I flung my arms out toward her. Mom laughed and leaned in to kiss me. I wrapped my arms around her neck and squeezed until Nibble squawked in the space between our bodies.

"Be careful. You don't want to make him shed his tail again." Mom rubbed Nibble's cheek against mine. He was scratchy like a toothbrush, not soft like the cats the rich girls talked about.

I giggled and pulled away. Sandcat hair can be poisonous, but Nibble's fur had been treated to make him safe. I could pet him, but Mom said I shouldn't do that to any old sandcat I see.

Mom put Nibble back on the bed. "We need to get you ready for school, little mouse."

"Can I bring Nibble?"

"You cannot." Mom put a clean uniform on my bed and got my brush from the top of the bureau. "Put that on, and I will brush your hair."

I made faces in the mirror while Mom yanked the brush through my hair. Mom's hair was long, too, but not as long as mine.

She laughed at my expressions. "Be glad it isn't curly. This would be a lot more painful."

"Will my hair get curly?"

"That's up to you." She looked at my reflection over the top of my head. "My hair is not, and your dad's hair is not. What would your science teacher say about that?"

"It's not in my genes."

"Is curly hair dominant or recessive?" Her reflection looked sad.

"I don't want to talk about science now. Is it my birthday yet?"

"You know your birthday isn't until next month."

"And I'll be seven."

"How many days until your birthday?"

I did the math in my head. "Thirty-three."

"How many hours?"

Gaul turned around in space every twenty-two and a half hours. "Seven hundred and forty-two point five."

"Good girl." She put the brush back on the bureau and kissed me on the head. "Say goodbye to Nibble, and we'll get you some breakfast."

Mom made pancakes and reminded me to eat them all up. There were kids in the central city who didn't get a good breakfast every day, and I needed to honor them by eating well. My parents lived there before I was born, and that's how they knew that.

We took the lift up to the rich floors and walked down the tunnel to the bus dock. "What will you do today?" I said.

"What I do every day." Mom leaned against the wall. "I'll work until it's time to come home. Your dad will be here in time to walk you inside."

"I could walk myself. All the other kids do."

"I happen to know that all the other kids do not," Mom said. "And it makes your daddy happy to walk with you and see you when you come home. Doesn't that make you happy?" She put her hand on the back of my head and stroked my hair.

Seeing him there made me happy but sometimes it made me feel bad. Sometimes the boys on the bus teased me about him. They said his clothes made him look like someone from *La Merde*. "What's *La Merde*, Mom?"

Her hand stopped moving on my head. "That's not a nice word. Where did you hear it?"

Her voice made me scared and excited at the same time. She was upset because I knew something I shouldn't. It was a secret word. I drew a circle on the window with my finger. "From a boy on the bus."

"Don't talk to that boy again, okay? And don't use that word."

"But what does it mean?"

"It's a mean way to talk about the people in the central city."

"The poor kids?"

"Yes. And we don't say bad things about people just because they don't have a lot of money, right?"

The door to the outside hissed open, and the bus snuggled into the hole. I let go of Mom's hand as soon as the inner door opened.

"Have a good day," she called after me.

The inside of the bus was as colorful as a magic carpet and soft as a cloud. It rocked a little as it wiggled free of the dock and floated up and away from my building.

I walked to the back to find my friend, Anki, so I could sit next to her. She was near a window, playing a game on her backpack. My backpack was only good for holding things, so I pulled out my reader. "Can I play, too?"

She shook her head. "It's a new game. I just got it."

Anki always had new things. Her backpack was new. Her game was new. She almost always had new clothes. She had the best toys, too.

The reader in my hand looked ugly and worn. I'd had it since kindergarten, and it still had stickers on it from back then. I put it away and slid closer to Anki. "What kind of game is it?"

She scooted closer to the window. "I'm playing with Greta."

Greta was a girl in my class. She didn't like to play with me and had never wanted to play with Anki, either.

"Let me see." I tried to see the screen on Anki's backpack, but she pulled it away. "I just want to look at it."

"You can't," she said. "It's mine."

"I just want to see."

Anki pushed me. It wasn't a hard push, but it hurt my heart. She turned her back on me and sang too quietly for the other kids to hear, "Baby, baby, little *La Merde* baby. See the baby cry."

I pulled her hair.

She screamed! The tangle field came on, pinning us to our seats. It made the light all weird and felt like tickles on my skin. I couldn't turn my head, but I could hear Anki's game beeping and her angry sobs. The other kids on the bus were whispering and giggling about us. The tangle field had been used on other kids, usually boys, but no one had ever used it on me. I was one of the good kids!

The tangle field held us in place after the other kids got off the bus. I could wiggle a little but not enough for me to scratch the itch on my cheek from where Mom had rubbed Nibble.

"Turn them loose," a deep voice said over the bus intercom.

The light went back to normal, and I could move.

Anki swung around and glared at me. "You got me in trouble."

I bit my lip.

The bus driver shooed us off the bus and into the school dock.

"What happened?" the owner of the deep voice said. It was Mr Brahl, the school principal. I had seen him at assembly but never up close. He had a thick mustache that looked like it would tickle his nose. "Did Anki slap you?"

I scratched my cheek. It felt hot and bumpy. "My sandcat–"

"She pulled my hair and tried to take my backpack!" Anki said.

"I did not!" She was such a liar! "I just wanted to see it."

"Why did you pull Anki's hair?" Mr Brahl's mustache made his frown look even angrier.

I didn't know what to say. It seemed silly now. Why had I gotten so mad? All she'd done was sing a song.

"I can watch the surveillance recording if you make me," Mr Brahl said. "Why did you pull her hair?"

I started crying. "I want my Mom." Adults were usually nicer to crying kids, but it didn't work on Mr Brahl.

"We're going to be calling your mother, no doubt about that," he said. "But I want to know why you thought it was okay to pull Anki's hair."

Mom had pulled my hair just that morning, while combing it, but she didn't mean to. Then she stroked it until–

"She called me a *La Merde* baby, and she sang a song about it."

Mr Brahl looked at Anki for the first time. "Did you do that, Anki? Did you call her that and make up a song about it?"

Anki turned red and nodded. Her chin quivered, and I knew she was about to try the crying thing. I could have told her it wouldn't work.

"I can't hear your head move, Anki," Mr Brahl said. "Did you call her a name?"

"I did." Her face scrunched up, and she started crying for real. That was better. She deserved it. If she had only let me play her dumb game, none of this would have happened.

Mr Brahl patted her shoulder. "Thank you for being truthful, Anki. You shouldn't have done that." He turned back to me. The look on his face made my stomach feel hot. "But that's no excuse for what you did, Hisako. You girls are supposed to be friends. This isn't how friends behave."

Anki's sobs turned to sniffles as he looked back and forth between us.

"I want the two of you to apologize to each other and give each other a hug," he said. "Can you do that?"

I held my arms out, ready to forgive. I usually took the bus to Anki's house once a week or so to play. I could try her game then. "I'm sorry I pulled your hair."

Anki gave me a quick squeeze. She put her mouth close to my ear like she was going to tell me a secret. "You're not my friend anymore," she said. "Greta is."

Mr Brahl put his hands on our shoulders and pulled us apart. "Good job, girls. Put your things away and get to class. Don't let me see this happen again."

Anki's first class was at the opposite end of the school from mine. I watched her stupid backpack as it moved away from me and waited for her to wave. What did she mean we weren't friends? We'd always been friends.

"Give her some space, Hisako. You hurt her feelings and that needs time to heal." Mr Brahl patted me on the back again. "Get to class. I let Ms Gemunder know you'd be late."

My first class every day was math. I had a special teacher named Ms Gemunder. She only taught math and only worked with gifted kids. Math was really easy, but I didn't like it much. I wish I were gifted in something else, but all my other classes were the regular kind.

The kids all looked up when I came into the room, and Ms Gemunder waved me to my seat. There were only seven kids in my math class, all of them older than me. The oldest, Franco, was in fifth grade, but I got the right answer more often than he did. Franco was having a hard time keeping up. I had heard Ms Gemunder talking with his mom about moving him back into regular math class.

So far, calculus was pretty easy. I did all the practice games Ms Gemunder loaded into my reader. The kids in the special classes got all kinds of extra help like that. I took an extra math class on Saturdays, and my parents were supposed to give me problems to solve. Mom doesn't know calculus, which is why she gave me easy stuff like the number of days until my birthday. She tried though. Dad didn't try at all. He read me stories and poetry instead, which I liked better than math anyway.

"Hisako, can you help Franco out with the answer to this problem?" Ms Gemunder said.

I didn't know what the problem was, because I wasn't paying attention. I squirmed in my seat, embarrassed. The screen on my desk flashed to remind me. It was an easy one, and I solved it quickly. I said the answer, my face hot.

Ms Gemunder frowned at me. "I know this comes easier to you than to some of the other children, Hisako, but that is no reason to let your mind wander."

Franco looked angry. It would have taken him a lot longer to solve the problem, if he could have at all. It wasn't my fault I was smarter. I was just born that way. I looked back at the desk screen, determined not to mess up again. Ms Gemunder sent a report to my patron every day, Mom said, and too many bad reports would result in bad things. We might not be able to afford to keep Nibble!

Class lasted an hour, and Ms Gemunder dismissed us herself. We were supposed to take a five-minute break before going to our regular classroom, so I went to the fountain down the hall to get a drink. I was bending toward the water, when I felt a hand on my head. It pushed my face hard into the fountain! I pushed back as hard as I could, but the hand was too strong. My nose smushed into the metal bottom of the fountain. I took a deep breath to yell, but water came in and I choked. Then I peed myself! The hand let me go, and I fell on the floor.

It was Franco. He still looked mad. I was on the floor coughing. My face and pants were wet.

"You're disgusting," Franco said. "You splices think you're so smart, taking up all the space in the good classes. But if you make me look stupid again, I'll get you. You'll never see it coming."

He walked away, and I ran to my regular classroom to tell Mrs Marchand. She was at the board. She caught me by the arms and held me away from her. "Did you– Did you have an accident, Hisako?"

Anki laughed. "I told you she was a baby. A little hair-pulling pee baby."

Mrs Marchand pushed a button on her desk. "We'll get you to the nurse and get you cleaned up, Hisako."

I wiped my eyes with my sleeve, but it was wet, too. "Franco pushed me into the fountain. He said he was going to– to– to hurt me."

The door slid open. "Is she causing trouble again?" Mr Brahl said.

"She just came in like this," the teacher said.

"She peed herself!" Anki yelled. "She's a baby."

"That's enough, Anki," Mr Brahl said. "Hisako, come with me."

"Make sure you get her some clean pants!" a boy laughed. "She might need a diaper change."

"Find out who said that," Mr Brahl said, "and send them to my office."

No one else said anything as Mr Brahl led me out of the classroom and down the hall to the nurse's office. The nurse was a fat woman who I saw when she checked my hair for lice every week.

"What happened to you?" the nurse said.

"Get her cleaned up and find her some dry clothes," Mr Brahl said. "I am going to go check the cameras. She said one of the older boys roughed her up."

The nurse pulled a towel out of a cabinet and used it to dry my face and hands. She sent me into the bathroom with a t-shirt and a pair of shorts. "Take your clothes off and put them in this plastic bag. Then put on the gym clothes."

"I don't have any clean underwear," I said.

"You can get a pair of disposables out of the dispenser in there. When it asks you what size you are, pick extra small."

The bathroom had a line of smiling ducks halfway up the wall. I wanted to scratch their faces off. It was all Anki's fault. If she had just let me play her stupid game, none of this would have happened.

I glared at the ducks as I took off my clothes, daring them to say something about my wet underwear, and put everything into the bag the nurse gave me. The disposable underwear was scratchy thin like paper, and even the extra small was too big. They sagged and drooped inside the shorts, which were too small. The shirt fell over everything like a dress. I padded barefoot back into the nurse's office. "Where are your shoes?" she said.

"In here." I held up the bag. "They were wet from…"

The nurse gave me a pair of slippers to put on. "You can wait here until Mr Brahl comes back. Do you like to color?"

She put a box of color sticks and a reader on the table. I looked for pictures of sandcats on it, but all it had were real cats, which were too expensive. Greta had one. When I showed her a picture of Nibble, she said he was an ugly lizard and that I should get a real cat.

I was trying to make a picture of a real cat look like Nibble, when Mr Brahl came back in. The color was right, but I couldn't hide the pointed ears and long tail. Nibble had no ears, and his tail was flat and stubby. Mr Brahl put my backpack on the nurse's desk. "You've had quite a day, Hisako. First you pull Anki's hair and now you start a fight with an older boy."

"I didn't start a fight!"

Mr Brahl held up his hand. "Franco said he got mad after you called him stupid."

"I did not! He was mad because I'm better at math than him."

"That's not what he said, but I don't have the recording to prove it either way." Mr Brahl looked tired. "I'm sending you both home to cool off." He spoke to the nurse. "Can you run her home?"

"Yes, Mr Brahl. But it may take some time."

"Take the rest of the day. I won't expect to see you back here until tomorrow morning."

The nurse smiled and grabbed my backpack. "Let's get you home, Hisako. Don't dawdle."

I followed her out to the dock and squeezed into a transit capsule with her. The capsule went on the road, so it took longer than usual. Then we sat in the capsule waiting for my father to get home.

"What's taking so long?" the nurse said. "I sent a message just before we left school."

"He works on a machine. Maybe he couldn't hear it."

"What about your nanny?" she said. "She should be here."

I didn't say anything. Some of my friends had nannies, but I didn't.

The nurse opened the capsule door for me. "Go right inside. I hope you have a better day tomorrow." She closed the door, and the capsule drove away, leaving me on the street.

From the window of my room, the ground looked pretty and clean, but really trash was everywhere, and the sidewalk was all broken up. There was a burned-out transit capsule lying on its side in front of the building.

A man was outside the capsule cooking something over the fire. It smelled like meat. He saw me and pointed to the meat roasting over the fire "You want a bite of this, little girl?" He smiled. He would have a hard time chewing food with so few teeth. "Come over here, and I'll give you a piece. Show me what's inside those shorts, and I'll give you half of it."

I shook my head. All I had inside my shorts was saggy disposable underwear. "I'm not hungry." I remembered my manners. "But thank you. What is it?"

The man closed one side of his nose with his finger and blew boogers out of the other side. They landed in the fire, just missing his dinner, and sizzled. "Big ugly lizard. Caught it right here." He motioned with his hand. "Come over here. I'll show you. I have some cachaca if you want a drink."

A big hand closed on my shoulder. I followed it up to my dad's face.

"What are you doing outside?" he said. "You know you shouldn't go down to the street."

"The nurse let me out here. I was just about to—"

"It's not safe." Dad let us in with his key and put money in the lift to take us to our floor. He looked tired.

The message light on the refrigerator was flashing, and Dad put his hand on the screen. It was my mother. She sounded upset. "Hisako's sandcat got out somehow. It must have been when we left for the bus. I can't find it anywhere, and I have to go to work. Can you look for it when you get home?"

I ran to my room. Nibble was gone.

HOW WE GOT HERE

by Hisako Sasaki, fourth grade

The Chin and India left Earth without even saying goodbye. They lifted as many people as they could to their mining asteroids and launched them into space. We haven't heard from them since. Maybe they have found a new home; maybe they are still traveling. Some people say the Chin made a new dynasty and will rejoin us someday. They will solve all of our problems or maybe they will take over.

The United Americas decided not to leave by themselves. They had mining asteroids, too, but used them up to build the evacuation ships. Every country that helped out with people or money got at least one evacuation ship. Some of the United's allies got worm-drive ships and went off to scout for planets we could live on. There were only about twelve worm-drive ships.

The important families left Earth on the fastest ships. At least one ship per colony had a mass-grav system that let it go faster than the other ones. They got to the new planets first to begin working. The rest of the families were frozen and packed into cargo pods. Some families worked as wake crews and stayed awake for hundreds of years to make sure the evacuation ships kept going.

Billions of people were still on Earth when the sun flared. They probably all died, but we have not gone back to check. The colony on Mars probably burned up, too. At the end, people left Earth any way they could. They put rockets on space stations or tried to escape in private ships. Even today, a thousand years later, some of those ships make it to us.

The first plan was to settle on one planet, Freedom, but the scientists were worried about diversifying the species, and people argued about who would live on what part of Freedom and who would be neighbors. So, instead, the evacuees from Earth colonized six planets The EuroD settled Gaul; the RussD settled the water and ice planet Nov Tero; Makkah was settled by evacuees from the Caliphate; the AfriD and BrazD settled Imbeleko; the United Americas worked with Australia, Israel, and the Kingdom to settle Freedom; and countries like Korea, Japan, and Vietnam went to Guatama.

Makkah and the United Americas destroyed each other in the Two-Day War and some of the other colonies are failing. Many of the survivors are coming here to live. We call those people refugees.

My mother is a EuroD. Her family came from a place on Earth called Turkey. My father's father was a refugee from Guatama, and my father's mother is from Imbeleko. I am an only child, which means I don't have any brothers or sisters. We live in an apartment near midtown. I had a sandcat once, but somebody ate him.

And that's how we got here.

ADEM

Qamata Station, Imbeleko, 3248

Adem opened the door to the captain's suite. "Sorry I'm late. I was—"

"Don't worry. You weren't the latest." Lucy came up behind him and ducked under his arm to get into the room first. "But now you are."

Lucy and Adem took seats across the table from their parents while the captain's new steward served breakfast. It wasn't a smooth operation. Their mother rarely dined in her quarters, so her steward didn't get a lot of practice. Most often she ate in the cafeteria with the crew or on the bridge.

"You're pulling out all the stops, Mother." Lucy loaded her plate with scrambled eggs and fruit. "You must have bad news to share. The last time we did this Uncle Rakin was buying his way back in."

Dooley ran a hand through his thinning red hair. "Rakin is partly why we asked you here. He's rallying support against your mother."

"He wants command?" Adem said. "He doesn't have any experience."

The captain moved the tiny pitcher of cream to the end of the table. She never used the stuff, no one in her family did, but her Gaul-born steward had insisted on putting it out. "He's claiming he can triple our profits."

"Which will make his investor pals happy," Lucy said.

"It would make everyone happy," Dooley said. "We're not exactly swimming in it, and we're behind on maintenance."

"Does he have the votes?" Adem picked up his coffee and wished he had something stronger. Family politics and business were among the least of his interests.

"No. But it would be better if I knew I had you two on my side when he tries." The captain leaned back in her chair. "And I need your help with something else."

"Ooooh!" Lucy said. "Is this when we find out the big secret?"

"Yes. I have a line on a worm-drive."

Adem aspirated his coffee.

"Impossible. There are only two or three still working in all the worlds," Lucy said.

"Four that we know of." Dooley leaned over the table like he was sharing a secret. "I've always suspected there were a few more under wraps. Maybe one or two scout ships repurposed as government couriers. I bet there's at least one among the Nov Tero syndicates."

Adem struggled to get his coughing under control. "It would cost a thousand times what the *Hajj* is worth, more than that probably, even if we could find one for sale."

"That's only a problem if we were buying it." The captain poured herself more coffee. "The one I have in mind is free, provided it's where I've been told it would be. Hence our course change."

Lucy's eyes narrowed. "Imbeleko never had a worm-drive ship, and there's nothing near here but the Makkah Cloud."

"Smugglers used to use the Cloud as a rendezvous. They'd meet to swap cargo, even hold festivals. One of them, an old friend of mine–"

"Old boyfriend," Dooley said loudly.

"–says he knows where the *Christopher Hadfield* is."

Lucy laughed. "We've gone from fairytales to ghost stories. This is ridiculous."

"It's no ghost story." The captain made eye contact with both of her children. "If Creighton said he found the *Hadfield*, he found it. He thinks the worm-drive might be intact."

"He could make a fortune off that, if it were true." Lucy's eyes rolled. "He shared this information with you because, what, you fucked him back in the dark ages?"

Dooley dropped the side of his fist on the tabletop, making the dishes rattle. "Lucy, shut up and show some respect." It had been years since he'd used his angry voice on his kids, but it worked. Adem and Lucy sat up straighter.

"I can handle this, Dooley, but thank you." The captain took a sip of coffee in the silence. "He doesn't want a fortune, at least not a big one. He told me about it because we were friends and because we have an agreement. He's a wanderer. Hasn't made planetfall in twenty years. Him or that android of his." She glanced at Dooley. "I told him if he ever found anything interesting out there that he should let me know. He did."

"How much are you paying him for it?" Adem said.

"Enough to pay for the next twenty years of wandering," Dooley's jaw tightened, "right out of our damned retirement fund."

The captain touched his arm. "Which is why we need your help. Your father and I have put ourselves in the hole for this. A deep one. If we can't refill it, we'll lose our shares and Rakin will take control. But if we had a worm-drive…" she paused, "there wouldn't be a ship in the worlds that could compete with us. We could make Nov Tero from here in six standard weeks, then another six to get all the way back to Gaul. Imagine it."

"Imagine what it could have meant for Hafgan." Dooley's voice was rough.

Adem imagined both things. Faster-than-light travel was a common fantasy among those who lived and worked in deep space; a pipe dream, but it could get deeply personal. Everyone had somebody they'd left behind in standard time. He'd nearly wept over how much Lucy had been changed by her years away. A wild, beautiful stranger had taken the place of the little girl who used to follow him everywhere, and Adem missed her. He missed his little brother, too. For Adem, only five years passed between the day Hafgan Sadiq left the ship and Adem's last visit with him. At that final meeting, Hafgan had been an old man, garrulous and shivering under a blanket with his wife sitting beside him. They'd offered Hafgan's oldest grandchild a share and an invitation to come aboard, but the girl had looked at them as if they were crazy. Give up the open sky for the corridors of an ancient ship? Even the grandchild might be dead now, but Adem had family pictures and saw his little brother peeking out of every set of dark eyes. Relativity could be a curse.

"What do you need us to do?" he said.

The captain laid her napkin on her plate. "I need you to go get it."

HISAKO

Age thirteen

My school uniform felt like it was too small, and my neck itched. But it might have just been nervousness. I bit my lip and waited for my friends' reactions.

Afet leaned across the lunch table so she could get a better look at the picture. "I think he's cute."

"Says he's just a little under two meters," Colette added, after perusing the profile information. "That's pretty tall."

Charo popped her gum. "What's with his hair? It's shaggy on one side and really short on the other."

"That's just the style," I lied. "All the Traders wear it that way."

Charo's mouth twisted. "That's not true. I meet Traders at my parents' parties all the time."

"Remember relativity. Maybe it's the style in the future or something." Afet stroked the screen of my reader to get a different angle on Adem's head. "Will you have to cut yours?"

"I think it's just for the men." I didn't know a thing about Trader culture. I just hoped it was a style and not some kind of weird thing only he did. Mostly it looked accidental.

Colette said Adem's eyes were spooky and romantic, like he had spent so much time looking into space that he had lost his soul. Charo said he had nice lips but needed a shave. Then the lunch bell rang. The reader went into my backpack as I headed to class with Afet. My neck wasn't itching anymore. It could have gone worse.

In the week since Mom told me I was in an arranged marriage, I'd been trying to figure out who Adem Sadiq was. I read his profile over and over again. He was pretty old, twenty-six, and had a sister. He lived on a spaceship and liked music. He was good at fixing stuff. He was an atheist and practiced jiu-jitsu. His birthday was in March, a month before mine.

That stuff was important, but the profile didn't help me with the important questions. I wanted to know if he was nice, what we'd have to talk about, and what his whiskers would feel like when he tried to kiss me. "Like a sandcat."

Afet tilted her head. "What did you say?"

"Nothing."

Surprises can be fun, like the party Mom and Dad threw last week for my thirteenth birthday. I came home after my violin lesson and my friends were waiting in the living room. The next day, Mom surprised me again: I was legally bound to marry a spaceman in eleven years. Fun? I wasn't sure about that one.

Dad was supposed to have been home to help her with the announcement and my questions, but he was at one of his political meetings. "Does this mean I can never date?" I said.

Mom's eyes got wide. "You're too young to be worried about that!"

Little did she know! The kids at school were always talking about dating and going out and sex. Afet had been going out with Henrik Birky for two months. They talked on their readers all the time, she said, and had gone to the stims together twice. At my party, they kept drifting off to make out.

And Henrik was just a skinny boy with big ears. Adem would be interested in a lot more than kissing. What if I didn't want–?

Afet elbowed me. "Madame just asked you a question."

"Huh?" A long, polished fingernail tapped on my desk. Tick-tick-tick. My heart seized. Our history teacher Madame Stavros had a long list of rules, but the most important one was: if the class ever got too loud to hear that tap, we would all get detentions and an extra assignment. I guess the class had been quiet before, but now, in the wake of the tap, I could hear air molecules brushing together.

"That is not the answer I was looking for, Ms Sasaki."

My face burned, half because I'd been caught not paying attention and half because of what had distracted me. "I'm sorry, Madame." I ducked my head.

"Please see me after class."

Ze moved on to torment Afet, who didn't know the answer, either. Afet didn't care about Gaul history any more than I did, but unlike me, she didn't have to worry about keeping her grades up. My jaw got tight as I watched Madame move through the classroom. I wouldn't need history in space anyway, no matter what my father said.

"History affects us every day," he told me the last time I had complained about the class. "Look around you. It's why people who look like your school friends live in *La Mur* and people who look like you live in *La Merde*." My father was full of theories like that. He went into *La Merde* for a lot of his so-called meetings, and his refugee friends there preached that their colonies had been designed to fail so Gaul and the other rich worlds would have cheap labor. "We thought we'd be free men on our new worlds, but now we're all slaves again."

That wasn't in the history Madame Stavros taught. Imbeleko and Guatama were failing, sure, but it wasn't part of a plan; they just hadn't been run correctly. Gaul had opened its doors to the refugees and gave them a safe place to live and food to eat. Every day there were new people coming down from orbit and asking for a handout. They weren't even from here, and they wanted more and more every week.

Madame Stavros finished prowling and broke us into groups to work on a project. I tried not to think about anything beyond schoolwork. I made it about ten minutes, thanks to Julio Odland, one of two boys in my assigned group.

"I heard you have a husband lined up." Julio was gross but super rich, so no one made jokes about him in front of his face. Behind his back though, Colette wondered if he could see his penis well enough to pee. She called him Sit-Down. "May I see the picture?"

I opened the picture and held out my reader. Julio studied it, his pink tongue sticking out of the corner of his mouth. "He looks like a rapist." He looked down his nose at me. "He bought you. Your parents will get a lot of money, and you'll have to fuck him. That makes you a prostitute. A space whore."

My stomach started twisting like it wanted to kill me, and I couldn't get enough air.

Julio licked his lips and raised his voice a little so all the kids in my group could hear him. "If you give her parents some money, she might fuck you, too." He winked.

Bonar Saiz, the other boy in my group who Charo said was a good kisser, leered at me. "How much would it cost?"

Colette punched him on the shoulder. "Shut up. Julio is just being an ass. It's an arranged marriage."

"She's still doing it for money," Bonar said. "I just want to know what else she'd do."

"It's not like that," I stammered. I suddenly wasn't sure what it was like. I felt like I was going to be sick.

"He's, like, forty. You're thirteen." Julio's lip curled. "That's sick enough, but your parents are getting money for it."

"The money is for school."

"School sucks. I wouldn't have sex with an old man just to come here." He looked at Colette. "Would you?"

"No." Her face turned pink. "Of course not." She didn't look at me.

"But it's okay for your friend? My mom says arranged marriages are wrong. It's like slavery."

"I don't want to talk about this." I spoke above the prescribed whisper, and I felt Madame Stavros come up behind me.

"Is there a problem, Hisako?" ze said.

"We are having trouble getting organized," Colette said. "Hisako was getting frustrated."

"That's something else I suppose we'll have to talk about after class." Ze brought hir hand down to my desk. Tap-tap-tap. "Let's try to get some work done before that."

Madame Stavros busied hirself with another group, and Colette brandished her fist at Bonar and Julio, daring them to say something else. We spent the rest of the period working at the proper decibel level, but I didn't contribute much.

Even Colette rushed away when the end-of-class bell sounded, leaving me to the never tender mercies of Madame Stavros. Ze assigned a punishment essay on the torrid relationship between Gaul's second prime minister and Parliament and directed me to move all the desks back into neat rows.

Madame's long skirts swished up behind me as I worked. "Many marriages resemble whoring, you know. Many things do. We all sell what we must to get what we need. Arrangements are not just for people like you, Ms Sasaki."

My breath caught. I'd had no idea Madame had heard us talking. I turned to see hir.

"Julio's new nickname for you is going to stick better than you would want it to." Hir hand floated up to one of hir ornate earrings. "Were I you, I would stop sharing that photo. It's hard enough being different without drawing attention to it."

My throat ached, and I felt so, so stupid. I had nearly convinced myself that it was exciting and romantic to have an arranged marriage. But, really, in eleven years, I would leave all of my friends and fly into space where a disgusting old man would be waiting for me to have sex with him. "Madame, have you known any others? Girls in arranged marriages, I mean."

Madame's hands fell to hir waist and came together. "Several. There are more than a few in this school right now. Brides and grooms. Though it's possible their parents have not told them about it yet. Most wait until after secondary school, although I don't understand why. My mother told me when I turned ten. I never knew my father, so he didn't raise any objection." Ze answered the question on my face. "Yes, I was in an arranged marriage, though I expect my mother sold me far more cheaply than your parents did you. I grew up very poor, you see, and I've never quite gotten the smell out of my skin."

"What happened?"

"I had a life, children. Then I grew tired of it. I asked for a divorce, sold my shares, and came back. And here I am." Madame peered at me through hir antique-style reading glasses. "We won't speak of this again, Ms Sasaki, and I trust you won't speak of it to anyone else."

"But—"

Tap. Tap. Tap. "Make sure you are better focused in tomorrow's class."

I caught the late bus home. My reader was full of messages from Colette and some of the other girls, but I didn't want to talk to anyone. They'd seen my home; now they knew I was in an arranged marriage. I might as well have just announced I was *La Merde*.

The shuttle stopped in front of our building. I stepped over a man sprawled in the doorway and I dropped some coins into the lift. The front door hissed open on our tiny living room. It had seemed cozy that morning, but now everything looked worn. The entertainment system only filled one wall instead of three or four like at my friends' houses. The paint looked dirty. The apartment smelled bad, too, like the ghost of old food and skin flakes. The couch was older than I was. How many pounds of our dirt and dander had soaked into the dingy cushions? I couldn't believe my parents had invited all my friends here. It was disgusting.

"How was school, Sako?" my mother called from the kitchen.

I didn't want to talk to her, but I wanted to know the answer to a question I'd been chewing on since I left Madame Stavros's room. I put my backpack on the disgusting couch and went into the kitchen.

"Was it worth it?"

"Was what worth it?" Mom was rolling out dough for pastels. "Let me put these in the fryer." She wiped her hands on the apron she wore over her work uniform. She worked for the Transit because she was good with languages. She spoke six and could understand three more, but she had never been good at understanding me. "Are you hungry?"

Now that I really understood how we were paying for the food, I didn't think I would ever be hungry again. "Was it worth it to trade me for this crappy apartment and our crappy life?"

"Who have you been talking to?"

"The least you could have done was to get more money. This place sucks. Couldn't you get a better deal?"

Mom put the back of her hand to her forehead, leaving a smudge of flour. "It's not like that," she said. "If we hadn't done it, you'd never have been born. They would have made me get rid of you."

"Maybe that would have been better. Did you ever think of that?"

"No. I never thought that, and neither did your father. We wanted you to live and—"

"You had no right!" I was yelling suddenly, and I didn't care that my father could hear me and that I would be robbing him of his sleep. He had made a deal that would cost me my life. "I didn't ask to be born!"

"No one ever does, Sako. Sit down and let's talk about this. Let me get you some tea."

"I don't want tea! I don't want anything from you!"

The door to my parents' bedroom slid open, and my father walked through it, blinking sleep out of his eyes. "What's all the yelling about?"

"I hate you. I hate both of you."

I rejoiced in the stricken look that appeared on their faces and wanted to hug them both and say I was sorry. I turned on my heel and disappeared into my bedroom.

ADEM

Two weeks out of Imbeleko

The survey ship was older than the *Hajj*, and it hadn't been built for comfort or beauty. Adem lifted his eyes from his reader and checked the controls for warning lights and alarms. The console was all grays and hard edges, like the rest of the little ship. The mass-grav systems were not as well-tuned as those on the *Hajj*, and the weeks at near *c* were making his joints ache. Still, the ship was Imbeleko's pride and joy, and the planetary government hadn't let it go cheaply. The load of foodstuff and building materials from Gaul went right into the hole with Creighton's finder fee.

Lucy dropped into the seat beside him and put her feet up on the control panel. "This is the worst trip ever."

"Good thing I have that panel locked down. You might have just killed us all."

She rolled her eyes. "Better than this. I'm so bored!"

"You're supposed to be sleeping." Adem's eyes drifted to a projection of the debris field they were approaching. "It looks pretty wild in there."

Lucy winced. "It looks worse to the sensors. Be glad we don't have to fly into it."

"It's hard to believe it used to be a planet."

History called it the Two-Day War, but, really, more than a

standard month had passed between the attacks that had destroyed two cultures.

"What the hell was Creighton looking for out here?" Adem said.

"The Chin." Lucy tugged at her lower lip. "Mom told me about him. He thinks they're, like, a super civilization that can save us from ourselves."

"We could use it." Adem pointed to the projection. "We must have had family there."

"Probably. And if great-grandma hadn't won the draw and assumed ownership of the *Hajj*... Pow!"

The colony on Makkah had been less than fifty years old when the Two-Day War ended.

"Who do you think shot first?" Adem said.

There wasn't much more than academic value in pointing fingers. The war had come to an end more than nine hundred standard years before. A suicide pilot in a small scout ship had turned the United Americas settlement on Freedom into a crater. The UA had either responded with or had already been on its way to a planet-crushing assault on Makkah.

"The Americans never liked us," Lucy said. "I think it was them."

"But it could have been the Caliphate," Adem said. "It happened before."

"It doesn't matter now."

The siblings looked out the cockpit window for a time. Lucy checked the readouts on the control panel. "Go back and bunk for a while."

"It's your turn." Adem's words turned into a mumble as he smothered a yawn.

"Mateo is snoring. There's no way I'll be able to sleep."

The towheaded engineer was easy to get along with when he was awake but hard to live with asleep. Adem stretched. "Alright, I'll take you up on it."

"We'll either make contact with the *Hadfield* in eight hours, or we've been suckered. Either way, I'll make sure you're awake for it."

Adem kissed the top of her head. "Catching that thing isn't going to be easy."

"Not in this ship. But I didn't become a pilot because it was easy." She swatted him on the hip. "Sleep."

The hallway between the cockpit and the crew's bunkroom was broken only by the door to a small refresher unit. Adem stopped to wash his face and hands.

Mateo Rojas wasn't the only one snoring, but he was by far the loudest of the three. Adem crawled into the open bunk and lay on his back, his head resting on his hands. The room was humid with exhalations and sour with body odor. The survey ship's hygiene resources were overtaxed with a crew of five, and the quarters were starting to show it.

Good thing it's only three weeks back. Adem closed his eyes against the sight of the upper bunk forty-five centimeters above his face. A boot thudding into the side of his bunk woke him up sometime later.

Mateo rubbed his hands together. "Your sister says there's something on the scope."

Adem nearly brained himself trying to sit up but caught himself in time and rolled off the bunk to the floor. "The *Hadfield*?"

The *Hadfield*'s orbit was erratic and decaying, Creighton's data showed. It didn't emerge from the debris cloud often.

"She said it's the right size. Wants us to get ready."

"How long do we have?"

"She said you have enough time to eat something and take a piss, but that's about it."

Adem pulled on his boots and woke the comm on his collar. "What can you tell me?"

"Resolution isn't good enough, yet," Lucy answered. "We'll start with Plan A and see what happens."

Plan A was an attempted docking at the derelict's forward airlock. Plan B involved attaching to the warship like a leech and cutting through its armored hull. Plan C hadn't been written yet, but any version relied on Lucy getting the survey ship very close to the *Christopher Hadfield*. "How fast is it moving?" he said.

Lucy snorted. "Speed isn't the problem. It's tumbling every way it can. Shut up and let me figure this out."

Adem grabbed a meal bar from the ship's little galley and washed it down with cold water. He waited in line for his turn at the refresher and came out in time to see Mateo again.

"Do you think this is going to work?" he said.

"What part?"

"Any of it. Docking. Salvaging the derelict." Mateo shrugged. "It seems like a big risk. The captain doesn't like big risks."

Adem tried to remember how long Mateo had been on the *Hajj*. "She doesn't like them, but that doesn't mean she won't take them."

"It just seems like a long way to go for some old records."

The cover story within the secret mission. News traveled fast on the *Hajj*, and the captain wanted to keep knowledge of the worm-drive out of Rakin's hands as long as possible.

"People will pay good money for anything we can pull off the ship," Adem said. "You might be able to retire early." Adem wasn't much older than Mateo, but interacting with him now made him feel ancient.

Mateo grinned. "Sun, sand, and girls on Freedom."

"Think about those later. Survive the operation now."

The ship lurched. Mateo already looked a little green. The little ship's mass-grav system was fine in a straight line, but it was having trouble keeping up with Lucy's twisting, turning course.

"It's going to be worse on the derelict," Adem said. "Remember not to puke in your helmet."

Mateo was a good kid; he'd get the job done and build a nice life off the proceeds. The ship wobbled again, and Adem reached out a hand to steady himself on the wall. He tapped his comm. "We crashing?"

"Just about," Lucy said. "Next maneuver should do it. Make sure you're hanging onto something."

The ship's overhead lights changed to red, letting the rest of the crew know to hang on, too. Adem braced his back against the hallway wall and wedged his feet against the junction of floor and wall on the other side. Mass-grav strained to keep up with a ninety-eight-degree twist.

"We're in position," Lucy announced. "About twenty minutes until we dock. Plan A looks good."

Adem forced himself to take his time but still made it to the airlock before the rest of the excursion crew. Once in his pressure suit, he checked the salvaging gear as the rest of the crew filed in and got ready. He sealed the airlock behind them.

Adem hit the comm switch in his helmet with his chin. "We're in place."

"If I pull this off without killing us, I expect a lifetime supply of booze and great sex," Lucy said.

"I'll talk to Mateo."

"Don't you dare!" She opened the comm channel to the entire crew. "Hold on everyone. This is where it gets interesting."

Adem wondered if he would feel more or less tense if he was in the copilot seat, watching his sister try to make contact with the tumbling warship. The survey vessel was more mobile than the *Hajj*, but Lucy's link with the little ship's nearsmart wasn't nearly as comprehensive. She was moving mostly on instinct and talent. He closed his eyes and concentrated on his breathing like his mother had taught him in martial arts class. *With breath there can be no fear.*

The survey ship dropped like a dead bird and twisted sharply to the left. Adem tightened his grip on one of the handholds along the wall. A sharp impact threw everyone in the airlock to their knees.

"Made it." Lucy's voice sounded small and sweaty. "Let's not do that again."

"No promises," Adem said. He performed a spot check of the salvage team and pronounced them shaken but ready. "Let's see if we can get the door open."

His fingers cramped as he forced them off the handhold, and he struggled past Mateo to get to the airlock's outer door. He slid it open to inspect the docking ring. "Seal looks tight. Are you picking up any leakage?"

"Nearsmart says it's holding," Lucy said.

"You getting anything from the *Hadfield*?"

"There was no handshake. It's not saying 'hello' nor telling us to get lost. I'm getting limited power readings."

Adem scanned the derelict's outer door with his multi-tool, hoping to get a sense of whether the ship's mechanical security measures were still in place. "I got nothing, either."

He put his hand near the big door, waiting for the arcing spark that would prove the security system was still awake and lethal. The spark failed to appear, and Adem reached for the door handle. "It's not locked." He twisted the handle. "I'm opening it."

The door opened into a dark corridor. "I'm still alive," Adem said.

"Good to hear it," Lucy said. "You have about thirteen hours before this thing slips back into the debris field."

Adem activated his helmet light and peered into the ink beyond the door. The illumination didn't penetrate far, but Adem could make out the walls and floor panels of the passageway beyond.

"How many were on board?" Mateo said.

"Seventy-two according to the history books." Adem stepped over the threshold, the first human to do so in nine centuries. "And a dozen androids."

Mateo stepped up behind Adem, crowding him. "Do you think we'll find bodies?"

"Depends how they died. If mass-grav failed, they were all crushed to jelly. If life support went out…" Adem nodded even though he knew Mateo couldn't see it through his helmet. "Yeah, we'll see bodies." He cleared his throat. "Split up. Mateo and me to the engine room. Charlie and Odessa to the bridge. If we can get some lights on it will make this whole thing a lot easier." Adem shone his helmet lamp up the hallway toward the bridge access then back to the airlock. "Check in every ten minutes or so."

The mass-grav systems were still working well enough to define the corridor's floor as down. Adem lightly magnetized his boots and headed in the opposite direction of the bridge, knowing Mateo would be right behind him. Their footsteps echoed dully. "There's air or something in here. Enough to carry sound. Get a sample and send the data to Lucy. Maybe she can tell us what we're walking through."

"I've played stim games like this," Mateo said. "This would be about the time the aliens spring out and attack."

"We'd better hope not. We won't last long defending ourselves with toolboxes."

"It's a warship." Mateo twisted his body to shine his headlamp down a corridor they passed. "There must be weapons here."

"Lots of them. And they're staying here. Captain says we're not bringing anything back that shoots or explodes."

"Bet your Uncle Rakin was happy about that."

"We're not here to make Rakin happy." Adem opened the group channel. "Check. Mateo and I are alive and well, about two hundred meters along the ship's axis toward engineering.

"Check," Odessa said. "Charlie and I are on the bridge. It's in pretty good shape." She paused. "There are bodies here."

"Try not to wake them up. You'll be okay. Out."

"How much further?" Mateo said.

Adem looked at the map on his reader. "Another fifty meters or so, then up. Engine room access is two levels above this one."

The comm beeped. "Adem, we're going to try something," Odessa said. "Stop moving for a couple of minutes."

"Acknowledged." Adem and Mateo stopped moving forward.

"What do you think–?" Mateo said.

Adem held up his hand. "Wait for it."

The lighting bars embedded in the ceiling flickered, died, and then came to a steady glow at about three-quarter strength.

"Did it work?" Odessa said.

"We got lights. Good work. Emergency power?"

"We just reset the cutouts. The reactor must still be working."

Adem whistled. "They weren't screwing around when they built these things."

"It's going to be a few hours on the nearsmart. The interface is just like the one on the *Hajj*, but I don't want to start it up too fast."

"Once you get it, start dumping every piece of information you see into portable storage. We're about twenty minutes from the engine room. Maybe we can get a little thruster power and slow the tumble. Out."

The hatch to the engine room access tube was stuck. "Come up the other side of this ladder and help me move this." Adem shuffled to the left to make room.

Mateo set down the equipment he was carrying and climbed the opposite side of the ladder. "I don't have a lot of space to work."

"I don't think you'll have to do much. It feels like it's catching on something."

Mateo climbed a little higher and got one hand on the hatch. He held onto the ladder with the other.

"Push!" The hatch resisted then came free. Adem followed it into the crawlspace. "Lights are not working in here." He inhaled sharply. "And we got bodies. At least three or four of them."

"Are they dead? Let me see."

Adem climbed the rest of the way up the ladder and tried to find room for his boots among the bones and fabric scraps.

Mateo's waist came even with the hatchway. "I thought they'd be better preserved."

Adem turned his helmet lamp on again and panned it up and down the sides of the narrow space. "What were they doing in here?"

"Maybe they were using the crawlspace after the power cut out."

"Maybe." Adem bent and fumbled in the debris. He held up a long bone and squinted at it through his faceplate. "That look gnawed to you?" He held the bone in front of Mateo's helmet.

"Someone ate him?"

"I think we're in someone's trashcan. A nice long tunnel to get rid of the garbage." Adem let go of the bone. It fell lazily, drawn down by mass-grav and sideways by the centripetal force generated by the ship's tumble. "Let's go up." He put his boot on the first step of the ladder and began to climb.

The slight tug downward wasn't enough to slow them much. It had barely been enough to make the remains collect in the bottom of the crawlspace. About halfway up they encountered another body, its arm hooked on the ladder. Adem looked it over carefully. "It's a woman. This one didn't get chewed on."

"Maybe they weren't hungry enough yet," Mateo said.

Adem freed the corpse's arm and let her drift down toward her crewmates. They had a lot of catching up to do. "Let's keep going." He opened the all-channel. "Check. Mateo and I are fine, about halfway up the access shaft to the engine room. We've found some bodies."

Mateo cut in. "Somebody ate them!"

Adem twisted his body to frown at him. "Looks like they lived for a while after the planet went to pieces. What's going on up there?"

"Reactor's at eleven percent," Charlie said. "Can't see from here if it's a malfunction or if someone dialed it down on purpose. We found an android that Odessa's trying to reboot with the codes the captain gave her. She thinks it might be able to help us wake the nearsmart."

"Be careful," Adem said. "It will probably demand a clearance code or something before it does you any favors."

"Odessa says she wasn't born yesterday, oh Great Leader, but thanks for the advice. Out."

Mateo and Adem climbed in silence until they reached the hatch to the engine room. "Climb back down a couple of steps," Adem said. "There might be a pressure difference on the other side."

Adem waited for Mateo to move then slid the hatch open. The equalizing air pressure hit Adem at gale force. He rocked back, clutching for the ladder with his free hand. He felt Mateo come up behind to keep him on the ladder.

"Looks like there was a pressure difference," Mateo said.

Adem got his breathing and heart rate back under control and climbed the last few steps of the ladder and into the engineering section.

He woke his comm. "Lucy, how's it coming on that gas analysis Mateo sent you?"

"It's air," she said. "But nothing you want to breathe. It's full of toxins, probably just from outgassing. If you got the power back on, it might filter clean in a couple of days."

"Is it touch toxic or only a problem if you breathe it?"

"There's a good chance it would give you a bad rash and burn your eyes out of your head. It's real cold in there anyway. No way could you warm it up in time."

"Looks like we're stuck in the suits. Out." He turned in time to see Mateo pull himself out of the crawlspace. "I'll check the thrusters. You check mass-grav."

The engine room layout was similar to the one in the *Hajj*, so Adem had little trouble finding the thruster controls. The control board lit up with a little prodding. "Check," he said. "Mateo and I are in engineering. Looks like we might have thruster control."

"Mass-grav is at minimum," Mateo said. "If you do anything, do it slow and careful."

"Odessa says the android is in love with her," Charlie said. "I think they're getting married, but first it's helping us get the nearsmart online. Thirty minutes."

"Ten-four. The automatic controls look okay. I'm going to wake them up and let them do their thing on the rumble. You still secure over there, Lucy?"

"Tight as a tick," she said. "Just don't get crazy."

Adem activated the thruster system's automatic controls. The floor underneath his feet vibrated as the warship worked to steady itself.

"The tumble is slowing, little brother," Lucy said. "I can almost look out the window without puking."

Adem felt the tumble's effect on the ship diminish. In minutes, the strongest pull was the weakened mass-grav system. He hopped experimentally. "Feels like ten percent gees. Probably as good as we're going to get it. Mateo, start looking for spare parts. Pack up anything we can pull off without blowing anything up. Lucy, lock the survey ship down and start working on Mom's laundry list. I'm going to check the engines."

"Before you do that," Mateo said, "I think I found the cannibal."

The cannibal had made its nest in the pressure-suit locker right off mass-grav control.

"I was just checking to see if there was anything in there worth packing up," Mateo said. "Scared the hell out of me to see him looking out at me like that."

There were two bodies in the locker, but the one who had propped himself against the wall and shot himself in the head had been male. The corpse stared balefully through slitted eyelids, its brain matter and blood signing the suicide all over the wall behind it. Adem prodded the second body with the toe of his boot. "You think she was dinner or a girlfriend?"

"I'm betting girlfriend."

"I wonder how long they lived."

"The whole story is probably on here." He handed an ancient reader to Adem. "This was beside him."

Adem slipped the reader into his thigh pocket for later. "I'm guessing these guys weren't techs. Everything is in good enough shape down here that they could have kept things going for a good long time. Reactor went into emergency mode, stopping everything non-essential. Most of the system failures seem to be due to automatic cutoffs."

"Maybe the squeezer caused an EM pulse. Fried or tripped all the circuits."

"We'll know more when we've downloaded everything." Adem checked the time. "We have about twelve hours left. Focus on anything small and expensive. I'll wake the reactor up a little more so we can use the lifts."

"We bringing the bodies back?"

"Maybe we'll try to get them all in one place so they can rest together, but that's a low priority."

"Might be some hard feelings there if this guy ate some of them."

"We'll let them work it out." Adem opened the group channel. "Check. Mateo and I are fine. He's starting salvage down here. I'm going to play with the reactor a little then head up your way."

"Ten-four," Charlie said. "The nearsmart is rebooting. Odessa is babysitting it. This thing is in pretty good shape. If the engines work, we could probably fly it back to Imbeleko and sell it."

"I'll let you know when I check the engines." Adem chewed his lip. "My vote is to cherry-pick the thing and use the thrusters to crash it into the cloud's center of mass. It's too haunted."

Mateo feigned a salute. "There's a cargo scooter over there. I'll charge it and load it up."

"Keep an eye out for androids. They're probably the biggest bang for the buck. Don't try to activate them." Adem left Mateo to scavenge and ducked into the corridor that led to the engine control. The big room beneath it was full of shadows, but there was more than enough light to see that the *Hadfield* would never fly again. He triggered his comm. "She's open to vacuum down here, and the engines are twisted off their mounts. Nothing we could fix."

"Anything in there worth packing up?"

"Not in the time we have left. I'll poke around the control room for a minute, then we'll steer clear." Adem activated the overseer's control panel. The telltales and screens flickered half-heartedly before coming to attention. A light blinked on the message panel, and Adem stroked the activation button. The message screen lit up to show a young woman. He synced his comm to the message output so he could hear her.

"Unless blowback happens soon, we're not going to make

it, captain. The engines are starting to run hot and the gravity fluctuations are pulling them out of alignment." Something on the left side of the control console caught the woman's attention. "Hold on to somethin–!" The screen went dark. Adem wondered what had scared her. Blowback, maybe, whatever that was. He downloaded the message to his reader to study later.

"Mateo, I'm through down here," he announced. "I'm going forward to help Lucy."

"Ten-four. Hey, do you have a schematic of the ship's systems and locations? It would make scavenging a lot easier."

The captain had deliberately kept that sort of thing scarce to lessen the chance of side missions to the *Hadfield*'s armory. Rakin was three weeks away and by the time he learned anything useful, the *Hadfield* would be back in the cloud. "I'll send you what I have. Call me before you go anywhere dangerous."

HISAKO

Age fifteen

The room was musky with dirty socks. The boy on the bed beside me reached for my breasts. I pushed his hands away.

"Why don't you want me to kiss you?" he said.

"I don't kiss with those."

"They're hanging out of your shirt like you want somebody to touch them."

I pulled the shirt both up and down for better coverage. It was the only piece of clothing like it I had, the only one I could afford, which was funny because it used less material than any of my other clothes. It folded down into a square the size of a meal bar and fit into the outer pocket of my backpack fortunate, because my mother would have never let me out of the house wearing it. "It's a style," I said. "Not an invitation."

Or maybe it was. It was something. I'd worn it because I knew I would end up at Maki Hakala's house after school. It was either go there or go home, and I was never going to let Maki, or anyone else from school, see where I lived. Maki lived in *La Mur* in a mansion and had proudly shown me a thousand year-old, non-functioning android named Trevor that Maki had gotten grounded over when he'd drawn a mustache on its face. "It came right off," Maki assured me.

I had never seen a corpse, but Trevor sure looked like one to me. Yet, there he was, sitting in the Hakalas' formal parlor in his very own chair. Creepy. "Touch him!" Maki had urged. "Go ahead. He's still warm!" Super creepy.

Maki was bad at nonchalant. He leaned back on his pillows. "Hey, whatever. You're the one who wanted to come over here."

Buying the shirt had eaten up a month's allowance and left me nothing for a stim or a meal or anything else we might have done. Maki had plenty of money, but I didn't want him to get the idea that I owed him something.

"Are you hungry?" he said. "We have one of the only working food assemblers in Versailles City. All it can make are, like, chicken bars, but they're okay."

Food assemblers and androids were United Americas technology, which meant no one knew how to make or fix them anymore. Even trying to take them apart resulted in a meltdown or explosion, or so my Intro to Engineering teacher said. The food assemblers, back when they worked, had been able to make food out of reclaimed proteins and algae and shit.

"I'm not hungry," I said. "We could do our homework. That was sort of the point of this."

"Was it?" He leaned toward me and smirked.

"That's what lab partners do."

He flopped backward on the bed. "I don't want to."

"Let's clean this place up then." I reached for a pillow but spotted several things on the floor, even on the bed I was sitting on, that I had no interest in touching. "Or we can watch something." I woke up his entertainment system and told it to play the action movie channel out of New Berlin.

Maki sighed. "Get up for a minute." He straightened his comforter and bedspread and lined up the scattered pillows against the headboard. I let him put his arm around me as we watched the film.

It was really stupid. Some guy was running around in a torn shirt fighting robots. There was a woman in it, too, but she didn't do much more than get in trouble and throw herself on torn-shirt guy whenever the robots showed up. I was barely paying attention to it, but I hadn't realized that Maki wasn't either until he cleared his throat and started reading.

Nibble
Hair like bristles,
sharp like spines
Scales ran down his body,
but there was no greater love than mine.

Tail like a paddle,
tiny ears slicked back,
he made a little squawk,
when I snuck him in my pack.

He was beautiful,
but not as beautiful as a real cat.
He was charming,
but not as charming as other pets.
But I still love him.
Though he Nibbled at my socks.

"Give that back!" I said.

"You're the one who left it unlocked." He rose to his knees and held my reader over his head. "Did you write that?"

I lunged for it, getting my chest in his face.

"Nibble, nibble!" Maki twisted and somehow ended up on top of me, the reader just out of reach. "Did you write it?"

"I wrote it a long time ago. Give it to me!" I squeezed my fingers into a fist. "I'm going to hit you so hard!" He laughed and handed over the reader. EuroD boys like Maki had good manners, as long as they thought they were relating to someone within their own social class. Mine were less refined. I really would have hit him.

"I had a cat once," he said. "The maid forgot to feed it or something. We got home from New Berlin, and it was dead under my bed."

"Is that why your room smells so bad?"

"Funny," he said. "Mother fired the maid and recorded a video of me crying to go in her personnel file. She probably never worked again."

"What was its name?"

"Meghan something. I can't remember her last name. We usually just called her The Maid."

"No, the cat's name."

Maki stared blankly for a few seconds. "I can't remember. I didn't get a chance to play with it much. It was always sleeping. I just remember being upset when it was gone. I was on medication for a couple of months until I got over it. Mother said she was tired of seeing me snotting around."

"I was upset about Nibble, too. He got out by accident and someone ate him."

He put his hand to his mouth. "Sandcats are basically lizards, right?"

"I wrote the poem a couple years later. My dad liked it. He used to read me poetry when I was little."

"Weird. Is he a teacher?"

My father was currently in jail because his drinking buddies were political radicals and wanted terrorists. "He does a lot of things."

"I don't really know what my father does. Some kind of business. He makes a lot of trips to Versailles Station and New Berlin. He has a mistress there and another son."

"He has four kids?" I didn't know anyone who had more than three children. Maki's sister was two years older and an absolute termagant. His little brother was twelve.

Maki crossed his arms. "He's very rich. He can have as many kids as he wants."

"I bet your mother's happy about it."

"She has a lover somewhere. I heard them talking once." He very obviously cast about for a new subject. "Do you still write poetry?"

"I'm more into music. I play a few instruments."

His eyes brightened. "I always wanted to learn how to play something. I asked my father for lessons, but he said it would be a waste of money."

"There are programs you can put on your reader that would help," I said. "I can show you."

"There's no one to play for. My father is never home, and Mother barely notices I'm here." Maki's mouth twisted. Somehow we'd gotten back to his family troubles, and he wasn't happy to be there.

"You got a new maid, right?" I elbowed him. "Play for yourself, silly. Play for Trevor. Play for me. We can start a band. What do you want to learn?"

"Drums, maybe? Every band needs to have drums, right?"

"You could do drums. Or we could use a program for that, and you could learn guitar."

"Let me show you something." Maki told the entertainment system to stop the movie and summoned his personal channel. "Play Spaceman Thirty-Seven," he said. The screen changed from explosions and computer-generated blood to a man sitting in a hallway with a guitar. The image quality wasn't great, like it had been broadcast at low power or had traveled a long way. The man was handsome but melancholy, his hair dark and curly.

"I know him," I said.

It had been a few years since I had looked at Adem's picture. I'd even deleted it off my reader.

Maki's jaw dropped. "You're a Spacehead?"

"What?" I couldn't take my eyes off the screen.

"This is an old, old song called 'The Midnight Special.' It's from Earth." Adem sang in English. He wasn't great on guitar, but he had a good voice. The song was a yearning, lonely thing even though the lyrics didn't make a lot of sense to me.

When the video ended, Maki told his system to display a list of all the vids on his channel. "I'd never guess you were a Spacehead, too." He licked his lips. "I only have a few dozen of them, but I know a guy who says there are more than a hundred."

"What are you talking about?" His excitement irritated me.

"The Spaceman!" He made an effort to calm down. "He works on a freighter. He makes these recordings every once in a while and broadcasts them. People who collect them call him the Spaceman, so we call ourselves–"

"Spaceheads," I said. "Clever."

"I know, right? Do you want to hear some more?"

Adem's face was frozen on the screen. I was his, bought and paid for. I'd read the contract. It didn't require virginity like some did, but it strongly suggested I avoid serious relationships. It would keep me from ever falling in love. I leaned back against Maki's pillows, my hands gripping his bedspread.

Maki started another video. This one was more playful, about a man whose father had given him a girl's name. It was more talking than singing, in French this time, and I listened closely to hear if he said anything that sounded like Hisako. He pronounced the "s" in "Sue" without a lisp or whistle.

"Like I said, I have more," Maki said when the "Sue" song was over. "Dad lets me use his nearsmart to look for them sometimes. It's kind of cheating, but–"

"Why do you collect them?"

"I like the music. Most of it. He does different stuff all the time." He studied the image on the screen. "Mostly it gives me something to do that a lot of the other kids don't."

"Do you want to learn how to play like that? I can teach you, and you can make your own videos."

His smile was adorable. "Really? There's a fan site where people post covers of his songs. I visit it all the time."

"I can teach you to play better than him."

"I don't care about that. If I could just do it good enough–"

"Better." That was suddenly very important to me. "You can be better. Play another one."

My fiancé started singing another song. I pulled my shirt off over my head and dropped it on the bed. Maki's eyes widened. I had his full attention. "This is an invitation."

NEARSMART DOCKING HANDSHAKE:
Trader Ship Hajj x773 to
Victoria Station x252, Freedom

Ship Length: 400 meters
Ship Width: 53 meters
Engine Type: Fusion, MK IV
Crew: 87
Registry: The Trader Union, Sadiq family, 2207
Captain: Maneera Sadiq
Chief Medical Officer: Abdul Sadiq
Pilot: Lucy Sadiq
Cargo: Helium, smelted aluminum, rice, pharmaceuticals, refugees.
Ship History: Constructed in Earth orbit by the United States of America, 2127. Granted to the Caliphate. Launched as the *Biriir ina*, 2129. Named changed to the *Morgan Freeman*, 2263. Name changed to the *Hajj*, 3000.
Flight Plan: Docking and unloading, Victoria Station. Expected departure to Gaul in thirteen days.

ADEM

Freedom, Jan 21, 3252

Adem put his hands behind his head and studied the ceiling, trying not to disturb the woman sprawled in bed next to him. Vladlena Mullova, Vee for short. She'd joined the crew at Imbeleko, and they'd ended up in bed together after drinking far too much.

"Your bed is huge. I love it." Vee's voice was partially muffled by a pillow. She twisted around and propped herself up on one elbow. "Morning, Spaceman."

"Want me to play you something?"

The second time they'd talked, she admitted she was a fan of his music and had collected all of his recordings, even the old ones that had come to her homeworld before her parents were born. She showed him the files on her reader.

Adem leaned out of bed to get one of his guitars and checked the tuning. Vee leaned against the wall to face him. "Smile," she said.

She was morning beautiful, sleep and sex tousled, and it was hard not to comply. His lips quirked. "What are you doing?"

She winked at him and held it a little longer than normal. She tapped the metal stud in her eyebrow. "Taking a picture for the fan sites. I've never seen a shirtless one before. It will go viral if I ever get a chance to post it."

Adem squinted at the stud. "That's a camera? I thought it was just a piercing."

"That's what it's supposed to look like. It stores to my reader, or I can broadcast it."

Broadcast? He imagined his mother and sister watching from the bridge, his mother with a disapproving twist on her lips, his sister grinning and taking notes to harass him with.

"Worried that we made a movie last night?" She winked. "No. It comes in handy if I need help with a diagnostic or something."

Adem settled the guitar into place. It was an Earth-made Martin D28 he'd found in a storage locker when he was fourteen. He cleared his throat and started with a G chord. His voice was rougher and deeper in the morning. The gravel in his throat added gravitas to his performance. His fingers reached for the next chord.

"You did that one last night," Vee interrupted.

"Sorry." He was sorrier for himself than for her. When he played, he felt like he was channeling something bigger and more important, and Vee had just pinched off the connection.

"What do you want to hear?" He tried to keep the irritation out of his voice.

"How about 'Here Comes the Sun'?" She lay back down and rested her head on his knee. "You cut that one about fifty years ago."

A half century standard. Though for him it had only been a couple of years. It was a good song for someone raised on a planet. In space, a home sun was just another star. "I don't think my voice is ready for it." He hummed to himself for a moment then played a song written by a member of the *Hajj*'s wake crew during the evacuation from Earth. It was a lonely song, but Adem liked lonely songs. It fit his morning voice, too, deep and sad. "I haven't recorded that one yet," he said when it was over.

"You should. It made me feel so hollow. Gave me the shivers."

"I'll get around to it one of these trips." He hung the guitar back on the wall and rolled his shoulders. "You can take the first shower. I want to take a peek at the to-do list before my feet hit the floor. Like to know what I'm in for."

She kissed him on the mouth. "Thanks for such a good time last night. It was just what I needed." Vee climbed out of bed. Adem's eyes followed her to the bathroom door. He'd never had a groupie before.

The first item on his chore list was flashing urgently. A bridge fill-in shift starting five minutes ago. He swore. The shower was going to have to wait.

Adem pulled on his utilisuit and stuck his head into the bathroom. "I gotta go."

Vladlena peeked through the shower curtain. "See you tonight?"

"We'll see how today shakes out."

She threw the shower curtain wide. "You know where I'll be."

"We're in range, Mother," Lucy said.

The captain turned to the communications station where Adem was filling in for a crewman who had called in with a stomach ache. "Sync us up."

Adem poked competently at the communications board and opened the ship's computer to the flood of data coming from the Freedom worldnet. "Done."

"Run the search," the captain said. "Usual parameters."

More than thirty years of updates in laws, popular culture, politics, economics, and science poured into the *Hajj*'s database. The nearsmart would sort through the public feeds and paid channels and tag anything worth noting. Any important changes would be brought to the captain's attention, and she'd let the shareholders know about potential problems at the planetfall briefing. As Dooley liked to say, events on the ground had a way of making a Trader's life complicated. The more time they had to figure out problems, the better chance they had of maintaining their profit margin.

"Red flags?" the captain said. Their business partners on Freedom were supposed to flag the biggest events – natural disasters, coups, surprising election results – anything that could change the price or demand for goods and services.

Adem shook his head then remembered that his mother was likely not watching him. "Not so far."

"Any problems with offloading the refugees?"

"They're starting a new settlement near the equator. They'll need workers for that," Adem said. "Looks like Rothman's daughter has finally taken over the business. The old man retired to his private island."

"I always liked Tessa better anyway," the captain said. "Send her something for me."

Adem made a note to send Tessa a fruit basket from Gaul, care of the *Hajj*. "It looks like that's it for now. Permission to get back to work?"

"Permission granted," she said. "Match later?"

"After you talk to the board? I'll start taking painkillers now."

"Good idea. I may need to work off some emotion."

"Before we hear the planetfall briefing," Rakin folded his hands on the conference table, "I would like to know what you found on that warship."

Adem and Lucy glanced guiltily at each other.

"You have someone in your pocket," Lucy said. "I'm guessing Mateo or Odessa."

"Nothing so gauche." Rakin waved his hand. "I don't need spies.

Word gets out. Someone talks to someone talks to me. It's a small ship."

"Historical artifacts," the captain said coolly. "Logs and records. All the spare parts we could grab. We left the weapons, if that's what you're wondering about."

Rakin's lips pursed. "I could have gotten you a good price for them on Nov Tero. Maybe a better price on Gaul what with the political climate there."

"We don't run guns or instigate revolutions. I already have buyers lined up for what we salvaged. Private collectors. Museums. Good money."

"And you accuse me of being cagey. There aren't enough private collectors in the worlds to pay the rental price of that survey ship, yet you sent your two surviving children into the dark for historical records and spare parts." Rakin held up his hand. "Don't protest. I like a good plan. If it pays off, I make money. If it doesn't..." He smiled at the women representing the crew and the investors. "If it doesn't, it might be time to consider new leadership."

"Call the vote," the captain said. "It might go better for you this time."

Rakin chuckled. "Oh, not me, sister. I am too old to captain a Trader ship. I just want a nice place to live out my remaining years."

"That's bullshit," Lucy said.

"There's a lot of that going around this table." Rakin leaned back in his chair. "Anything else? I motion we hear the captain's report."

Adem slapped the mat to spread out the impact, but the fall still hurt.

His mother bounced on the balls of her feet. "And that's two for me."

Her throw had twisted Adem's gi half around. He rolled to his feet and tugged it back into position. "Nice one."

"I thought you had me." She swung her arms in circles. "Been a long time since anyone took it to three falls."

Adem winced. "You always say that. Where were you hiding that last throw?"

"I taught you everything you know but held a few moves back for myself. Walk back with me." She nodded to the gym attendant as they passed by. One benefit of being captain was that she no longer had to wipe down the mats after a workout. "How are you holding up?"

Adem massaged his neck. "Nothing a hot shower and a couple of aspirin won't cure."

"Wasn't talking about that. You're getting married. How is that sitting with you?"

"I haven't thought about it much."

"That blonde girl going to be a problem? We can't keep buying off your playmates."

"It's nothing serious."

The captain slung her towel around her neck. There was a sprinkling of gray in her short, dark hair. Otherwise, she looked much as she had for all of Adem's life: strong-featured, stocky, and stronger than any two people on the ship. She spent a lot of time in the captain's chair, but she didn't scrimp on her workouts. The pain in Adem's back and shoulders attested to that.

"That's good to hear," she said. "But you might want to think about having a little less fun. You're meeting your wife in less than four months."

"Did you stop having fun for Dooley?"

"I got very drunk with a man from engineering the night before the wedding. Nearly didn't get up in time." She smiled. "Your wife might not be as flexible as your father."

"I'll think about it."

They paused at the doors to the locker rooms.

"Speaking of Dooley, you should talk to him," she said. "Let your friend fend for herself for one night. Let him give you some advice. You don't have to follow it, but he might say something you can use. He's always been better at this parenting shit than me."

Adem shifted his feet. "That sounds incredibly awkward."

"Do a gig together. Break the ice."

"It's been years since we played for anyone."

"Years for your father, maybe." She reached up and pushed the hair off his forehead. "I see every transmission that comes and goes from the ship. I know about your night job."

Adem looked away. "I'm just fooling around."

"I have all sixty-three videos."

"There might be a few more than that."

"I'll have the nearsmart dig them out of the archive," she said. "I'm going to shower. You find your father. He's not the kind to seek you out, but I know he wants to talk to you."

Abdul "Dooley" Sadiq could usually be found in one of two places on the ship – the med center or Terry's Place, the tiny pub he'd cobbled together out of storage boxes and conduit space at the bottom of the engineering section.

At the beginning of a run, the menu at Terry's included snacks, Dooley's highly experimental cocktails, and whatever cheap beer he could pick up planetside. By trip's end, the selection was often down to meal bars and the rotgut that engine room distillers like Adem produced. Some years before, on a run to Nov Tero, prune juice had been the only mixer to survive until planetfall, and the crew spent the last three weeks of the trip swilling "Moonblasts" and shitting its brains out.

Dooley didn't drink, but he believed that ministering to the crew's emotional needs was just as important as tending to its flesh. When Adem ducked through Terry's low doorway, his father was standing behind the bar talking gently to a crewman hunched on the other side.

"You can keep drinking all you want, Tom, and I'll keep pouring. But there'll be no miracle cures coming out of my pharmacy for your hangover. I'll keep you alive, my friend, but you won't enjoy it." Dooley affected an Irish brogue whenever he tended bar. He waved to Adem over the man's head and leaned in to hear something Tom mumbled. He poured the man another drink. "Tom is suffering from a broken heart," he told Adem. "What can I get for you, son?"

"Just a beer," Adem said.

"It's early for you to be down here."

"Mom just beat me into a paste. Thought I'd come find some painkiller."

"That's why I don't spar with her anymore." Dooley put a frosted glass on the bar and lay a packet of beer next to it. "Got just what you're looking for. It's what all the lowlifes were drinking on Gaul. Tastes like cold piss, and I'm down to my last case."

Adem decanted the watery beer into his glass and winced at the first sip. "I know you can afford to stock this place with better booze."

"But that might make fine fellows like yourself drink more of it, and then where would we be?" Dooley winked. "It's poison, you know. Kills the spirit. Might as well make you feel it die."

"And taste it." Adem put the glass back on the bar, hoping a few minutes of aging would make the next sip more palatable. "I was wondering if you wanted to do a gig with me."

"Nah. It's been years since I've been able to keep up with you." He laughed. "You said it yourself."

"I was seventeen and a horse's ass when I said that." Adem looked away. "I'm sorry I hurt your feelings."

"You were right. You kept practicing, and I didn't." Dooley picked up his bar cloth and wiped up spilled beer from around Adem's glass. "It was a good lesson. I can't always get by on my native talent and charm."

"So, you want to try it? Maybe in a couple of weeks?"

"There are better ways to sow your oats. I've seen that lass you've been squiring around. Seems sweet enough."

"Oddly enough, she likes me mostly for my music."

"Well, it's certainly not for your face." Dooley rubbed his hands together. "Looks too much like mine. It's a good thing you got your mother's hair and eyes. All that darkness makes the girls think you're mysterious instead of just confused."

"Feckless, you used to say."

"I used to say a lot of things. Some of it was important. Most of it wasn't."

"So, will you play with me?"

"Give me a set list and a couple months to practice. I'll put it on the calendar." He pointed to the blank wall behind the bar. "Looks like I have a couple of spots open. Maybe I'll get your lady friend panting after me, too."

"She's not panting. She's actually pretty cool, but—"

"You're nearly a newlywed and can't get too involved." He nodded slowly. "I know the feeling. I had a lover when I left Freedom. I knew it was a bad idea, but there it was."

"Her name was Terry, right? I knew the name had to come from somewhere."

"You think your ma would let me name my bar after an old girlfriend?" Dooley slapped his hands together. "Terry was the name of the dog."

"Since when was your family rich enough to be able to afford a dog?"

"Never was. We had a bunch of them in the Gap, all clones, to keep the weevils away. Little slimy bastards, the weevils were. This big." He held his hands about six inches apart. "They'd climb up on you while you were sleeping and lay eggs in your face. Disgusting. Terry was common property, lived anywhere in the village that she wanted." He grinned. "But she liked me best."

"Asking you this was Mom's idea, but any advice for a soon-to-be husband with an interesting girlfriend?"

Dooley grunted and turned to the small counter behind the bar. "I want you to try something." Adem heard the bustle of a mixed drink being prepared. "It's new."

"Make sure you use my stuff," Adem said. "The booze Tully turns out always tastes like he strained it through one of his socks."

"That's because he does." Dooley turned, drink in hand and placed it on the bar in front of his son.

"I can't believe you keep inflicting these things on us without ever trying them yourself."

"It's haram." Dooley crossed himself. "My sainted mother paid good money to raise me Muslim. I promised her alcohol would never pass my lips."

Haram and halal. Adem's childhood had been full of those words. Asking questions, halal. Defying orders, haram. Picking on younger siblings, haram, unless it was fun to all parties, then it was halal. On Earth the words might have had the force of law, but on the *Hajj* they'd been Dooley's shorthand for how to be a good person.

Adem picked up the drink and sniffed it. "Smells spicy." He took a cautious sip and held it in his mouth. His eyes and nostrils flared, and he swallowed hard. It was hotter than rocket exhaust, and swallowing made it worse. The drink traced a line of fire down the back of his throat. When it hit his stomach, the heat turned to instant nausea.

"What the hell did you give me?"

Dooley chuckled. "Wait for it."

The nausea and shakes subsided quickly and were replaced by a warm glow that seemed to fill Adem's entire body. He felt relaxed and rested.

"Think I should put it on the menu?"

"What the hell is it?" Adem wiped sweat off his face.

"I just invented it. I call it An Arranged Marriage, because that's what it will be like if you're lucky. If not," he picked up his bar cloth again, "it will be hard on both of you. She'll be leaving everything she knows and casting her lot with a bunch of strangers. Worse. Her parents cast it, and there's bound to be some resentment over that. I wouldn't expect to be getting along with her right away. You'll have to win her over."

"Sounds like I have it pretty easy."

"You haven't had much of a life." Dooley's right eyebrow went up. "You've spent what? A year off this ship? And most of that was in dry dock when you were thirteen, and we needed an overhaul. She's been living on a planet that's been growing and changing all along, surrounded by new ideas and new people coming in and out of her life." He polished the bar unnecessarily. "We'll be like dinosaurs to her. Or ghosts, maybe. Your great-grandmother was on one of the last boats off Earth. That was a millennium ago. Ancient history to your bride, but to you it's family. The way we do things up here is going to seem impossibly new and incredibly old at the same time. How's she going to feel when she finds out one of her husband's last sweeties was a boy?"

Adem sputtered. "You can't possibly think she'll be a fundamentalist!"

"Maybe not, but she's been bound to one world and things

change fast down there. What might be okay one decade is frowned upon or forbidden the next. And she hasn't been living in a box all this time. She's a teenager now. Who's to say she hasn't been finding lovers and love of her own? She's likely to have as much baggage as you do by the time she boards."

"I don't have baggage."

"Says you. I think you were sweeter on Sarat than you let on." He hung the bar cloth on the sink and untied his apron. "I have to close and do a shift in the med center. You want another drink?"

Adem eyed his cocktail glass fearfully. "I'm all set."

Dooley came around the bar and handed the apron to Adem. "Take over. Make sure poor Tommy gets back to his cabin."

"You make it seem impossible that any of this is going to work."

"Guess it's too late to run, isn't it?"

HISAKO

Age seventeen

The stillbirth of my fairytale stained my dress crimson
And I will be dragged to the Underworld with it.
Let the Greek tragedy begin
Without comedy or wit.
I am the passive daughter of Mother Nature
Spotted in the fields by a cradle snatcher.
Was it six pomegranate seeds or three?
Will winter fall in my absence,
Or did Demeter forget her empathy?
Now I stand at the altar still as a painted corpse.
The hollow space buried in my ribcage may ache,
Yet I will smile in ivory tulle and champagne silk.
I won't shiver with each breath I take.
My eyes won't fill with glitter and stars like the other girls.
I can't speak any louder,
Nor cry underneath pretty pearls
And Zeus could not be prouder.

I closed the hand-bound book. There was a song in there somewhere,
but fuck proud father figures. Mine was in jail again, hauled in as

part of a random sweep. Wrong place, wrong time, he said. My mother disagreed: wrong place, wrong company. They hadn't talked since they locked him up, so my father sent me a message asking me to take care of his book. He was afraid Mom would trash it. I'd been carrying it around ever since. It was stupid, but it felt like a talisman. If I kept it safe, he'd find his way home.

Johnny took a drag of his cigarette. "It's got to be you, Sako. Maki can't carry a tune in a cargo pod. He's holding us back."

Maki and I had been on-again, off-again for years. He played better when we were on, but there are only so many sacrifices a girl should have to make for her band. Johnny was taller and had more tattoos. His grin was infectious and made parts of me want to smile along. Not my heart though. It was in the contract. I leaned back against his legs. He was sitting on the couch, and I was on the floor in front of him in case he wanted to play with my hair. He said he liked it long. "If I take over the guitar, who is going to play keyboards? You?"

"I could learn." Johnny failed to blow a smoke ring. His name wasn't really Johnny, but he preferred it to Jean-Paul and got touchy if anyone called him that. Johnny was more punk, he said. His parents were loaded and had bought him an apartment on the other side of the crater from them. It was a good place to hang out and practice.

Ramona laughed, making her green mohawk shake. She held out her hand for Johnny's cigarette. "Sako's been playing for years. It would take you at least that long to get as good as we need you to be. Stick with the drums." She puffed on Johnny's cigarette and watched the smoke as it rose to the ceiling.

Smoking was new to me, and I hadn't decided if I liked it yet. My brand was odorless, but Johnny preferred the cheaper, old-fashioned variety. I could taste it on his breath whenever he kissed me, and I wasn't sure if I liked that either. I scratched the corner of my eye, careful not to smudge the heavy eyeliner I'd started wearing last year. I wasn't sure why I bothered to try saving it. I'd have to scrape it all off before I went home, or I'd get an earful from my mother.

Ramona stubbed out the cigarette. "We could go into *La Merde*." The snarl she usually wore tended to look fake, unlike the smile that lit up her face when she wasn't paying attention. "I hear they have some radioactive guitarists down there. I saw a documentary on it."

I'd seen the same documentary. A well-heeled camera team had gone into the squalor to reveal the "Magic of the Square," a place in the center of *La Merde* where the refugee kids went to make art, love, and music. Already one of the bands featured on the documentary had a rich patron and was recording in a studio uptown.

"We'll get shot then stabbed," I said. "Bad idea."

Johnny flexed a well-muscled arm that had seen no work other than the gym or holding a drumstick. "No one's going to mess with us. We're way too badass. I vote we do it."

"We're not even old enough to cross the checkpoint alone."

"Fake IDs," Johnny said. "I know a guy. I can have some for us by next week. I just need a photo and a copy of your biometrics."

"How much?" Ramona said.

Johnny flapped his hand lazily. "I'll take care of it. We'll aim for going in on a Saturday afternoon when it's not so crazy."

"It doesn't work like that," I said. "They either work all week there or they don't work at all. There's no way to predict a quiet time to visit."

"Look who's suddenly an expert," Johnny said. "Have you ever been there? I have. Lots of times."

"Doing what?"

The edge of *La Merde* was now right up against my apartment building, but all I knew of the area was what my parents had told me. My father had been mugged half a dozen times on his way home from his meetings. He might have been dumb about some things, but he always made sure his drinking money was the only thing they could steal off him.

"Parties, mostly," Johnny said. "Crazy ones. No one complains if anything gets broken or killed. I've had a couple of girlfriends out there, too. You'd be shocked if you knew what they'd do for a couple of credits."

Ramona laughed like a stripped gear. "Those weren't girlfriends, honey." She flashed a look at me. "You better have him tested before you get too close to him."

"Do I look diseased to you?" Johnny flexed again. "They were girlfriends. I just helped them out with rent or groceries. Bailed one girl out of jail once. Small shit."

"What happened to them?" I said.

"Stuff," Johnny shrugged. "One died, I think. Just disappeared. Another one got pregnant. She claimed it was mine and wouldn't get rid of it. My parents sued her, then I don't know what happened."

"Probably nothing good, you asshole," Ramona said.

"Wasn't my fault. I offered to sneak her into a clinic up here. Get her breasts enlarged while we were there." He sighed. "She told me to fuck off and die."

"Hey, let's get some practice in. We're a band not a therapy session," I said.

Johnny was an asshole, but that made it easier. I could have loved Maki if he hadn't been such a puppy. With Johnny there was no chance.

He picked up his drumsticks and twirled them, nearly losing them in the process. "So, are we doing the *La Merde* thing?"

"Yeah. I'll get you the information by this weekend. Ramona?"

The tall girl stretched and walked to the mike. "I'm in. But

Johnny better come through with the bail money if this goes bad. I don't want my parents finding out."

Johnny laughed. "Nothing is going to happen when you're with me. They love me down there."

I filled in for Maki on the guitar. I was way better than he was, but it wasn't my first choice. Johnny was a shitty drummer. I caught Ramona's eye after the first song, and we switched our monitors to the output from her reader and played along to the drum machine. During shows, we sometimes cut Johnny's mikes so the audience couldn't hear his playing. He was so rhythm deaf he never noticed. We played through our entire set list twice and broke for the night.

"That was awesome." Johnny wiped sweat off his face with a hand towel. "We should bring all of our shit down to the Square and show those dirty birdies how we do it uptown."

Ramona's eyes widened. There was probably no better way to get us laughed at and chased out than to play with a drummer who couldn't keep time.

"Maybe later," I said. "This is a scouting trip. We're looking for someone good, not showing off."

"Suit yourself. You staying over tonight?"

"My mother would shoot me."

"Is she like two hundred years old or something?" Johnny said. "Tell her you're going to stay with Ramona."

I put my hand on his chest. The sweat on his body was starting to cool so it felt clammy instead of slick. "Tomorrow night, okay? I'll tell her Ramona and I are having a sleepover and come over here." I looked at Ramona for support. "Is that all right?"

She shrugged. "So long as you cover for me when I want to fuck someone."

"No problem." Ramona had never been to my house, and, if I had anything to say about it, she never would. "You ready to go?"

Ramona picked up her bag and coat. "Can we split the cab back? If I go over budget again, my mother is going to ground my account."

I tallied all the money I had in my pocket. I had just enough to make it to midtown where I could grab a shuttle the rest of the way. "Sounds good."

Ramona used her reader to summon a cab. Johnny and I fooled around while we waited. He was a good kisser. He swatted me on the ass as I walked out of his room. "Better see you Friday, Sako. Johnny might get a little restless if he doesn't get a chance to play." He tried to grin it off, but he was serious. He had plenty of money to throw around and could easily get a dozen girls to come back to his grotto with him.

"Wouldn't want that to happen, stud." I stood on tiptoes to kiss him again and grabbed his testicles hard enough to let him know I was serious, too. "You get lonely, I start looking for a new drummer."

His face was still. He knew I could do him a world of hurt with just a little more pressure. "Friday, then," he said.

"Friday." I turned to Ramona who was fighting to keep a straight face. She'd seen me handle guys before. Drummers were plentiful, and, while Johnny was hot, he wasn't so sexy that I was going to put up with a lot of bullshit. "Late Friday. I have a science fair I have to win."

Ramona finally let herself laugh when we were safely in the cab. "I thought he was going to shit himself when you grabbed him like that."

"My band. My rules," I said.

"Are you really going to stay with him Friday night?"

"Probably. It's not like we haven't had sex before."

"When have you had time?"

"We were fooling around on Maki. That's what got him so upset."

"Maki's in love with you."

I lit one of my odorless cigarettes. "I hear that happens."

She threw her head back. "Are you really cool with going into *La Merde* for a talent search?"

"Sure. A lot of kids go down there. It will be like a safari."

"We're hunting wabbits," she said. It was a line from one of the songs she wrote for the band. She'd based it on an ancient cartoon she watched as a kid. It was about this guy with a giant head who wanted to kill and eat a furry. It was probably a sexual thing. Ramona bummed a drag off my cigarette and made a face. "I don't know how you can smoke these."

"Maybe we should work as an all-girl band. Change the name to something better."

"I've been thinking about that. There are way too many dicks in this band. How does The Sandcats sound? It's like people think we're pets, but we're really poisonous."

"I like it."

"How 'bout, if Johnny survives the trip to the Square, we broom him at the first opportunity?"

"Works for me."

Johnny was lucky on Friday, or maybe I was just bored. I don't know. I liked sex. Sure, it could feel good, but there were ways to get that without putting up with someone else. What I liked about it was how vulnerable the guy got when I put my hand on his cock. No matter how much bravado they had before, they turned into little boys afraid I was going to laugh at them. It was a stupid kind of power, but I didn't have so much of it that I wasn't going to enjoy the little I had. Johnny and I fucked and then we watched a movie. I slept in his bed and asked him to sleep on the floor. He was all "I've tamed the she-beast," but he was the one sleeping under a blanket on top of ceramic tiles. I gave him a pillow.

I had a bunch of projects due, so we didn't get together in person during the next week. We had one rehearsal via our readers, which made it easier to ignore Johnny's shitty drumming and met up Saturday afternoon in the commercial district, a couple of blocks from the border.

The commercial district wasn't impressive, no matter how many of my classmates were panting for a job there. It was just a bunch of tall, ugly buildings with unkempt parks crammed in every couple of blocks. There were people sleeping in a few of them. I wondered if we should call security, but Ramona said we should let them sleep. She said they looked peaceful.

We waited on a bench in one of the empty parks until Johnny sauntered up. He was dressed in a dusty-looking black outfit and the ugliest boots I'd ever seen. "You ladies ready?" he said. He winked at me.

I covered a yawn.

"Do you have the passes?" Ramona said.

He patted the pocket of his vest. "Aren't you worried you look a little too nice for this trip?"

"We look normal," Ramona said. "You look like someone from a Fall-of-the-Earth stim."

The material of his vest was so thick it was nearly armor. "This is how they dress in there. I'll blend in."

"Where did you get those boots?" I said. They were gray, and bumpy like they had acne.

He propped one up on the bench so we could get a closer look. "Like them? They're real sandcat. My dad got them for me."

"They're beautiful." Ramona elbowed me in the ribs. "I think I saw some just like them in a museum gift shop."

"Was it the Museum of Bad Ideas? I think I saw them, too."

"Fuck you," Johnny said. "Do you know how much I had to pay for these passes?"

"Let's see them."

Johnny pulled the ID sticks out of his pocket and handed them around. They looked okay to me, but Ramona laughed again. "These cases are at least twenty years old. You think we're all going to pass for our late thirties?"

Johnny flushed. "The guy did say we'd be better off going through with a group."

"This isn't going to work," Ramona said.

"Only way to know is to try. Look," I pointed out a group of young-looking people crossing by the front of the park, "let's go through with them."

We hustled to not quite catch up with the group and spy on their conversation. They were all university students, heading into *La Merde* for a wild time. The border guards waved us through without looking at our IDs, but I saw one guard smirk and say something to his colleague, pointing out Johnny. The man nodded and said something like "ass kicked for sure."

Johnny put his arms around our shoulders and strutted like a pimp. "I told you it was going to be okay. They have everything here… drugs, booze, sex. My brother told me about going to a show and watching this girl having sex with–"

"We're here for the Square and a guitarist. In that order," I said. "Then I'm headed back."

"If you want to stick around after that, it's up to you." Ramona looked back at the checkpoint. "I bet they check IDs more closely going through the other way."

"We'll deal with that when it comes," I said. "Which way to the Square?"

Johnny let go of us and waved vaguely toward the group of college kids. "Follow them. I'll catch up in a minute."

"Where are you going?" Ramona said.

He grinned. "See a guy and get high. Don't worry your pretty little tails. I got this." He stuck his hands in his pockets and legged it down a side street.

"Should we wait?" Ramona said.

I grabbed her arm and hurried after the college kids. "Let's just hope they're going to the Square and not to one of Johnny's sex shows."

We got back to eavesdropping distance again. Unlike Johnny, they were dressed normally. One guy asked about music, and a girl said there'd be plenty of it and advised the guy to avoid eating any food sold on a stick.

"I think we're on the right track," I whispered.

We followed the kids about seven blocks before we started hearing it. It started low, like a bass note, and filled in slowly as we got closer. I started to make out individual shouts and cheers. Finally, we heard laughter as we got within sight of the tall fence that enclosed the Square.

"It doesn't sound so bad," Ramona said. She looked nervous.

According to the documentary, the Square covered four square blocks. A hundred years ago it was supposed to have been midtown housing or office space, I forget. When the refugees started coming in, whatever company had planned the project pulled out, leaving a big fenced-in area. The refugees poked holes in the fence and took over.

We followed the college kids in through one of the gates. They kept going, but Ramona froze in place. "It smells incredible."

Dozens of little carts were set up inside the walls like mobile kitchens. People were queued twenty deep at some of them, talking in half a dozen languages. They were skinny and grimy, but they were laughing harder than I'd ever heard anyone laugh before.

"Do you think that girl was right about not eating anything here?" Ramona was practically drooling.

"They're eating it. Some of it should be okay."

"Did you bring any cash?"

"Let's see what they have."

We wove in and out of the food stalls, squinting to read the menus. Most of the vendors had written them out by hand, the script laughable. Others featured languages I couldn't begin to understand.

"What do you think that means?" I pointed at one stall with a particularly illegible sign.

"It probably says 'rat burgers'." Ramona grabbed my hand. "Come on. Let's go back to the frito stand we passed. At least we know what that is."

No one talked to us as we stood in line, although a couple of little kids tried to pull us into a game of peek-a-boo between their parents' legs. The kids were scrawny, and their clothes weren't much better.

"What do you want, city girls?" the vendor said when it was our turn. His French was strongly accented.

"Alpim frito." Cassava fries, or whatever they were substituting them with. My New Portuguese was really limited, but I had read somewhere you'd have more street cred if you tried to speak the local lingo. He asked me what we wanted on top of the fries, and my vocabulary failed me. I was reduced to pointing and nodding.

We steered clear of the meat sauce because there was no way of telling what it was. The cost of the meal took about a quarter of my cash.

"He charged you at least twice as much as he charged everyone else," Ramona said.

"I can afford it." The line had grown behind us. "I don't think they can."

We sat to eat the fritos, which were delicious by any standard, and resumed our search for music. The Square was really a square within a square. Only the outside edges were used for the perpetual festival. The inside square was a community garden. The gates to the inner greenery were guarded, and the gardens were divided into family-sized plots.

"This was in the documentary," Ramona said, apparently forgetting I'd seen the film, too. "It's like a co-op. They pay for a plot and share responsibility for the water supply and the guards. It's not licensed or anything."

"Do you think the frito guy had a license?"

The next corner of the Square was like an outdoor shopping mall. Everything in it was either used or handmade. Ramona picked through a table of obsolete electronics. She squealed and held up something that looked like a dead baby. "It's a Terry Talker. I had one when I was a kid."

She tugged its arm, and the baby started singing a song about friendship.

"You want?" The woman behind the table was old in a way people in *La Mur* never got. Without money for injections, hormone therapy, and skin transplants, her face had wrinkled into deep brown furrows.

"We're just looking," I said.

"Ask her how much it is," Ramona said.

"You don't want it."

"Ask her."

The old woman gave me a number that would take everything else I had in my pocket.

"Too much. Let's go."

"But I want it," Ramona said.

"You don't have any money, and I don't have enough. Let's find the musicians and do what we came here for."

"Music." The old woman pointed at the singing toy. "You want?"

"We want to hear some live music." I pantomimed playing a guitar. "Music."

She smiled, showing a sunny mixture of missing and dead teeth. "I tell you."

Ramona put down the toy, which immediately stopped singing the stupid song.

The woman looked back and forth between us, still smiling.

"Why is she not telling us?" Ramona said.

"I think she wants money," I said.

"Give her some."

"If we keep walking, we'll find the music. The Square only has four corners."

"She could save us time," Ramona said. "Give her some money. She needs it more than we do."

I handed the woman a few coins, and she tucked them into her pocket. She pointed in the direction I had already planned to go. "That way."

The music was not in the next corner, which was full of ragged tents and ramshackle huts. As soon as we got within sight of the place we were surrounded by children, arms outstretched and begging in a dozen languages. The kids were filthy, and they smelled like they had never taken a bath in their lives.

"It's my worst nightmare," Ramona said. "Do they live here?"

"I think so." The huts and tents were child-sized. "I think they're *illicite*. This is like a camp or something."

"They must have parents somewhere."

"They might be in prison. Refugee births are pretty tightly controlled. Any government aid you get requires sterilization."

"You try to live free you get this." Ramona crossed her arms over her chest to keep her hands away from the kids.

"Please, madam," one girl said. Her hair was matted. Had my parents made different choices, she could have been my little sister.

"What's your name?" I said.

The girl's face lit up like she'd found a treasure in the back of her memories. "Chuchu," she said. "My name is Chuchu."

"What kind of name is that?" Ramona fended off the grasping hand of a little boy.

"It's probably something her mother called her," I said. "It means 'darling' in New Portuguese."

"Can we go?" Ramona said.

I took the smallest coin out of my pocket and pressed it into the little girl's hand. "Get some food. Don't let anyone know you have it."

The coin disappeared like a magic trick.

"Let's go," I said. "I don't have enough to help them all."

"Why would you want to?" Ramona said. "They're like a swarm. They're barely people."

I wanted to punch her. "They're people. They just don't have what you have. It's not their fault."

"It is their parents' fault," she said. "They knew what would happen."

"It's not always a choice." It sounded like something my mother and father would say, and it felt strange coming out of my mouth. "They don't have the options we do."

A few of the kids followed us partway down the next corridor, but they stopped at some point that meant something to them and went back to their little village.

"They weren't in the documentary," Ramona said.

"Putting a bunch of *illicite* on film would be a great way to get the Square raided, don't you think?" I said. "They probably thought of that."

"If the company that owns the land found out they're using all this for free, I bet you they'd try like crazy to come up with a way to charge rent."

"Yeah. Let's hurry up and find a guitarist before it happens."

The walls along the way were filled with stalls of people selling handcrafts of various kinds. Ramona noticed one selling shoes made out of old vehicle seats, and we giggled when we saw a pair that looked exactly like Johnny's survival boots.

We heard the drums first, and then the wail of something that sounded like the world's angriest guitar. The path opened up into the last corner. There was a stage and a rickety sound system that bands seemed to be taking turns on.

The guitarist was a girl about our age backed by a boy on a simple drum kit and a long-haired guy playing bass. Their music sounded like nothing I had ever heard before. It was fast and jangly. Angry and loud. Sloppy but completely under control.

"I think we lucked out," I said.

"You can play better than that."

"Better, maybe. But not like that."

The drummer began an awkward solo, and the girl picked up a bottle of water. She drained it and flung it at the audience. She picked the song back up with a riff that sounded like post-argument sex and screamed into the microphone. She was rail thin, her hair cut into a wedge. She had more tattoos than Johnny.

"I think I just came," Ramona said.

I nodded, utterly entranced by the girl on the stage. She took up all the room and light.

The band played a short set, six songs, no encore, and then started unplugging to make way for the next act.

"Is this the one?" Ramona said.

I was already headed for the stage. "You're pretty good," I said, looking up at the girl.

She looked like she'd been about to smile at the compliment but scowled instead. "You don't belong here. Better go home before someone notices."

"We have a band, and we're looking for a new guitarist." The look on her face told me I was on the wrong track. "Correction, we had a band. It fell apart, and we're building a new one."

"What have you got?"

"Just the two of us." I brought Ramona into the conversation. "I play four or five instruments. Ramona is good on vocals, a little keyboard. Next weekend we're going to put some people together and see how it sounds."

"What do you play?"

Ramona and I rattled off our influences, a lot of Earth stuff and a couple of bands from the asteroid belt.

"Not bad."

"We can get you a visitor's pass," Ramona said. "Pick you up at the border and escort you to my house."

"Worried I might come in and steal something?" She laughed. "Because I will. Anything small enough to fit in my pocket will be going home with me."

"You don't have to steal," Ramona said. "I can—"

I narrowed my eyes. "Steal from us, you might not make it back."

The guitarist grinned. "You might belong here after all. My name is Marjani Conteh. Leave me a pass and the directions at the border. Maybe I'll drop by." She pointed at the two boys packing up her gear. "Leave us all passes. I don't go anywhere without my boys."

"Give me their names." I looked at Ramona. "Will your mother sponsor them all?"

Marjani laughed. "You hear that, boys? We're going to have a rich-bitch sponsor. Our dreams have come true."

Ramona flushed. "She will. At least for a day pass."

"See if you can make it a weekend. We might need it."

We left before the next band's set. Ramona had a curfew and breaking it would not have helped to convince her mother to fork over the sponsorship deposit. We exited back at the food stalls but didn't stop for more fritos.

"That wasn't so bad," Ramona said. "I wonder what all the fuss was about."

Johnny was waiting for us when we came out. "Where the hell have you been?" His voice was high and scared, and the blood on his face told us why. He was being held, nearly held up, by three guys.

"Jesus, Johnny, what happened?" Ramona said. She took a step toward him, but I grabbed her arm.

"Don't," I said. "What do they want, Johnny?"

"Money." His voice was shuddery, his shoulders slumping in defeat. "I told them you had cash. If you give it to them, they'll let us go."

"What will they do if I don't?"

The men around Johnny laughed. "Find out," the smallest rowdy said.

"How much do you want?"

"Just give them everything you have!" Johnny grimaced in pain or fear. He was missing a couple of teeth in the front. An easy fix for his dentist, but it looked like it hurt.

"Okay. Okay." I reached into my pocket for the rest of the coins I had brought along. It wasn't much. One of the boys stepped forward, and I dropped the coins into his hand. He brought them back to show the guy who had spoken.

"Not enough." He punched Johnny in the stomach. Johnny doubled over and threw up on his stupid boots. "You want him, pay some more."

"I don't have more."

The lout hit Johnny in the face with the back of his fist, sending him sprawling. Johnny made a noise like a scared kid and started sniffling.

"Maybe we can make some sort of a deal," I said.

He pulled a knife out. "No deals. Payment or pain."

"Give 'em a break, Carlito." Marjani stepped through the gate with her band. "They're going to make me a music star. Can't do that if you kill their boyfriend." She curled her lip at me. "He yours?"

"Sort of."

She laughed. "See? Take the money. Maybe take his clothes. Then let these fools go the fuck home."

They talked in a language I didn't understand, back and forth for about thirty seconds. Finally, Carlito threw up his hands in disgust. "Get his clothes," he said. "He can keep the boots."

Carlito's friends pulled off Johnny's clothes. He fought feebly, but was quickly stripped down to his undersuit.

Carlito stabbed a finger at Marjani. "You owe me, *irmazhina*."

She blew Carlito a kiss. "Front row tickets to my first show in *La Mur*, baby!"

I yanked Johnny to his feet. "Come on. Let's get this idiot home."

ADEM

Two weeks out of Freedom

"We're definitely slowing down." Lucy contradicted herself somewhat by flipping two more pancakes onto her breakfast plate. "I ran the numbers last night. We've lost .03 percent of c since this time last year."

"Did you tell Mom?"

Lucy answered through a mouthful of pancakes. "She says the you-know-what will solve everything."

Adem rubbed his face. A drop from .9997 of the speed of light to .9994 was huge, even if not an immediate emergency. It was still a long way to nine-tenths c, a speed at which their current loop – Gaul to Imbeleko to Freedom and back to Gaul – would be a ten and a half relative-year slog instead of the ten month jaunt they were currently on schedule for, but the downward trend was concerning.

"How long have we got?" Adem said.

"There's no way to predict. I'd love to be able say we'll lose .03 percent every year of use, but that's not the way it works. At some point the engines are just going to stop working. There's nothing we can do about it."

They'd be lucky if that's how it happened. If the mass-grav system failed first, they'd all die before they knew what was happening. So, maybe that was the lucky way.

"Well, it probably won't happen today, and I need to get to work." Adem rose from the table. "Chef says the burners on his stove are operating at different temperatures. He wants me to calibrate them so they match exactly."

"It's not wise to piss him off. Fly, be free, or we'll all be eating nothing but meal bars for the rest of the trip."

"Are you coming to the gig tonight?"

"Wouldn't miss it."

The job required taking the old stove to pieces and scrubbing every square inch. When Adem got it all back together the chef tested the burners and acknowledged that it was good enough. He promised to make Adem's favorite breakfast – gravy over biscuits – sometime in the next week. Adem chalked the day off as a win and went back to his suite to wash up.

Vee was in his bed when he came out of the shower.

"We said we weren't going to do this anymore," Adem said.

"We said that." She stretched, and the thin sheet slipped down her body. "Things change."

"I have a gig to play in about an hour."

"Ninety minutes. I checked. You'll even have time for another shower if we share."

He pulled the Martin off the wall. "I was going to restring this."

"Don't. You know that will make it sound flat." She got to her knees and grabbed him by the towel he'd wrapped around his waist. "Come here."

Adem sat on the bed next to her. She kissed his neck. "I love how you smell coming out of the shower."

"I smell like soap. You're lucky I wasn't working in waste management today." He'd had to scrub like a madman to get all the cooking grease out from under his fingernails.

She stroked the short hairs at the base of his skull. It was his "spot," maybe the most erogenous of his zones, and it bothered him a little that she knew it. He pulled his head away. "You know, you'll have plenty of money after this trip. You could get off at Gaul, sell your share, and set yourself up nice."

"Worried that I am going to be a problem for you and the new wifey?" She smiled. "I'll go if you do." She put her finger on his mouth before he could say anything. "I'm just kidding. I know you won't leave the ship. But I'm not leaving, either."

"This can't keep happening." Almost unbidden his hand slid down the length of her back. "It's wrong."

"Wrong by what measure?" She reached for the back of his neck again. "She'll be here soon, and I'll find someone else to keep me occupied. Shut up and stop worrying."

Adem barely had time for that second shower, but he made it to Terry's in time for a quick sound check.

"You want one?" Dooley waved a glass at him. It was glowing gently from whatever cocktail he'd created for the evening.

"Just a beer."

Dooley put a glass on the bar and slapped a package of beer beside it. "We're getting short. We'll be down to piss and vinegar in another couple of weeks."

Adem made his thousandth mental note to try his hand at brewing beer. It couldn't be much harder than distilling spirits and might save the crew a few hangovers. "Good thing we'll be making planetfall soon."

"Be real interesting to see what happens after that."

"Depends on whether the Sasakis held up their end," Adem said. "She could be a poet for all we know."

"A poet with a face like a bulldog." Dooley grinned.

"Sounds like a song."

"Write it fast, and you can sing it at the wedding." Dooley nodded toward the door. "Your girlfriend is here."

Vee slipped through the door. She waved to a group of friends and sat down at their table.

"Ex-girlfriend. I called it off."

Lucy came up behind Adem and stole his beer. "Was that before or after you fucked each other's brains out in your suite a few minutes ago?"

"Voyeur," Adem said. "Both. This time it's going to stick."

Lucy pouted. "Where is the fun in that, little brother? I was hoping to bond with my new sister about what a brat you can be."

"I'm sure I'll give her plenty of fodder for that without committing adultery."

"Oh, I'm sure." Lucy flipped the tab off the beer pack and filled the glass. "Oh, was this yours?" She walked off and joined a table of friends.

"And she calls me a brat."

"You are," Dooley said. "But you don't have the market cornered. You ready to go on?"

"Let me check the sound and the recording gear one more time. Pour me another beer, will you?"

The acoustics in the little bar left a lot to be desired, but the audience would help. Nearly everyone who was awake and off shift had packed into Terry's Place for the show and many of those still working would tune in. There weren't many recreation options on a ship the size of the *Hajj*, and the crew seized every opportunity for something new.

Someone at Vee's table chanted, "Spaceman! Spaceman!" and it spread. Adem told the nearsmart to start recording. Dooley handed Adem a glass of beer. They mounted the stools set up on the bar's tiny stage.

Dooley cleared his throat. "You need no introductions, even though it's been a few years since we played together." He forced his accent broader with every syllable. "But for you poor folks who only get to watch this on your wee vid screens, this is the Spaceman." He pointed his thumb at Adem. "And I'm the Spaceman's da."

There wasn't much room in Terry's for dancing, but they did their best. At the end of the first song, Dooley set down his drum and picked up a tin pipe.

"Before we play another one," Dooley said, "I'd like to make a toast." He waved to the woman he'd corralled to serve as bartender. "Give us a drop of that poison you're pouring there."

He held the drink to the light. "This is my first drink in all my fifty-two years of life, and I'm drinking it because we're about to expand this little band of ours by one." He waited for the crowd to settle down. "The truth is my boy Adem here is pregnant."

Adem heard his sister's cackle above the rest.

"Come up here, Auntie Lucy. It's sure to be an ugly baby, but I hope you learn to love it."

Lucy climbed onstage, and Dooley put his arm around her waist. "Adem, your sister and I want to wish you the best of luck. Marriage is a serious business, and you're getting into it for all kinds of wrong reasons. But if anyone can make it work, it's Mr. Fixit." He held up the glass. "To Adem and his missus." Dooley took a single sip and passed the rest to Lucy. "Now let's get back to the party."

Adem switched to hard alcohol midway through the show. They played a twelve song set with two encores then gave the stage over to anyone who wanted to give it a go. Once they'd rested, they went back on stage, and the music continued long into the night.

Waking up was a different story. Adem did not remember leaving the bar. His head was painful and thick, and his tongue seemed to fill his entire mouth. Vee was in the bed next to him, and so was one of the men from her table.

Adem ground the heels of his hands into his eyes. *Good thing I made the bed bigger.*

HISAKO

Age twenty-two

My newly minted master's degree disappeared under a pile of clothes as I emptied my closet onto my narrow bed. Two years living in a geostationary orbit above Versailles City was coming to an end.

"Are you looking forward to moving home?" Britt said.

Britt TerVeer, my extremely well-meaning boyfriend of convenience, sat in my single chair between two boxes. One of the boxes was marked "keep," the other was marked "trash." I had heard the question, but I didn't know how to answer just yet. "What?" I said, both stalling for time and sending him a message that I didn't want to talk about it.

"Are you happy about moving back down to Gaul?" He reached for the printouts I was holding and tugged them from my hands. "What are these?"

"Pictures of my old band."

His eyes widened as he leafed through the stack. "You were in a band with Marjani? How come you never told me about that?"

"It was a long time ago." I rubbed my temples, hoping to prevent the headache building there. Maybe I just needed some water.

"What happened?"

"Grad school. I'm contractually obligated to be an expert in useless things."

Marjani had stolen my band out from under me and went off to make it better than I ever could, but he didn't need to know that story. I still heard from Ramona occasionally. She and Marjani were expecting a baby. I reclaimed the pictures and tossed them in the trash box.

He looked down at them mournfully "You could probably get some money for those. She's getting pretty famous."

"Be my guest." I didn't wait to see if he picked them up. The next pile of crap beckoned. It was sort of amazing how much I'd accumulated in the little studio apartment. Mostly I'd been using it as a place to sleep between classes and time in the physics lab. Weird little souvenirs like my android finger went into the trash box; my growing collection of kitchen gadgets were diverted to "keep." After a moment's thought I moved the finger to "keep," too.

"What's this?" Britt held up a hand-bound book from my bedside. It had been there for two years, and he'd never expressed interest in it before.

"It was my father's."

Years of breathing silica in the oxygen works caught up with him at the end of my junior year, and he had died gasping. He'd insisted that I focus on my studies rather than come home from my semester in New Berlin to see him. I did not argue long or hard. My mother sent the book to me about a week after his cremation.

"It's in English," he said, thumbing through the slim volume. "I learned it for my thesis." He read to me.

I am the marionette
The doll all dressed in white
A blank smile drawn on a china face
Limbs posed perfectly at the altar
Thank you, Father

Your support has yet to falter
You praise my blank stare
Speak as I move red lips
I could never lie well
But I promise not to stutter.

"My father was nuts about poetry. He used to read it to me from that book when I was a kid."

"He sounds like a romantic." He flipped more pages in the book.

"It got him two years in prison. Not the poetry," I added, noting the question on his face, "the romanticism. He started hanging out with the revolutionary wackos in *La Merde* and ranting about how some of the colonies had been designed to fail in order to create a slave class."

"That's not such a radical theory. My brother wrote his dissertation on it."

"Your brother is a EuroD academic. He can afford to believe that."

"Now who's the conspiracy theorist?" He adjusted the cuffs of his tailored shirt. "We're not all bad. Some of us try to help."

Britt was a member of any number of do-good groups that provided aid to refugees, and he'd spent a semester teaching in *La Merde* and rebuilding homes after a sandstorm nearly buried the place a few years ago. He was handsome, healthy, tall, and came from a long line of EuroD wealth. He'd spent the six months living in his family's flat on Versailles Station to "gain perspective."

Britt slung his arm over the back of the chair. "You should spend the summer with me. My family has a private dome halfway between the cities. It's a little rough, but it's comfortable. It's a great place to relax, maybe fool around with your music. I know you haven't been playing much."

I avoided looking at the pile of instruments near the door. I hadn't spent more than a couple of hours on any of them since the beginning of the semester. I'd had the fortune to get the university's mad professor as my thesis adviser and did two years of hard labor trying to recreate the technology the UA used to manipulate gravity waves. We failed completely, but we shared authorship of a paper about it. "I need to go home. I haven't seen my mother since my father died."

"Spend a couple weeks with me, then." The smile on his face was heartbreaking. He thought he was in love with me.

My eyes rolled against my will. "I'm leaving the planet in two years, and I probably won't be coming back until you're in your fifties. There's no future for us, Britt."

His smile faded. Whatever flavor I delivered the reminder in, and I'd done it enough to serve it in several different ways, it always had that effect. But Britt TerVeer was nothing if not an optimist. He believed a little bit just might be enough, and his smile fought its way back to the surface. "That doesn't mean we can't hang out. Might help you get your head together between here and there. Or there and somewhere else if you want to see your mother first."

It was tempting. I couldn't imagine it would be easy living with my mother again. The shabby little apartment would echo with my father. "I'll think about it."

He picked up the poetry book again and started making scans of it with his reader. "Do you mind? Maybe I can use some of them in my thesis. Do you know anything about where it's from?"

"The man who gave it to my father used to be a teacher in *La Mur*, but he was living in *La Merde* for some reason. The poems were written by one of his students."

"Do you know his name?"

"It was French."

"A project will keep my parents off my back about getting a

summer job." He also scanned the picture stored inside the book and put the little volume in the "keep" box. He helped me finish packing, and I had sex with him to say "goodbye and thank you" and "maybe, but probably not." It seemed to satisfy him, and he was wearing a different sort of smile when he dropped me off at the top of the elevator.

I bought my ticket down and took a walk. The first four months I'd lived on Versailles Station had felt claustrophobic, but now it was almost home. The population was a mix of EuroD wealthy, students, and station maintenance workers. I stopped for a coffee at my favorite shop and visited the local parks and sculpture gardens. It didn't take long. Versailles Station had started life as a pair of evacuation ships parked above the city. Over time, thirteen more ships had been added to the structure. Retired Trader vessels mostly, although one of Gaul's battleships had joined the mix three hundred years before I was born. The sensitive areas had been sealed off, the weapons taken elsewhere, and the ship's rooms and hallways converted into luxury apartments.

The descent to Versailles City took two days, and I was stuck at the bottom for another six hours because a shootout had locked down the cabs and trolley service. When the smoke cleared, an armored taxi with blacked-out windows whisked me away. The driver asked me if I was serious about getting out at the address I supplied and sped away when I told her – twice – that I was.

A cluster of shacks and humpies had sprung up around the apartment building, narrowing the street to a single lane. I pushed through a crowd of beggars to get to the door. The lift was out of order, and I climbed through a family of six that had taken up residence in the second-floor stairwell.

My mother opened the door of the apartment in her work uniform.

"You look good," she said.

I don't know what she saw, but I found myself wondering when my beautiful mother had been replaced by a middle-aged woman. There had never been enough of her to thicken, but her body had solidified, almost like a brick in the efficient uniform. Her hair was cropped short, and grief or weariness had etched lines in her face.

"I have to go into work because of the attack," she said. "I made some dinner for you. It's in the kitchen. If you get up early, we can have breakfast together."

Her brusque energy felt like spurs rubbing against my fatigue. "I'm so tired I'll probably go right to sleep," I said.

"We kept your room as you were, not how you are now, but it's clean. I have to go. I've already lost money for being late."

I blinked, and she was gone, leaving only displaced air in her wake. The tidy little apartment was achingly familiar, but it no longer felt like home. I felt like a ghost, present but unable to affect my surroundings. My father's armchair beckoned. He'd plunked it in the corner when I was a kid, mended a few damaged spots with tape, and dubbed it his reading chair. Somehow we both fit into it, and we read together. Sometimes him to me and other times me to him. It had been retaped several times, but it was still the most comfortable thing in the house. I sank into it and almost felt his arms around me again.

On a packing crate beside the chair was a family photo taken for my fifteenth birthday. My mother had saved up to have it taken by a professional. She had wanted to throw me a party, too. She must have understood why I refused because after that initial flash of hurt in her eyes, she hadn't asked again. In the photo, my parents were dressed in their best, and I was exhibiting the first stages of my asteroid-punk phase. They were smiling, and I was wearing what passed for a pleasant smirk. My mother and I had two arguments on the way to the photo shoot and one knock-down, drag-out row in the studio. My father and the photographer sat and drank from my father's flask while my mother and I fought over whether the photo I was now considering would ever exist. I had not cared about the photo as much as I wanted to deny my mother a victory. She claimed the win in the end but not until making promises and concessions that I spent the next three years making sure she kept to the letter.

"Little bitch." Past Hisako didn't care or was beyond listening to anything I had to say.

I put the photo back down on the crate and stretched out in the chair. It reminded me so strongly of my father that I wondered if my mother didn't come home from work every day just to be held by it. In my earliest memories, my parents had been silly, almost giddy, around each other. I couldn't remember when they'd lost that.

My reader pinged, and I used my mother's cheap entertainment system to access the message instead of getting up. Britt's face smiled at me from the screen. "I translated one of the poems," Britt said. "I got home and didn't have anything else to do." He displayed the stanzas on the screen as he read it aloud in French.

I've wondered what it's like to fall in love.
Is it like gliding through clouds of cotton?
Or tumbling down a hill of thorns?

I want to know what it's like to make love.
Is it magical and romantic?
Is it savage and violent?

I want to know what it's like to have heartbreak.
Do you cry in anguish then forget?
Or do you hide what you feel and always remember?

I want to know what it's like to fall in love.
Will my heart race when I see him?
Will butterflies shoot from my mouth when he touches me?

I want to know what it's like to be loved.
Is it when he will bring me gifts of gold?
Is it when he will kiss me with the gentleness of a feather?
Is it when he cries out for me when I am away?

What is it like to love?
To feel loved?
I don't know.

"Teenagers, right?" He grinned. "I already have a lead on the writer."
He smothered a yawn. "I'm out. Get some sleep, Sako."

He looked like he wanted to say more – maybe "I love you" or "I
miss you" or "Thanks for the fuck" – but thought better of it. The
screen flickered to black, and I was grateful. I didn't want anyone to
love me. I pulled a blanket off the back of the chair and wrapped it
around me.

What is it like to love? To feel loved?

"A little on the nose, don't you think? Wonder why you picked
that one to translate."

My mother's entertainment system wasn't expensive enough to
respond. I closed my eyes and let the past few days of papers and
goodbyes and packing push me into sleep.

Some hours later, I woke up with a sharp pain in my neck and
my mother standing over me. She looked gray and tired. Her face
was hard.

"Your father adored you," she said.

My neck popped. It seemed impossible that I'd slept through her entire shift. "I loved him. He was a lovable man."

"And a fool." Her mouth tightened. "Even before you were born, he loved you. Before you were even a soul. He would have been happy to live in the worst part of the city to keep you."

I crossed my arms. "And you wouldn't have?"

"If it had come to that, maybe." Her jaw tightened. "Look at you. Clean. Healthy. Educated. You've never known hunger."

"I've been to *La Merde*, Mom. It's not that bad."

"You've been to the Square. As a tourist. That's like going to the air ballet on Nov Tero and saying you understand the entire planet." She loosened her uniform collar. "You'll never have to know real want, and that helps me sleep at night in spite of everything. Did you eat?"

It was an old fight, and I wasn't going to let her out of it so quickly. Not when I knew the next attack so well it was almost a reflex. "Your peace of mind comes at a cost."

Her reflexes were pretty good, too. "Two years," her face flushed. "If you don't want to stay married after that, the contract is void. Two years of your life in exchange for everything you have. You won the lottery before you were even born!"

My blood rushed. I only ever fought with my mother, maybe only really felt alive when we were at each other's throats. It was the only passion the contract had allowed. "I didn't buy the ticket! You don't think that I might have liked some kind of say into where I ended up?"

"The only choice I made in this life was to keep you." My mother's voice shook. "Everything before that was chance. Everything after that was governed by our efforts to give you the best life possible. Don't you understand that?"

I did. Mentally, I agreed with everything she was saying, but emotionally I still couldn't shake the unfairness of it all. She had chosen my father. Out of necessity and geography maybe, but she had made a choice. I couldn't choose anyone. I didn't pick Adem Sadiq any more than I had decided to be good at science and music.

"There's more, isn't there?" I said. "You've never told me the truth. Am I a splice? Did you have me hacked to fit the terms of the contract?"

"It was just a tweak." She avoided my eyes. "We took you up to the station for it. It didn't change who you were, just what you might be good at."

"Do you know what that could have done to me? What it still could?" Cancer. Lowered life expectancy. Mutation. Every health teacher I'd ever had swam into my head and shook a finger at me. It didn't even work! The tests showed I was only a near-genius.

"We were careful. It wasn't a hack job. Every cent we had went to the genegineer. Your father was on pins and needles the entire time I was pregnant. He cried so hard when you came out pink and perfect."

"You didn't leave anything to chance, did you?" My teeth ground together. "You gave birth to your perfect little cash cow and sold her off as soon as you could."

"How many times are we going to rehash this?" she said. "We gave you the best chance at a good life that we could. Maybe you'll always hate us for it. But maybe you'll realize that we gave you options that you never would have had otherwise." She rubbed her face. "I'm tired. I worked ten hours while you mooned around and slept. I'm going to get up in a few hours and do it again. What are you going to do?"

"I'm leaving." I picked up my reader to send a message. A few weeks in a private dome sounded perfect. "Thanks to you, Mom, I have options."

ADEM

Gaul, Sept 29, 3260

The *Hajj* reached out an electronic hand to the Gaul worldnet and began to download information. The ship's nearsmart sifted restlessly through twenty-four years of magazine articles, legal briefs, vid news programs, scholarly journals, and messages.

Adem was only interested in one thing.

Lucy put her hand on his shoulder. "If it's a vid, and she's naked, I want to see."

Adem ran the search again. "She didn't send anything. There's only a message from her mother." He opened it. "It's instructions for the wedding."

His bride was going to come aboard in less than a week, and Adem still had no sense of who he was marrying.

"Did you send something to her?" Lucy said.

"I didn't know what to say." Adem's knuckles were turning white on the communications console.

"How about you start with, 'I'm sorry. I'm an idiot. I should have worked out what to say a long time ago'?"

"I have no idea who she is." Adem read his future mother-in-law's message again to see if he had missed anything. "At least she has my picture and profile."

"She's had that since before she was born. Send her a note to remind her that she's not marrying some dirty old man."

"I'll do it when I get off shift. She doesn't even know we're in the system, yet."

"I want to see it before you send it out," Lucy said.

"Naturally," he lied. "What should I do with these wedding instructions?"

"Send them to Mother. Her partners on Gaul will take care of everything. Your job is to make sure your sweetie sticks around long enough to give me some nieces and nephews."

"Mom wants this woman for what she knows, not for her uterus."

"That's just her money talking," Lucy said. "What she really wants is for her baby boy to be happy and fill this old ship with kids."

Adem laughed. "Mom hates kids. Remember how she kept threatening to leave us on Freedom until we were twenty-five and worth talking to? Sometimes I think Dooley is the only reason we're still alive."

"She just doesn't like being nagged. She'll love having grandkids. She'll take all of the fun parts and leave you with the shit work."

Adem looked up at the view screen. Gaul was little more than a dirty point of light. "It doesn't bode well that she didn't send me anything, does it?"

"Maybe she saw one of your Spaceman vids."

Adem responded with the rudest gesture he knew, unmistakable in any of the languages spoken aboard ship. Lucy laughed. "She's the one who has to give up her entire world. Show her there's something here to replace it. Play her a song. She'll probably think it's adorable."

Adem tried to rush through his to-do list, but a tricky loading-arm repair tripped him up. He could have put it off – they wouldn't be docking for a few weeks – but he wanted some wiggle-room in case his welds didn't hold. It was late evening before he scrubbed his hands, grabbed a sandwich from the cafeteria, and sat down with his guitar.

He ran through a few songs he thought his fiancée might like and realized they were the same tunes Vee asked him to play. He'd steered clear of her the last few weeks, but she had made it clear that she was up for a sleepover anytime.

An icon flashed on his reader. The nearsmart had found a couple of new bands that matched his interests. The first one was an anti-folk group that had formed on one of Gaul's small moons. He listened to a few cuts: catchy but derivative. The second band was an all-girl proto-punk four-piece called The Sandcats. It was fronted by the most passionate guitar player he'd ever heard. She could make a song crawl in submission and rage like a beast in the same measure.

Adem directed the nearsmart to dig up information on the band's origins and lost himself in history and music. A year before The Sandcats found its patron, there'd been a roster change. Before that it had been a five-piece, and the second guitarist had a weird classical flair that he liked. Her playing softened the band's sound while making it sarcastic and subversive. The anger was still there, but it was more of a mocking smirk than a snarl. The guitarist had quit the band under a cloud and disappeared from the music scene.

Adem rubbed at the stubble on his face. His legs were numb from inactivity. He'd spent hours listening to The Sandcats and was no closer to sending a message than he had been when he'd left the bridge that morning.

He cleared his throat and ran his hand through his hair, which was a spiky mess from the work day and the hours spent listening to music. He told the nearsmart to start recording.

"Hello. I'm Adem." He looked right and left for something intelligent to say. "I'm looking forward to meeting you. I hope you like music. I play sometimes with my father, but he's only interested in a couple of different styles. Earth Primitive, mostly. It's fun but…" He looked down. The guitar was a dead thing in his lap. "Never mind. It will be good to see you. I hope you'll be happy here, and I will try to be a good husband. I'm pretty easy to live with. I hope you're interested in meeting me." He sighed. "I guess that's it. I'm going to send this now. See you soon."

He saved the recording before he lost courage and sent it to Hadiya Sasaki, the only contact he had. At this distance, she'd get it in an hour or so, but whether it would be her daytime or nighttime he didn't know. He could ask the nearsmart to look it up for him but decided it probably didn't matter.

Adem hung up his guitar and collapsed on the bed. He dreamed about The Sandcats. Marjani asked him to come up on stage to jam, but when he got there, he realized his guitar had no strings. "Play, Spaceman! Play!" the audience chanted while he stood there helpless. Adem stirred uneasily in his sleep but didn't wake up.

Lucy caught up with him at breakfast. He had opened his eyes to a splitting headache, and his joints hurt from lack of sleep. He propped his elbows on the table and rested his head in his hands.

"You look like shit, little brother. Did you go out drinking without me?"

"I worked late," he mumbled. "Then I was listening to a new band and lost track of the time."

"What did you play for your sweetie?"

"Nothing. I just talked. I can't remember what I said. It was pretty late when I sent it."

"You better hope you looked better than you do now, or she's going to think she's marrying a Bliss junkie."

Adem filled his mouth with eggs so he wouldn't be expected to respond.

"Have you looked at the guidelines for the ceremony?"

The eggs turned to dust in Adem's mouth. "Do I have to learn lines or something?"

"Nothing. The matchmaker will conduct the ceremony. No human sacrifice. No invocation of god. Not even a toast. You'd think she's not looking forward to getting married or something."

"Can you blame her?" Adem said.

"Come on, it's an adventure. A couple of years in space, a pocket full of money." She drained her juice glass. "Besides, you're not bad to look at, and Vee says you're decent in the sack. What's not to look forward to?"

"It's not funny. I thought she'd at least give this a chance."

"I'd throw a party or something for you two, but Mother probably already has one in the works. She's not going to let her baby go quietly into married bliss. You'll have a formal presentation of gifts and a shower of coins next thing you know."

"I don't want that," Adem said. "If she doesn't want that, I don't."

"Tell that to the captain. And you'd better tell her quick. She scheduled a call for," she closed her eyes to check the ship's time, "right about now."

Adem shoveled the rest of his breakfast into his mouth and ran for the spine. He resisted using the emergency boost to get to the bridge faster only because he knew he'd be the one making repairs to the lift. He nearly tripped and fell through the bridge doorway in his haste. "Don't change the wedding!"

"Why would I do something like that?" Adem's mother pointed to the screen where the image of a woman in a severe uniform was buffering. "I'm talking to Hadiya right now. There's a fifteen-minute delay so she has yet to receive proof that you're ridiculous."

"I thought…"

"That I would try to alter the ceremony? If the bride wants to keep it simple, there's nothing I would do to change that. However, Hadiya and I are talking about the reception, which is up to the parents to plan. And I don't believe we need your help." She nodded at the screen where the image was still buffering. "Give your regards to the mother of the bride then go."

Adem offered a formal bow to the screen. "Good day, Mother. It will be nice to meet you. I'm going back to work now."

Adem took the lift to the engineering section, his face burning. He checked his to-do list and got caught flat-footed by a message from Lucy. *Got you again, little brother.*

The teasing didn't diminish much over the next few weeks, but Lucy volunteered to come down the elevator with him and serve as Adem's witness. She insisted on taking a cab to the matchmaker's office rather than walk as Adem would have preferred. "We don't need you to get broody before you meet your new wife," she said. "By the time we got to the matchmaker your pockets would be empty and your mood soured for the rest of the day."

Adem didn't protest, and he let Lucy darken the windows. He mostly succeeded in not thinking about the boy he'd met the last time he was on Gaul. The boy would be close to thirty years old now or dead. "I feel like a stone skipping over the water," Adem said.

"If that's your way of saying you're excited and nervous, welcome to the club," Lucy said. "Mom says I have to help your lady acclimatize to the ship's culture. What if she's a handful? All you have to do is sleep with her."

In minutes they were parked outside the office building Adem remembered from his last trip. The sidewalk outside was littered with trash and the pavement riddled with cracks. Down the street, the little green park had become a campsite filled with lean-tos and tents, the statue broken off at the knees. The matchmaker's building was closed. Adem checked his reader. "She's moved further out," he said. They got back in the cab and rode for several more minutes before stopping in a better district.

"How do I look?" Adem said.

"Like you cut your own hair," Lucy said, "but I suppose you don't want to try to fool the poor girl into thinking you're a stim star."

Adem tugged at his collar. The suit he'd found waiting for him at the bottom of the elevator was stiff and uncomfortable. He wasn't sure he'd gotten all of it on correctly, and Lucy had been no help. She'd watched him dress, not bothering to smother her laughter.

"I've never even seen this color before," Adem said. "How does it look?"

"Watch her face when you walk in. If she looks horrified, Mother made a bad choice."

Madam Toulouse met them in her office. She looked older, but not distressingly so. She'd settled into herself rather than aging. She patted Adem's arm familiarly. "It's good to see you again. It's not often that I get to see this part."

"Is she here?" Adem said.

"Right inside. Is this your mother?" She smiled at Lucy.

"Younger sister." Lucy frowned. "My mother is probably yelling at everybody at the reception venue."

Madam Toulouse lost a few degrees of unflappability. "Thank you for serving as a witness."

The matchmaker led them down a short hallway. The door slid open on a medium-sized room with chairs lined up inside. "It's a little ad hoc," the matchmaker said. "We don't do enough of these to make it worth maintaining a proper chapel."

Adem was barely listening. Two women were sitting in the front row with an empty seat between them. Hadiya Sasaki had aged in a way that the matchmaker had not. Life had worn at her, and she had grown more solid in response. Adem bowed. "Mrs Sasaki, it is good to see you again." His Turkish was poor, but he'd been practicing the phrase all the way down the elevator so he wouldn't mangle it too badly.

Mrs Sasaki answered in Trader Esperanto. "I am no longer the uneducated girl you met all those years ago, Mr Sadiq. Is this your sister?"

While they introduced themselves, Adem almost absently let his eyes drift to the other woman. She was maybe a meter and a half tall, with a long face and strong nose. Her skin was a little lighter than her mother's. She wore a fitted red dress, and her dark hair was up in a bun. Adem tugged his collar. It felt like it had tightened, but he'd given it no such instructions.

"I sent you a message…" Adem ran out of vocabulary.

"I don't know much Turkish," the woman said. "I speak French, New Portuguese, and a little German. I am also, per the terms of our contract, fluent in Trader Esperanto."

Adem wrung his hands. "How are you? Who are you?"

"You'll have your whole life to figure that out." Madam Toulouse took his arm. "Adem Sadiq, this is Hisako Sasaki. Shall we begin?"

HISAKO

Age twenty-four

The matchmaker led us through the vows in French. I spoke at my cues; Adem spoke at his. Somewhere, the last payment slid into my mother's savings account. She had offered it to me as a wedding present, but I refused so she'd have enough money, provided she kept working until she retired at eighty, to keep her little apartment, although I expected *La Merde* to claim it long before then. All her neighbors who could would move further out, and my mother would find herself among people she believed she'd escaped before I was born.

The matchmaker hugged everyone at the end of the ceremony. The fuzzy tang of her perfume made me want to sneeze. There was more hugging and handshaking, but I'm not sure who was doing what to whom. I felt like I'd had a stroke. My arms were numb, and the smile on my face threatened to melt without constant support. It was exhausting.

Adem sort of loomed over everything, swaying back and forth slightly. He looked younger than I'd expected. He took a position slightly behind his sister and stayed there like it was an assignment. My mother left early for the reception, and Lucy summoned a cab for the rest of us.

"How did your dissertation go?" she asked me once we'd settled into the seats. She was in her early thirties, pretty, and spoke good French. I'd have bet she had lived on Gaul for at least part of her life.

"There was some talk of publishing it. We'll see. It really didn't come to much." UA physics and engineering was more of a parlor trick than an actual discipline, something for idle EuroD to drink coffee over and speculate about. *However did those crazy Americans do it?*

"Have you ever been off-planet?" Lucy said.

I rubbed my forehead like a punch-drunk boxer. It felt cloudy in there. Too much, too fast. "I lived on the space station for a couple of years and went out to the asteroid belt twice for research. I don't expect ship life to be much different."

"When everything works right it's not. One fault in mass-grav though…" Lucy faked a shudder. "But that won't happen. It's a good ship. Old, like all Trader ships. But she's sound."

"Have you spent your entire life on board?"

"I spent about a dozen years on Versailles Station to study navigation and get fitted with these." She slid her headscarf aside so I could see the link ports installed in her scalp.

"What's it like being linked to the nearsmart?"

"Sometimes it's pretty boring. Other times, it's better than sex." She grinned. "You should try it."

"I haven't had the nanosurgery."

She slipped the scarf back in place. "The link makes it a lot easier and quicker, but I can show you how to use my mother's old rig. It's almost as good." She frowned. "Well, it's not bad." She kicked her brother in the ankle. "Adem, talk to Hisako. Prove to her that she hasn't married a goon."

Adem flushed. "It was a nice ceremony."

"Was it?" Adem and I had held hands through part of it, and the physical contact failed to open previously undiscovered channels of agape and eros. "It went by so fast I think I missed most of it," I exhibited the ring on my left hand, the key to my two-share wedding gift and the deeds that listed me as part owner of an ancient starship, "but it looks like it worked."

Lucy patted my arm. "I apologize for my little brother. He doesn't get off the ship much, and he is apparently afraid of strangers."

Adem squared his shoulders. "Not true. I get off ship every planetfall."

"Doesn't count," she said. "You go down and take a walk and moan about how much things have changed. Then you come back to the ship, and you're moody for weeks."

"Where do you walk?" I said.

"Depends on the planet," Adem said. "Mostly just from the elevator to somewhere else I need to go. The refugee areas have kind of grown up along the route I take here."

"It's like cancer," Lucy said. "I was on the station when they really started to grow. Before that the EuroD kept a tight rein on it. Lots of low-income housing developments spiraling in from midtown."

"They're just trying to make a home." Adem fought with his collar like it was trying to strangle him. "It's happening on every planet that accepts refugees. Nov Tero. Freedom. Gaul. They just call it by different names."

"Why do you walk?" I said.

"I've seen a couple of centuries of this planet's history first-hand. That's a lot of change over time. I've met people who don't exist anymore, people who no one else remembers." He let go of his collar, and it arranged itself back into its original position. "I guess I'm bearing witness."

"Which is why he is always in a bad mood," Lucy said. "If you ever lose track of him, let me know. I will point out all of his little hiding places. You're sure to find him in one of them, moping and playing his guitar."

The conversation hit a lull, and my head started spinning again. If I kept everyone talking, I wouldn't have time to think. Lucy had just said something about Adem's guitar, so… "I was in a couple of bands when I was a kid."

Adem brightened. "What did you play?"

"Punk-classical fusion. Then proto-punk. I gave it up when I got serious about my studies."

"Science makes the worlds go round," Lucy said. "I have a couple of advanced-science degrees. Adem has one in aerospace engineering."

"And one in Earth History," he said. "Mom has a couple of doctorates. She gets them for fun."

"Life can get a little dull out there," Lucy said. "If you're not working, you might as well be learning something. The classes are run by the nearsmart, so they might not be as good as you're used to, but they're all certified."

"I just got out of school," I said. "I don't know that I'm in a big rush to go back in."

"Of course not," Lucy said, "but it's an option. You're going from large to small pretty quickly. Ship life can be limited, but it's not prison. We even have a pool. Two, if you count the leak Adem still hasn't found."

"It's not that big a leak," Adem said. "Maybe twenty-five gallons so far. Every ship has a leak or two."

The cab pulled up to a building uptown. Lucy put her ID stick into the pay slot. "My treat. I programmed it to take the long route so the Moms had some extra time to set things up."

We entered the building and walked down a long hallway. Lucy slid open a door with a flourish. "Welcome to your party, little sister," she kissed me on the cheek. "Come on in and meet the family."

A small crowd greeted us on the other side, clapping and smiling. My mother was in the front with one of her sisters. Most of the others were strangers: Adem's family – my family now – and crew from the *Hajj*. Someone put a drink in my hand.

"Hey, Sako." A tall man in worn clothes clinked drinks with me. I blinked. He'd put on about fifty pounds, but it was definitely Johnny. He waggled his eyebrows. "Your mom invited me."

I had never let my mother meet my friends. "How did–?"

"She must have gone through your contacts."

My stomach clenched. If that was so, there was no telling who was going to come crawling out of my past. Now that I knew what to look for, a few of the guests' faces started to look chillingly familiar.

"I know we haven't talked in a while." Johnny's skin looked waxy and damp. "But your mom said there would be food and an open bar."

I forced a smile. "What have you been up to?"

"Nothing really. I got into some trouble a few years ago. My dad pretty much cut me off after that. He still pays for my flat, but that's about it." He drained his glass. "Hey, is the bar free the whole time?"

"No idea. I had nothing to do with this. Are you still doing music?"

"Films mostly. I don't make them, but I let them use my place to make pornos. Sometimes I–"

I cleared my throat. "This is Lucy Sadiq and this… this is my husband, Adem."

Lucy said something polite, and Adem stuck his hand out. "Pleased to meet you," he said. "Didn't catch the name."

Johnny gripped Adem's hand listlessly. "Sako and I used to hang out. Hey, do you know where the bathroom is? I need to piss."

"We just got here," Adem said.

"I'll ask someone else." Johnny clutched his crotch and stalked away.

"Interesting," Lucy said. "I see this party is going to be a lot more amusing for me than it will be for you." She looped an arm around my waist. "Let's introduce you to the captain."

Adem made a sound that rode the border between acceptance and panic and trailed after us as Lucy led me toward a short woman who looked like she could break me over her knee. "Mother," Lucy said, "this is your new daughter, Hisako Sasaki. Hisako, this is the captain."

The woman took my hands and stood on tiptoe to kiss me on both cheeks. Her smile made her stern little face beautiful. "Call me Maneera when we're not on duty. Welcome to the family."

I offered her the formal bow from my grade-school etiquette lessons. "It is an honor. Thank you for my life and education."

"This is awkward, I know," the captain said. "But beginnings always are. I'm glad we could help your family out. Hopefully, you won't find life with us to be too much of a burden."

I felt a hand on the small of my back. "Don't mind my daughter, Maneera. She takes a little while to warm up." My mother's dress uniform flattered her while still making her look like a martinet.

"I have some thoughts about your guest list, Mom," I said. "I keep wondering what new horror is going to appear out of the crowd."

My mother shrugged. "We worked with what we had. I asked you to make a list, but you said you were too busy. I used a parental override into one of your old readers." She gestured to the guests milling around the room. "This is what you get."

"I haven't seen some of these people since grade school."

"Then I am sure you have a lot to catch up on," the captain said. "Adem, don't just stand there. Go get your mothers a drink."

"I'll have one, too, little brother," Lucy said.

Adem just about looked at me. "Hisako?"

Getting drunk seemed like the best defense. I agreed and watched him thread his way to the bar.

"Is he all right?" the captain said. "He's acting like someone we just unfroze."

"He's just being Adem," Lucy said. "It takes him a while to adjust to new things. He's like a cat."

"Do you have one?" I said. The Sadiq family seemed to have ridiculous amounts of money. Surely they could afford a real cat.

"My grandmother did." Lucy smiled. "It died when I was a kid. I always wanted another one, but Dooley said he didn't want all that hair in the air filters. Do you have one?"

"I had a sandcat for a while. He got eaten."

"Animal?"

"Neighbor."

We chatted. Adem was taking a long time with the drinks. I had visions of him being regaled with stories by Johnny and Maki and all the other regrets and bad decisions my mother had so thoughtfully invited to my wedding reception.

"Did you have a good summer?" my mother said. "I haven't seen much of you since you graduated."

"Good enough. Dr Martineau helped me revise my dissertation for publication."

Francis Martineau had said a lot of things over the summer, mostly when we were both naked in his tiny apartment. He had *La Mur* tastes and a midtown budget. Dulled by cognac and afterglow, he'd once offered to buy out my contract with the Sadiqs but never mentioned it again after I told him how much it would cost.

"Did I hear my name?" Francis swept past me and bowed to my mother. "There is no doubt it will be published. It is only a question of where and when. Lovely party, Mrs Sasaki. Thank you so much for the invitation."

I glared at him. "You didn't tell me you'd be here." He'd had plenty of opportunity, including that morning when I crawled over him to get to the shower.

He spread a paternal smile across his face. "I wouldn't have missed this for the world." He took the captain's hand. "You are running away with one of my best students. She could have made a good living in research."

The captain smiled. "She still can. What better place to research physics than onboard a starship?"

"Point taken. Maybe I'll sign on, too." He tried a leer on Lucy. "Are you married? Would you like to be?"

"Silly boy." She smothered a yawn. "Buy a share, and you can sign on as crew. We can have you back here in twenty or thirty years."

Adem returned with the drinks. We hadn't told him what we wanted, but he'd made good choices. He greeted Francis and stuck his hand out. "Adem."

Francis shook the offered hand. "I have heard nothing about you. Dr Francis Martineau. I taught little Sako everything she knows." He put his hand on the small of my back in a gesture meant to tell Adem that he had been there first. Adem didn't appear to notice.

"I skimmed a paper you did on using natural singularities for FTL. I couldn't follow the math, but it seemed like an interesting theory. The other side of the singularity has to show up somewhere, right?"

"Right." I'd actually written most of the paper, but Francis had judged me too junior for a co-authorship. "The problem is, it's completely random and—"

"Seems completely random," Francis said.

I acknowledged his point. "And in an infinite universe, the exit point could be anywhere. None of our probes have reported back yet. Which means—"

It was Adem's return to interrupt, "Which means they could be so far away that the signal won't get here for years."

"Or your probes were destroyed by the gravitational forces," Lucy said, "and you'll never hear back from them." She sipped her drink. "I read the paper, too."

"Interesting work," the captain said. "We try to keep current on anything that could save us some time. The *Hajj* isn't cheap to run. We're always looking for a shortcut."

Someone cleared his throat noisily behind us, and we turned to see an older, thickset man approaching. "Someone should introduce me to my new niece," he said.

"Hisako," Lucy said. "This is Rakin Sadiq. My uncle and now yours."

"Rakin is from Nov Tero," the captain said. "He only recently bought back into the crew."

"Crew? I own three percent of the ship," Rakin said.

"When you ran away to Nov Tero you had ten percent, Uncle," Lucy said. "You lost some standing in the transition."

Rakin kissed my proffered hand instead of shaking it. His lips were moist. "Don't listen to them, my dear. I trust you will be as good an investment for the family as you will be a wife to my favorite nephew."

"I will certainly try, Uncle."

The captain slid her arm through mine. "Let's leave the business for the conference room, Rakin. This is a party and the banquet is ready. Shall we? I had to guess what you'd like, but we carried some of this all the way from Freedom for the occasion. I hope you enjoy it."

The banquet was amazing, but the party stayed awkward. At one point Francis asked me to dance and spent the entire song with his hands on my ass. I returned to my seat next to Lucy with my face flaming. "I hope your brother didn't see that."

"Even if he did, don't expect him to ask the good doctor to step outside to settle it. First, he's not the jealous type. Most Traders are pretty open about that kind of thing. The men don't have pissing contests over us because they know we'll do what we want anyway."

She took a sip of her drink. "Second, Adem could break your professor in half without trying. He doesn't fight unless it's for fun or deadly serious."

I looked around the reception hall. "Where is he?"

"Probably taking a walk or sitting in a corner somewhere. He's not the most social of men, and he's not a fan of crowds. This may be the largest one he's ever seen."

"I thought he was a musician."

"He's fine on stage. He knows his role there. At something like this…" She adjusted her dress. "Who is he supposed to be? The groom? The *Hajj*'s jack of all trades? He'll downplay everything he does to the point no one thinks he does anything, but the ship wouldn't fly without him. The captain decides where we go. I get us there. Adem holds the whole thing together." She pointed toward the bathrooms with her drink. "There he is. You should grab him and spend some time with him."

"I don't know what to say."

"Tell him about yourself. He's a good listener, but don't expect him to share much at first. Everything you are is exotic to him, and he'll think he has nothing interesting to offer."

"Okay." I gulped the rest of my drink. "Wait, what's he doing?"

Adem had pulled one of the event staff aside and was whispering to him, gesturing. The waiter nodded and jogged toward the kitchen.

Adem put his back to the bathroom door and redirected Francis who approached it. Denied his chance to pee, Francis came looking for me.

"Quite a party," he said, sliding into a seat next to me. "Hubby says there's someone passed out in the bathroom. He spent the last twenty minutes bringing him back to life."

"Who is it?"

"He didn't know. One of your guests, I imagine. The parameds have been called, so we can just drink and watch the–"

I lifted the hem of my dress so I could make better time and ran across the dance floor to Adem. "What's going on?" He seemed sharper, more focused than before.

"Someone overdosed," Adem said. "I got him breathing again and put the docbox on him. I don't know how long he'd been out before I found him."

"Who is it?"

"Maybe you can tell me." Adem opened the door. "Let me know if he's gone down again. The doc should keep him alive, but you never know."

Johnny was lying on the polished tile floor with a docbox strapped to his chest. It was breathing for him and keeping his heart beating. I didn't know what good brain activity looked like, but none of the telltales on the docbox were in the red.

"Johnny, you idiot." I dropped to my knees as if there was something I could do that the doc wasn't already. Johnny opened his eyes.

"Sako, is that you? What happened?"

"You overdosed. What did you take?"

"Just had a couple of beers."

"Don't bullshit me. The parameds are on their way, and they're going to want to know what you're on."

Johnny fumbled a Bliss inhaler out of his vest pocket. "I was holding it for someone else and wanted to see what it was like."

"You need help, Johnny." He'd needed it for years, probably needed it when I was dating him, and it had never occurred to me to tell him that.

"I'm fine. Just need a little rest."

"You're lucky to be alive."

The door swung open. "I heard someone in here needed a doctor," Francis said.

"He needs a medical doctor."

"I needed to piss anyway." Francis stepped over Johnny and crossed to the bank of urinals on the far wall. "Do you want to help me out with this for old time's sake? Your husband's guarding the door. No one will come in."

"You're an ass."

"And you're married, which, for some reason, is really arousing me right now. Where are you staying tonight?"

"In your dreams, Francis. Why did I sleep with you again?"

He tucked his penis back into his pants. "Convenience, probably. And the publication opportunities." He looked at Johnny. "Is he going to die?"

"No."

"Good. Shitty thing to happen at a party." He stepped over Johnny again. "I think I'm going to go. Big day tomorrow. Interviewing a new thesis candidate." He winked. "Have a good life, Hisako. Look me up when you come back this way."

Johnny was crying. "I'm such a waste, Sako. This wasn't how it was supposed to be."

I smoothed his hair back. "I know. Rest. Everything will be all right."

The door opened again, and Adem came in with a man wearing a plaid skirt. "This is Dooley, my father. He's a doctor."

"Hello, daughter," the red-headed man said. "Imagine meeting a lady like yourself in the jakes." He went to his knees and squinted at the telltales on the doc. "Bliss?"

I nodded.

"A bad batch goes right for the brainstem." He tapped the docbox. "This is the only thing keeping him alive. Might need to get used to this thing, boyo."

"Where are the parameds?" I said.

"Delayed," Adem said. "There was an attack on the elevator. Some refugee rights group took down one of the access towers."

Dooley snorted. "If so, they've done a lot more damage to themselves than they did to these *La Mur* assholes. They can repair the tower, but there's no telling how many people died when it came down." He stood. "You need to find a way to recharge the doc. It's got maybe ten minutes left. I'm going downtown to see if I can help."

"Do you want me to come?" Adem said.

"Soon as you're done here." Dooley ran his hand through his hair, making it stand up like rusty fire. "I'll grab some of our people from the party."

"Bring some lifter operators," Adem said. "They might be able to run some of the rescue equipment."

"Unless I am very much mistaken, the authorities are going to be more concerned with crime and punishment than in digging anyone out." Dooley frowned. "We'll see what we can do. Get him stabilized and come down. Don't tell Rakin. He'll have a conniption about using ship resources for something like this. Maybe pack up the leftovers from the buffet."

The charge light on Johnny's life-support system dropped to red, and a buzzer sounded. "Docboxes are supposed to last for hours," I said.

"Twelve hours, but only if they're maintained. The dust was so thick on it I doubt it had been touched in years." Adem pulled a multi-tool out of his suit pocket and used it to pry open the charge port. "This thing is older than me."

"I don't want to die!" Johnny said.

"Don't worry," Adem said. "Tell me how you met Hisako." He handed me the multi-tool. "Go get me three or four of the power units from those food warmers out there."

Lucy was standing guard outside the door. The party was breaking up as news spread about the attack. "Your mother had to leave," she said.

"She'll have to work." I grabbed Lucy's arm. "I need some help."

Lucy spotted the multi-tool in my hand and pulled one of her own from the small clutch she was carrying. "Never leave the ship without it."

It was the work of only a couple of minutes to get the power units. They were built right into the warmers, but the laser cutter on the multi-tool made short work of the casings. One of the waiters squawked but shut up when Lucy pointed her cutter at him. We carried the units back into the bathroom. The light on the docbox was flashing rapidly, which wasn't doing anything for Johnny's calm. Adem was talking to Johnny and poking around inside a wall-mounted hand dryer with a bent fork. He took the heating units from us.

"Perfect." He pulled a handful of wire out of the hand dryer and squatted beside Johnny. "These heaters run on broadcast power. I'm going to hook them into the doc's power supply."

"Won't that just heat everything up?"

Adem passed me a handful of small metal strips. "Not anymore." He used the multi-tool to connect the heating units to the docbox. "Johnny tells me the two of you used to date."

"It was a long time ago."

The light on the docbox stopped flashing, and the charge bar started creeping back up toward green.

"Stay with him," Adem said. "I'm going down to the elevator to see what I can do to help. Lucy, check in with Mom. We're going to need to use the elevator in New Berlin if we want to keep to our schedule."

She nodded. "Stay in touch, and don't do anything stupid."

Adem dashed out the door. Lucy closed her eyes, and the implants on her forehead blinked. "This is going to screw everything up. We might have to get some of the crew up with shuttles." She stood. "I'll be back."

The door swung wildly behind her. Johnny made a rattling sound, and after a moment of panic, I realized he was snoring. All of the lights on the docbox were green, and the hodge-podge charging system Adem had made with heating units, a hand dryer, and a fork hummed happily beside him.

And – oh, yeah – I was married. The gray nightmare I'd been having for the past eleven years had come true.

Johnny blinked sleepily. "Thanks for inviting me to the party, Sako. It's good to see you."

"Yeah. It's good to see you, too, Johnny."

ADEM

Versailles City, Oct 22, 3260

Adem hot-wired a delivery scooter to speed up the trip, but Dooley already had a triage area established and was covered in dust and blood by the time his son arrived at the elevator depot. The attack had taken down one of the four lattice towers workers used for maintenance of the system.

"How did you get past the security cordon?" Dooley said.

"Walked. They stopped me on one street so I went three blocks over. What's happening?"

"Death and destruction. All east of here." Dooley wiped his forehead with the back of his hand, leaving a dark smear on his fair skin. "The damned tower was three klicks high. I'm just grateful they only took down the one."

"City's not doing much to help."

"We're it for the moment. Bunch of rubes fresh from a party." Dooley handed Adem a first-aid kit. "The thing fell across something the locals call the Square. Get in there and see what we're up against."

Adem slung the kit over his shoulder and followed the debris. The explosion had gone off at the tower's base, toppling the structure like a giant tree. Gravity had been kind enough to lay some of it on the roadway. Mostly though, it had fallen into apartment blocks and squats.

Adem climbed the tower's now sideways framework to get through the fence surrounding the Square. The struts and guy lines, a mixture of aluminum, synthetic-diamond weave, and carbon nanotubes, scraped through the knees of his thin wedding trousers and into the flesh beneath. He took a moment to inspect his wounds and gave both knees a squirt of insta-bandage.

The tower had flexed as it fell, missing a cluster of food carts and smashing through a low wall and into a large garden. Adem followed the destruction past neat rows of vegetables. A hutch full of lizard things had been smashed flat, and the survivors were meeping pitifully to be let out. Adem kicked it open, wincing at the impact through his thin, shiny shoes. The five or six survivors scurried into the plant growth on either side of the impact zone.

"Ought not to have done that," a woman said. Adem twisted to see who it was and nearly fell against the tower's lattice again. She pointed at the departed lizards with her chin. "People will be hungry. You cut loose their food."

"I'm sorry," Adem said. "They were trapped and—"

"It's done now." She squinted at him. "You lost? *La Mur* is that way. Might want to get back there before folks start looking for someone to blame."

Adem brushed at his clothes. "I was at a party. My wedding. We came down to help."

Tears streaked paths down the woman's dust-caked face. "Help won't help," she pointed farther east, the way she had come, "it came right down on the Children's Village."

"Show me," Adem said.

He followed the woman to the far corner of the garden and helped her over the remains of the interior fence. The tower had fallen across a cluster of huts and tents.

"What is it?" Adem said.

"*Illicite*. We keep them safe when their parents run off or go to prison. Feed 'em, put a roof over their heads."

Adem surveyed the rubble. It seemed impossible that anyone could have survived. "How many were in there?"

"Dozens." The woman's hands rose to her face. Her fingers were scraped raw, two of them nearly to the bone.

"Let me see your hands." Adem coated her fingers liberally with insta-bandage and helped her to a seat against the wall. "Stay there and rest."

He walked carefully into the rubble. Here and there, a small hand or foot protruded from the piles of cloth and wood. Each time, Adem dropped to his knees and checked for signs of life.

"Hello!" he shouted. "Is there anyone here?"

He tugged a handmade stuffed animal from under a beam and held it in both hands. He shouted again. A low cry made him drop the stuffed animal and stumble toward the outer wall. He heard it again.

"She's dying!" the voice said.

Adem heaved at the rubble and succeeded in lifting a large portion of roof up. The fallen roof had created a small zone of protection where three children crouched: two boys and a little girl. The older boy blinked dust out of his eyes and pointed at the girl. "Her arm. She's dying!"

One of the children had tied a rough tourniquet around the girl's arm, which ended in a mass of pulped flesh and bone. Adem checked her pulse. He sprayed the rest of the insta-bandage on the girl's arm and strapped the first-aid kit's small docbox to her tiny chest.

"There's a woman near the garden wall," he told the older boy. "Take her back to the elevator and look for a man named Dooley. He has red hair. Tell him I'm coming with the girl. Okay?"

The boy took the younger one's hand and pulled him toward the wall. Adem turned his attention back to the girl. Her skin was gray from blood loss and shock, but the telltales on the docbox said she was stable. It hissed as it administered some drug or other.

"What's your name, honey?" Adem said.

The girl's eyes fluttered open. "Chuchu."

Adem slid his arms under her and lifted. She weighed next to nothing. She leaned her head weakly against his shoulder. "Okay, Chuchu. Let's get you somewhere safe."

HISAKO

I gave up waiting for Adem and his father to return and took a cab to my mother's apoartment. She came home four hours later and made me breakfast. She was exhausted. Even though Transit didn't run during emergencies, she'd been out straight with her public-relations duties, fielding questions and complaints the best that she could.

"It was probably that group your father used to drink with," she said. "I'll be lucky to keep my job if that ever comes to light."

That group had never amounted to much. A few protests, some minor sabotage... Most of its members had been rounded up when I was still a teenager, but I didn't see any point in arguing with her. As we ate, I tried to get her to talk about the past, maybe dredge up some warm memories and good feelings to take with me up into the dark. She didn't bite.

"Your father was the sensitive one. He'd be crying now, or reading some of his poetry." Her face darkened. "What did that ever get him? He drank, you know. He wasn't a saint."

He was not. Some nights he didn't come out of their bedroom because he was sleeping off a hangover. When he hugged me during my teenage years, all I could smell was the cheap, sweet liquor he liked to drink. It oozed out of him like sweat.

"He tried," I said.

"He should have tried harder," she said. "Maybe he would still be alive."

After I helped her with the breakfast dishes, I called a taxi. Lucy and her mother had already taken a shuttle up to the ship. The rest of us had to take a train to the elevator in New Berlin and get to the *Hajj* from there.

The train was near capacity. The attack on the tower had sent many who could running to second houses and family friends far away from the perceived danger. They didn't seem to care that midtown and *La Mur* hadn't been touched.

Dooley was already aboard the elevator when I arrived. He smiled wanly and invited me to sit with him. "Quite a night. None of us got any sleep. Adem's still working."

"Was it bad?"

"Letting people build right up against the elevator was a piss-poor idea. The city council will have a lot to answer for."

"They won't," I said. "Nobody important died. There are always more refugees coming. I bet you brought some with you."

"We did at that." Dooley was in his fifties, but exhaustion and the ghost of all he had seen the night before made him look older. "Another five thousand waiting in orbit to come down."

"You'd be surprised how few of your freezer pods ever make the surface. Most of them are probably still floating around up there."

Dooley rubbed his face. "Once they're off our manifest we don't think too much about them."

The elevator shook as it began its two-day trip up the tether. The acceleration was smooth, but many of my fellow passengers looked queasy. I recognized a few faces from my party and guessed alcohol consumption might be adding to their miseries.

"You ever been up to the New Berlin Station before?" Dooley said.

"A few times. Once for a long weekend with a boyfriend. His family owns an asteroid."

"How big?"

"A kilometer end to end. Nothing too grand."

"I'd like to have one of those someday. Dig it out. Spin it for gravity, maybe a nice, easy three-quarter g. Open a little pub and let the universe come to me for a change."

"Would the captain come with you?"

"If the *Hajj* was in good hands. Her mother passed it on to her like that. I think she'd like to pass it on to one of the kids."

"Adem."

"I think Lucy would be her first choice. She's hella smart and a fantastic pilot. Adem has a better heart, though. He's kinder."

"That doesn't always make a good leader."

"Or a successful Trader. But the Sadiq family has never been about making money, and don't let Rakin tell you different. We get through, make a living, and try not to fuck too many people over in the process." He smiled. "Hey, I like that. I'll try to get Maneera to let me paint it on the hull."

The elevator car trembled and accelerated again.

"Lucy told me that you were in an arranged marriage."

"Parents worked a kelp farm on Freedom. I was an accident of love, my da told me. Put us one kid over the quota. It was either find me a match or abort. I can't complain about the way it turned out. Maneera is a good woman. We've had three beautiful children and no jail time."

"I've not met the third."

"The youngest decided to get off on Freedom about five years ago. Maybe a hundred and twenty-five years ago your time. He got married, had a family. Died at a hundred and thirty." He reached for his pocket. "I have pictures on my reader if you want to see them."

"That's okay." I leaned back in the seat. "Relativity makes it all really weird."

He chuckled. "Adem is the oldest by three years. Then Lucy, but she spent a dozen years planetside so she's older than Adem now by about six years biological. Hafgan was the youngest. Said he wanted to live under the sky. He sold his shares to become a farmer and a historian. Wrote some books. We have copies, real printed copies, up on the ship."

"Have you read them?"

"Cover to cover more than once. We all have. It's the only thing we have of him now." He cleared his throat. "Don't tell Adem I said this, but I'd recommend you get your own suite at first. You two need to get to know each other before you set up housekeeping."

"Can I do that?"

"Course you can. The contract says you have to get married and spend two years with us. That's it. You don't have to like us. You don't even have to talk to Adem except for ship's business if that's what you want. But you might be missing out. He's a good boy."

"I didn't know I could get my own place. I thought…"

"That you were coming up to be ravished by Traders? Didn't you read the contract? Your parents were supposed to give you a copy as soon as they told you about the arrangement."

"I tried to avoid thinking about it."

"I broke into my mother's reader to get at mine. It was no secret that I was to be married off, but I wanted to get a look at the girl I was supposed to be making babies with. Scared the hell out of me. I read about her black belts and thought she would beat me to a pulp as soon as look at me."

"Your contract said you had to be a doctor."

"That was the only criteria. My deal was for six years, though. Medical school is expensive on Freedom, and Ma negotiated schooling for the other kids, too. By the end of it we had a lawyer, a doctor, and a horticulturist in the family." His smile faded. "I went back to see them a time or two, but it was hard. They'd gotten older, and I hadn't. My sister, the horticulturalist, was the last to go. I missed her funeral by five years standard."

The whistling sound outside the car dulled, and the ride got smoother.

"Will they pick us up with the *Hajj*?"

"Nah. Maneera will have got us stowage on some tug or other hauling between the stations. We might even be riding on the outside of it in suits. She's always looking for ways to save pennies, especially on this trip out."

"What's special on this trip?"

"Let's say there's a lot chewing into our profit margins this time out." He yawned. "I'm going to catch a few winks. You might be wise to do the same."

He got up and headed toward the bank of sleeping capsules that ringed the center of the elevator. Each coffin-sized capsule was kitted out with a sleeping pad and an entertainment center. Elevator passengers could rent them by the hour.

I had slept fine the night before, if not long, and I wasn't the least bit tired. I pulled my reader out of my pocket. The message icon was flashing. I pulled out the headphones so only I would hear the playback and pressed the "retrieve" button.

My mother's face blinked into focus on the small screen. She'd been crying. "I am sorry I was short with you this morning," she said. "I was tired and…" She shook her head. "That's not it. I was angry at you for going and angry at myself for making you go. We had such hopes, your father and I. We shared them with each other like prayers. So little in life was as we hoped. I always wanted to be close to you, Hisako. I think we were once, but you always seemed to prefer your father. I was mad at both of you for that. I knew we would only have you for so long…"

She was thousands of miles away and receding fast, but my arms suddenly ached to gather her in and hold her.

"This is not how I wanted to say goodbye," she said, "but it is better than this morning. Find me when you come back. Your father made a recording before he died. He asked me to play it for you on the day you left, and I nearly forgot." She smiled sadly at the memory card in her hand. "Maybe I tried to forget. I love you." She inserted the card into her console, and the screen flickered again.

I never realized how much the disease had taken away from my father. He had always been thin, but sickness made him gaunt and gray, what was left of his lungs fighting for any scrap of air. Through the video, he smiled at me.

"I know I look like shit. I don't feel so great, either, chuchu." He tapped the doc strapped to his chest. "Box says I'll be feeling better soon though."

He struggled to adjust his pillow and sit up straighter.

"My family died coming to Gaul. I told you that, right? I can't remember. The rest of us got to live for a while at least." He inhaled deeply, unleashing a round of racking coughs.

A past version of my mother stepped to his side to help. The coughing petered out, and my father was silent while my mother wiped blood from his mouth. "No time for small talk, I guess." He tried to smile, but it was more of a wince. "I love you, chuchu. I wish I could have come to your wedding. I know it wasn't your idea, but I'm sure you were the most beautiful, brilliant thing there. We did what we could with what we had. Don't think too badly of us." He looked off screen to my mother. "I want to sleep. I'm done."

The message ended. A flashing icon on the screen asked me if I wanted to replay it. I wiped my eyes and shut the reader down. I took my seatbelt off and walked to the observation gallery. We were nearly high enough to see the curve of the planet. My mother was down there, as were the bones of her parents and her husband. I rested my forehead on the window. The space outside refused to absorb my misery and guilt. My mother hadn't had much of me in the last ten years or so. I hadn't given myself to her like a good daughter should, and now she was alone. I made an effort to shake it off. There were at least a hundred people on the elevator. Mine couldn't have been the saddest story going into orbit that day.

I went back to my seat. The reports on the vid screens were all about the "countless lives lost to the senseless attacks." None of the talking heads admitted that there would likely never be a true count of those lives. It was *La Merde* after all; they were all just refugees, too dumb to live outside the shadow of the elevator.

I used my wedding ring to unlock my access to the *Hajj* records and accounts. I was rich, at least by my parents' standards. In two years, I could sell my shares and retire, maybe even set myself up in a private dome. I compared my fortune to the ship's operating costs and understood why the captain said she was living job to job. The profit margin was distressingly small. The ship had to fly constantly or no one made anything at all. The *Hajj* was three years overdue for an overhaul, a year overdue for an atmosphere exchange. The cost savings had paid for my education and upbringing.

Dooley returned from his nap in a few hours. "That's better," he said. "I hate having to take stimulants. That little nap will keep me going until tonight."

"I caught up on the news. It's a real mess down there."

"Probably worse than the news is saying. I never want to see that again, and I only worked with the ones whole enough to try to save." He pursed his lips. "There's a vid playing in about ten minutes. A comedy, I think. Want to catch it with me and then grab some dinner?"

Our ride from New Berlin Station turned out to be the cargo hold of an equipment shuttle. We squeezed in with the other commuters for the ride to Versailles Station. Dooley showed me how to prop myself against the packing crates so the sudden acceleration wouldn't send me ass over teakettle into the wall. While we were waiting for takeoff, he walked among the riders offering advice and first-aid appropriate to their various ills. Motion sickness was the big one. He spent a good bit of time talking to a group of riders heading back to the *Hajj* with us.

"It's the same every time we make planetfall," he said when he returned. "Someone falls in love and spends the first couple weeks of a run bemoaning that she'll be old and married by the time we come back this way."

"Have you ever been in love?"

"With someone other than my wife, you mean?" He rubbed his forehead. "No. I've been obsessed a time or two but never in love. It took Maneera and I a couple of years to get to that point, and it wasn't always easy."

The shuttle shook, and the acceleration pressed me against the crate I was leaning on.

"There we go. We'll be at Versailles in about an hour." He closed his eyes and, to all appearances, went back to sleep. This time I let myself join him. The sound of snores and murmurs around me faded into my dreams.

Sometime later, Dooley shook me awake. "Here we are, lass. You've been here before, so I expect you can find your way to the ship."

I blinked sleep out of my eyes.

"I've got to see a man about restocking my bar. I hope the cargo pod made it up before the attack."

He left me to fend for myself. The last time I'd been on the station had been for a long weekend with Francis. He'd tried to induct me into the "Freefall Club" on the shuttle to our rented orbital, but the whole thing had been so awkward that I gave up in the middle of it. The fact that he even knew how to use the Velcro straps we found on board squicked me out. The orbital had been dark and kind of damp. If someone had been religiously tending to its systems, it would have been nice enough, but as an occasional getaway it just wasn't getting the right maintenance. The environmental system was overgrown, and Francis had balked when I suggested we spend some of our time tending it.

"I didn't come up here to weed a garden," he said.

He ended up with a respiratory fungal infection, so I guess I proved my point.

The space station had started as a couple of the evacuation ships and a raft of shipping containers, and it had grown without much planning ever since. It served mostly as the endpoint of the elevator and, as such, had become the hub of off-world trading. There were always ships coming in and out. One Trader ship had been parked there for five years due to some kind of legal battle between the family that ran it and its investors.

No one had told me how quickly I needed to get onboard the *Hajj*, so I stopped in the food court for a box of noodles and sat down to eat. It was the first meal I'd eaten since breakfast with my mother. When I finally presented myself to the *Hajj* dockmaster and asked to board the ship, a tall, blonde woman came out to meet me. Her name was Vladlena "Call me Vee" Mullova.

"Can I carry anything for you?"

"I just have this bag. The rest of my stuff should have come up yesterday."

"Your closet made it up just before the shit hit the fan,"

she said. "You'll be able to get to it when you want to. Is there anything you need right now?"

I couldn't think of anything, so she sent my bag ahead and offered me a tour of the ship. "Just the fun parts," she said. "You'll get to know the boring bits soon enough."

Someone had tried to make the corridor we were in warm and friendly by painting it. The scheme was just a little off somehow, like the painter saw color differently than I did. Since humanity had now evolved for thirty generations under six different suns, that was probably true. But there was no disguising the fact that the paint had gone over bare metal, and the steel-grid decking and the pipes running overhead were less than homey.

"It smells stale in here," I said.

"Our air mass is overdue for an exchange, but it's safe. The air in your cabin will be fresher. Do you need something to eat?"

I told her about the noodles.

"We can see the cafe on the last leg of the trip then. How about a drink?"

"I could use one."

Vee took me along two unmarked corridors and down a ladder. We emerged in a small space that looked like a blind welder had banged it together out of shipping containers. The crazy color scheme continued in here, and someone had hung up signs and pictures representing all the human planets. A small stage took up the floor space at one end. It was strange but cozy.

"This is Terry's Place," Vee said. "Our home away from home."

The kid behind the bar was picking his nose. I was relieved to see him wash his hands before reaching into the ice bucket to make us cocktails.

"What is it?" I studied the murky fluid in the glasses he put in front of us.

"A Dooley special. I just followed his instructions," he said. "We almost never know what it is. It's bound to be strong though, so tread carefully."

It tasted like powdered lemon-drink mix and pepper, and it burned going down to tell me it was working.

Vee and I carried our drinks to a table near the wall. "I asked to be the one to meet you because I wanted to clear the air. Adem and I were in a relationship before you got married, and I didn't want you to hear that from anyone else."

"Were you in love?"

"It was purely recreational. Are you okay with that?"

"I barely know Adem, and we haven't even had a conversation that lasted longer than two minutes. The last time I saw him he was keeping my ex-boyfriend alive." I lifted my glass. "To clearing the air."

We clinked our cloudy cocktails.

"What do you do here?" I said.

"I work in the medical center. My parents bought me a half-share as a graduation-from-med-school gift. I grew up on Nov Tero."

"What's that like?"

"Cold. We only have the one city, but it's bigger."

I took another sip of the horrible cocktail. Things had started to soften around the edges, and that was just fine with me. "What do you do for fun around here?"

She unzipped the top of her utilisuit and tied the arms around her waist. The t-shirt she wore underneath revealed a lot of muscle. "It's a lot like university. We work. We drink. We hook up. Most of us study. I'm about a quarter of the way through a degree in computer science. I'm working with Odessa for that. We play games. I read a lot. Go to the gym. It's not so bad. Most of the crew only sign on for a few years. They work, make some money, and move on."

"But nothing is the same when they get back."

"That's the appeal of being here for a lot of people. You literally can't go back to whatever you were escaping."

"Don't you miss your parents?"

"They have their own lives, and I have a good excuse for not calling all the time." She pointed at my drink. "Finish that up, and I'll show you the rest of the ship."

I gulped down the rest of the cocktail. "I can't feel my teeth."

"That's how you know it's working. This way." Vee led me down another long hallway.

"I didn't expect everything to be so…"

"Don't say dirty or the captain will have us all down here scrubbing."

"I was going to say worn. It's clean but it looks used."

"The *Hajj* launched more than a thousand years ago. It's clocked a lot of kilometers. It's from the Middle East somewhere. Persia. Is that right?" She tapped her chin. "Something like that. The Sadiq family was part of the wake crew. The captain's grandmother got the ship when the crew's descendants drew lots." She slid open a door in the wall. "This is mass-grav control. You probably know more about it than I do. It's the one system the captain has inspected every time we stop. It's expensive but without it–"

Instant death. I patted a console and offered it friendly thoughts.

"You'll get to know it, I'm sure. You specialized in mass-grav theory, right?"

"United Americas physics and engineering. Mass-grav. Wormholes. All the fantasies of the past."

"I wonder why," she said.

Vee led me down a flight of stairs. The door opened to a multi-level room. "Life support," she said.

"Another thing I know nothing about."

"Maybe that's the captain's way of making sure you spend plenty of time with Adem. He's not an expert, but he knows more than most."

"I didn't see any of that on his profile."

"You won't see a lot of things there. He grew up on the ship, so he knows at least a bit about everything. He's the official generalist." She pointed to the far corner of the room. "There are a couple of stills back there. Adem makes the best hooch."

"Is that where the cocktails come from?"

"Dooley usually gets a pod of beer at the start of each run, but once it's gone it's all homemade."

"This does feel like university."

"Told you. Let me show you the medical center, and then we'll grab some lunch. Adem's not aboard yet, so it's up to me to keep you entertained."

Vee was doing a nice job of being friendly. "So, more cocktails, then?"

ADEM

Versailles City, Oct 24, 3260

The older boy Adem had rescued had put a big piece of wedding cake in front of an elderly woman. "Cake," he said. "It's good."

The woman pushed the cake around the plate with her fork and spouted something angry in a language Adem didn't recognize.

"My name is Raul." The boy took the woman's fork and ate a bite of the cake. "It's safe to eat. It's sweet." He handed the fork back to her, and she smiled mostly toothlessly at him. She wolfed the rest of the cake down.

"She didn't trust it. It looked too EuroD," Raul told Adem.

Gifts from *La Mur* always came with strings. Resettlement came with *La Merde*. Welfare came with sterilization or prison for *illicite* birth. Adem hoped the rich food from the wedding wouldn't make anyone sick. "She's going to be alright. That girl you helped. Chuchu."

Raul snorted. "That's not her name. It means 'darling girl.' It's probably something her mother called her. All the girls are 'chuchu' if you ask them. She's crippled. Might have been better if she died."

Adem frowned. "You can't mean that."

"She can't work. She'll end up a beggar. Maybe starve to death. She might not be thankful that you saved her, spaceman."

"How old are you?"

"Ten, I think. Maybe nine? My uncle said he can get me work in the mines when I'm twelve."

The younger boy Adem had pulled out of the toppled hut had spent one night on a triage cot then grabbed as much food as he could and ran back into *La Merde*.

"Did you get any of the cake?" Adem said. There'd been a surprising amount of food left over from the banquet but after two days of feeding victims and volunteers it was mostly gone.

"My father said sweets make you weak, although he never ate them and now he's dead." Raul rubbed his chin.

Adem pulled his reader out of his pocket and reset it. "Take this. Learn to read. Study. Maybe you can do better than the mines."

Raul turned the reader over and over in his hands. "I could just sell it."

"It might be worth more to you if you keep it. There are games on it, too."

Raul slipped it into his dirty clothes. "If the older kids see it…"

"Be careful. Be smart." Adem's sinuses were coated with dust. He ripped off part of his shirt sleeve and blew his nose into it. "I have to go. Will you be alright?"

"It's warm tonight. I've eaten. Tomorrow? Who knows? Maybe I will see my uncle and get my supper there."

"Where will you sleep?"

Raul perked up. "You looking for a date? How much do you have?"

"I just want to make sure you have somewhere warm and safe tonight."

"I have places. Some warm. Some safe. A few that are both. I'll go to one of them." He pointed at a pile of blankets the *Hajj* crew had scrounged and purchased on the way to the disaster scene. "Can I have one?"

Adem handed it over with some coins. "Take more food, too. And this."

Raul refused the money. "Give it to the old woman. I can work." He tossed Adem a jaunty salute and headed to the table where the *Hajj* rescue party had set up a supply cache. The wedding banquet had been supplemented by trips into midtown for basic staples. Adem watched Raul make himself a sandwich and stuff a bag of meal bars into his shirt. The boy waved goodbye and walked out of the range of the emergency lighting.

Adem stepped over to the old woman Raul had talked into trying the cake. Her eyes were closed, and she was snoring, her nearly toothless mouth hanging open.

"Grandmother?" Adem knelt down beside the woman. "Grandmother?"

"Let her sleep," someone said. It was the woman with the ruined fingers, which were now properly bandaged. Adem recognized his father's handiwork. "She's exhausted. She used to be the matron of the Children's Village. She came here as soon as she heard."

"How are you?" Adem said.

"The doctor said I was in shock. He gave me an injection. Did this." She held up her hands.

"Do they hurt?"

"Not anymore."

"I need to go soon. My ship will be leaving orbit." He jingled the coins in his hand. "Can you make sure she gets these?"

"Give them to me. I will make sure they are used well. She would only give them to me anyway. I am the matron now."

"What do you do for them?"

The woman gazed down at the trail of destruction the tower left as it fell. "Not enough. Food. Clothes. School. If the children want to stay in the Village, they need to take lessons."

"What about Raul?"

"He lives in the Village sometimes. He doesn't like school, but he's a good boy."

"Yeah, I gave him my reader so he could take lessons on it."

"He might." She held out her hand. "You can trust me."

Adem dropped the money in her palm. "I wish I had more."

"So do I." She counted the coins. "Thank you for your help. We can take it from here."

Adem nearly laughed at the thought.

The woman pulled a blanket off the pile and tucked it around the old woman's shoulders. She scrubbed at her forehead with the back of her wrist. "Why would they do this?"

"City security says it was a terrorist attack. Some local group."

The woman's laugh was dry and brittle, more like a sharp bark of pain than anything containing mirth. "They would say that."

"What do you mean?"

"Go back to your ship. By the time you return this will only be a memory. One disaster among a thousand others."

Adem looked around the triage area trying to estimate how much of the ship's budget he had spent on supplies and rescue gear. He'd catch hell from some of the shareholders at the next meeting.

The shuttle pad was six blocks away, and Adem covered the distance at a jog. The security guards at the door tried to refuse him entrance, but with enough waving of his ID stick and a couple of reminders about who he was, Adem made it onto the shuttle. He opened a channel to the *Hajj*. Lucy's voice was thin and tired.

"I'm on my way up," Adem said.

"Safe travels, little brother. You know it makes me nervous when you fly without me."

"It will be fine. They do this all day." Adem signed off and stretched his shoulders as far as the crowded shuttle would allow.

Along with the usual mix of tourists and tech workers, about a dozen well-heeled EuroD were waiting for the ride up.

"Happens every time there's an attack. Anyone with a vacation place on the station goes up to wait things out," the man next to him offered. He was sweating heavily.

"What's your excuse?"

"I work life support on the station. Keep everything running. My family owned a Trader ship. Engine went out about fifty years ago, and we leased it to the station."

"Is that where you work?"

"I work all over. But I still live on the ship. As long as one of us does we keep our ownership rights."

"But it will never fly again."

"There are worse things. The engines failed about a week out, so we were already moving slow. Got a tow in and sold everything that wasn't attached. We could have sold the ship outright, but we voted to lease the space. Now, every year we get a check. Most of the kids have jobs now, but it helps."

A tone sounded and a light flashed over the seating area.

"Launch warning," the man grimaced. His knuckles were white on the arms of his seat. "I really hate this part."

HISAKO

Three hours out of Gaul

My husband opened the door to his cabin the third or fourth time I rang the buzzer. He was shirtless and tall.

"I want my own place," I slurred. "Dooley said it would be alright."

"What time is it?" Adem scratched his ear. "Are you okay?"

I stomped my foot. "Did you hear me?"

"Yeah. Come in." He pulled a shirt over broad shoulders and a surprisingly well-muscled chest. "I'm sorry I haven't been here. I barely made it back in time for our launch window."

"Vee showed me around."

He froze.

"It's okay." I held up my hand. It wobbled. I felt wobbly. Vee and I had ended up back at Terry's Place for more terrible cocktails with her friends. She said it was my bachelorette party and that it didn't matter if I had it after the wedding. "It's oh-kay. She told me you'd been sleeping together."

"Is that why you want your own place?"

"No." Wobbly. I put my hand on the wall to steady myself.

Adem pulled the chair out from the desk. "Here. Sit down before you fall down."

"I'm not drunk." I sat carefully in the chair and crossed my legs.

"Sure." Adem smoothed down his hair with his hand. "You can

have this suite. I modded it with you in mind. Just let me get a few things out of it, and I'll move into one of the empty crew suites."

"No!" I shook my head too firmly. "No. This is your…" I nodded off. By the time I had opened my eyes, Adem had stripped the bed and stuffed the linens down the laundry chute. I watched him remake the bed. He was good at it. Tight corners. Smooth bedspread.

"You look like you need to sleep it off." He filled a big glass of water from the tap in the bathroom, put it on the bedside table, and pulled a guitar off the wall. "I'll just take this for now. And this." He plucked a reader off the desk and slid it into his pocket. "There's aspirin in the bathroom for when you wake up."

I was having a hard time sitting in the chair. Something was wrong with gravity. It was pulling me sideways. "You don't have to do this."

"I fixed this room up for you. It makes sense that you should have it. There are empty suites closer to the engine room. I'll take one of those. You sleep." He pointed at a half-sized sliding door on the wall. "Your closet has already been installed. I'll have mine moved by the end of day tomorrow." He stopped at the door. "I am glad you're here, Hisako."

A door closed somewhere. My head was heavy. I messed up Adem's beautifully made bed and crawled inside.

I woke up around four in the morning with a splitting headache and blessed Adem for leaving me the water. Then I cursed him for making me get up to get the painkillers. The bathroom was small but clean, and my bladder was thankful. I took my hangover back to bed. Adem had made the room cozy by hanging rugs and woven mats over the hard metal of the walls. There were three guitars and a mandolin hanging on hooks, obviously not as special as the one Adem had taken with him.

The next time I woke up, Lucy was shaking me by my shoulder.

I burrowed deeper into the covers to escape. Adem had good taste in beds.

"Rise and shine, spacer." Lucy flicked my ear. "How's your head?" She was enjoying this.

"Ugh. Did Vee tell you we went drinking?"

"I was there for the third hour. You were not, apparently." Lucy tapped the side of her head scarf. "Plus, I see everything the ship sees, and I don't have to be on the bridge to do it. I could fly the *Hajj* from the shitter, if I wanted. Mother just likes me on the bridge."

"Lovely. Does the ship's pilot usually serve as the wake-up service?" The pain in my head was more of a dull throb than a blinding spike, a vast improvement.

"Only to new members of the family enjoying their first morning aboard. And only if I like them. Besides, Adem said you kicked him out, so he wants to give you space. I am his proxy." She carried my empty water glass to the bathroom and filled it up again. "I'm sorry I missed the end of the party. It looked like you were having fun."

"I think I was. Today I'm not so sure."

"That's how everyone feels after a night at Terry's. People say Dooley adds something to the alcohol to make everyone's hangover worse. He wants to keep them from drinking quite so much the next time, but it never works."

"It might have this time. I am never drinking again."

"You'll keep that promise for about fifteen hours. Adem and Dooley are playing tonight, and it's my turn to take you out."

I pulled the covers up to my chin. "What am I supposed to do today?"

"Get to know the ship. Evacuation routes, safety protocols, that kind of thing. Make sure you won't be in the way if we have an emergency."

"I thought an emergency would kill us instantly."

"Most of them will, but we might get lucky and die slowly. It's an old ship. Adem keeps it running pretty well, but bad things happen. Tomorrow you start a rotation in engineering. Uncle Rakin is officially the chief engineer, but ignore him. He doesn't know his ass from a laser cutter."

She pulled my reader from a pile of clothes on the floor and tossed it on the bed. "Your schedule should be in here. Mother will want to meet with you soon and get you started on the project."

"What project?"

"Classified." She swatted my leg. "Move over. I have a little maneuver coming up, and it's hard to do astrogation and stand at the same time."

I wriggled over, and she lay down beside me. "Good bed. Adem spent some time on this. Go get a shower. I'll have it all squared away by the time you come out, and we can go get breakfast." Her breathing slowed, and she looked like she'd fallen asleep. Her eyes darted under her lids like she was having an intense dream. "Go," she said. "You're staring at me, and you smell like a sweaty distillery."

I climbed out of bed and swallowed more painkillers. The water pressure in the shower was fantastic, and a handy timer counted down the minutes of hot water I had been allocated. I had time to lather and rinse twice. I wrapped a towel around myself and went back to the main room. Lucy was still on the bed, her eyes closed. "I gave you a couple extra minutes of hot water," she said. "Go ahead and get dressed. This part is tricky."

My closet slid open to reveal the jumble of things I'd packed. No one had said anything about a dress code, so I put on the coveralls I usually wore when doing lab work. They sort of looked like an utilisuit with fewer pockets and D-rings.

"You'll have time to change before we go to Terry's tonight," Lucy said, sitting up.

"Is changing course always that hard?"

Lucy led the way through the door and turned right at the end of the hall. "Changing course was the easy part. The hard part was convincing Versailles Station that we had a good reason to. We're not supposed to deviate from the shipping lanes. Makes it hard for someone to come out to rescue us if we have problems."

"I'm surprised anyone would come."

"It would cost more than the ship is worth, but it beats death for some people."

"Only some?"

"Trader families can lose everything that way. Anyway, I told the station we'd been having problems with pirates, which is an enormous lie. We're kind of taking the scenic route." She waved me through the cafeteria door ahead of her.

Lucy had let me sleep late enough that we'd missed the breakfast rush. Only a few people were in the cafeteria lingering over coffee, and we had the buffet line to ourselves. I picked up a breakfast tray and tried to figure out which foods would make me feel the least nauseated. Lucy picked with more alacrity, and she was already fork deep in a plate of scrambled hash and eggs when I joined her at a table.

"Do you have to wear that scarf?" I said.

Lucy touched it. "Does it bother you?"

I sat down. "Not at all. Your mother doesn't wear one and–"

"And you wondered if it was a religious thing. It keeps my head warm. I had my scalp depilated when I got my implants. Plus, it keeps dust out of my ports. You wouldn't believe what a pain in the ass it is to clean them out."

"I read a little about, you know, Allah and all that when my parents told me I was marrying into a Muslim family."

"Did it freak you out? Gaul is pretty secular."

I tried the toast. "Not really. It seemed kind of like a fairytale when I was thirteen. All those rituals and rules."

"I think you'll find we're all pretty deep in the atheist-agnostic side of things. The wake crews gave up most of their religious baggage during the trip out here."

I steeled myself. I hated talking about this kind of thing but… "I didn't kick Adem out. All I said was that I wanted my own place for a while."

"I know. He knows, too. It was probably kind of a relief for him. We've been telling him horror stories about families that lock the bride and groom in a room until they fuck." She smiled. "Don't get me wrong; it's not the fucking that would bother him. It's the awkward silence before and after. He'd have no idea what to talk to you about."

"Me, either." Aboard the *Hajj*, my marriage made even less sense. Adem wasn't some lonely space weirdo. He was good looking, smart or smart-ish… Hell, he'd been hooking up with Vee for months. He didn't need a wife, especially not one who wanted her own suite. "So, why am I here? Adem has less interest in me than I have in him, if that's possible."

"Maybe I've always wanted a little sister." Lucy drained her coffee cup and refilled it from a spigot built into the table. "Alright, fine. I'm going to tell you something that only my mother, my father, Adem, and I know. Don't spread it around." She took a breath. "You're the closest thing out there to a worm-drive expert, right?"

"As much as anybody. The whole field is mostly just wishes and wannabes."

"There's not much use for a worm-drive expert without a worm-drive for her to play with." She plucked a slice of toast from the breakfast tray. "Get it?"

"That's impossible."

"That's what I said! You ever hear of the *Christopher Hadfield*?"

Madame Stavros floated into my head and pointed a gleaming fingernail at me. *You know this, Hisako.* "It's the ship that destroyed Makkah."

"Close. It was the backup to the ship that destroyed Makkah. It never fired a shot, and it's been out there floating in the Makkah debris field all this time. We boarded it and salvaged the drive."

"I thought nothing survived the squeezer."

"Nothing did," Lucy said. "The ship's dead. Her engines were tinsel. We met her as her orbit poked her out of the cloud and pushed her farther back in after we were finished. She's rubble by now."

"And your mother wants me to make the drive work for the *Hajj*." Which meant… "My contract was never about Adem."

She seesawed her hand. "You might be a good match for him. Mother usually has two or three reasons for everything she does. It wouldn't surprise me if one of her motives was to see Adem happy."

"But a working worm-drive was higher on the list." For this I'd spent my entire life not letting anyone get too close to me. "I've never even laid hands on a worm-drive. No one has, and no one knows how they work."

"But you've seen one," Lucy said. "Your mother told me you were on the *Sun King* for a couple of weeks."

Gaul's one and only warship. It hadn't fired a shot in anger in almost a thousand years. It had a worm-drive, but it was never used in case the one time proved to be the last time, stranding the ship and crew millions of kilometers away from home. "Just to read the user's manual and write a paper! Do you have any idea how complex they are? One bad calculation and the other end of the wormhole could open up in the middle of a planet!"

"You get it working; we'll make sure the math is right. Are you going to eat those crepes? Chef doesn't make them much."

"Keep your hands off my crepes." I pulled the plate away from her. "What happens if the drive doesn't work?"

"Rakin takes over and turns the ship into a slave hauler. I sell my shares and find something else to do."

"What happens to me?"

"You can sell and leave with a nice little nest egg, or stay aboard and make a living off human misery."

I pushed the plate of crepes across the table to her. "I can't believe this was the plan."

"The captain plays the long game. She has to. She's always looking twenty to fifty standard years out, trying to figure out what people will need by the time we come into port." Lucy attacked the crepes like they were her first course. "Based on the elevator attack, she figures there's a good chance Gaul will be in the middle of a civil war the next time we're back this way."

"Is she going to supply weapons?"

"She's a bleeding heart like Adem. She'll get some do-gooder group on Freedom to pay us to haul humanitarian supplies. It won't make much of a profit, but most of us will sleep better at night." Lucy made the last piece of crepe disappear.

"I need to warn my mother," I said.

"You're the one who spent the last ten years in an ivory tower, sweetie. Your mom struck me as someone who knows exactly what's going on. That's why she got you out." Lucy picked up the tray. "I'm headed to the bridge. I'll see you at Terry's tonight."

Talking with Lucy gave me mixed feelings. On the one hand, I wasn't on the *Hajj* just to play house with Adem the Lonely Spaceman, which was nice to know. If anything, my relationship with Adem seemed to be pretty low on everyone's agenda. Plus, they had something practical for me to do with my education, which I had never expected would happen. Still, I wasn't happy about being so casually manipulated. Every year of my life had Maneera Sadiq's thumbprint on it.

I finished my breakfast and linked my reader with the ship's nearsmart. It responded with a day-long guided tour of the ship's emergency systems, from the quick-close bulkheads to the fire-suppression protocols to the escape pods. The pods were basically fast-freeze capsules with heavy-duty transmitters mounted on them: fifteen percent chance of instant death, nearly zero percent chance of rescue. Use them and I'd likely float frozen forever... dead or alive. The last stop on the tour was the emergency pressure-suit locker outside the bridge. The helmets hung on the simple suits like broken dandiflowers. The nearsmart listed all the conditions that might force everyone to troop to a locker and don one of the things.

"This concludes the tour," it said. "Are you ready for your quiz, or would you prefer to review?"

My stomach growled. The meal bar I had looted out of one of the emergency lockers hadn't held me long. "I'll do the quiz tomorrow."

"Very well." The tinny voice made a good try at sounding disappointed. "At any time you can retake the tour during your off-duty hours."

"I think that might make me insane." I smothered a yawn. "I need dinner and drinks, and not necessarily in that order."

"Do you need directions to the cafeteria?"

"That's a good start."

When I returned to the cafeteria, Vee caught my attention and waved me to her table. She sent the towheaded man sitting next to her to the food line for me and introduced a lot of young, horny, over-educated people with in-jokes that would take me months to get. I did my best to smile at the right spots.

"And this is Mateo," Vee said, introducing the man who had just come back with a tray of food for me.

"I didn't know what you would want, so I got everything," Mateo said. "We can help you with it."

"She won't want these. I can tell." A prematurely balding man named Tobey reached across the table and grabbed a handful of protein strips to replace those he had just finished.

"You and Mateo will be working together." Vee smiled at him. "Sako is going to be on your team for a couple of weeks. You need to show her around and keep Rakin from molesting her."

"She might be safe," Tobey said. "She's family."

"You can't tell with that goat. He starts thinking his money's impressive enough that no one can see his outer ugly."

"Ship's rules are pretty strict about things like that," said a woman whose name I had already forgotten. "Tell him plain, and the captain will have his ass if he asks again. We haven't used the brig in a while."

Mateo laughed. "Since the last time Tobey was in it. He drank four of Dooley's experimental cocktails and ended up streaking on the ship. His last stop was the bridge. I have a recording of the dance he did for the captain if you'd like to see it."

Tobey's balding pate turned rosy red along with the rest of his face.

"Maybe later." I held up my hands. "Are all of you going to Terry's tonight?"

"It's either that or study."

"Or play stims. I got a couple of new ones on Gaul. Some of them look pretty good," Mateo added.

"Did you get the one about the Nov Tero cartels? We could ask Rakin for advice," Tobey asked.

"Not a good idea from what I've heard," Vee said. "He had to borrow money from a shark to buy his way back onto the ship."

"What did the shark get out of it?" I said.

"Same thing we all get." Tobey went on when I didn't nod.

"Money. I didn't spend six years in school to live out my golden years in *La Merde*."

"Are you from Gaul?" I said.

"Nah. Freedom."

"There are different names for it, but there's a refugee town of some kind on all the successful planets," Vee said. "Life can't have winners without losers."

"And the Traders keep moving above it all." Lucy walked by and snagged a cookie off Vee's tray. "And we don't look back because back was a long, long time ago. You guys ready to head for Terry's? It's a good idea to get a couple of drinks in before Adem and Dooley go on."

"Are they that bad?" I said.

"No. But a few drinks make everything better. I need more cookies. I'll see you losers there."

Vee plucked at the sleeve of my coverall. "Are you going to wear this? It's not a problem if you do. A lot of us are going in work clothes. I just figured…"

"That I might want to pretty up for my husband? I probably should." The sigh came out on its own.

"Why bother?" Tobey said. "Adem'll be coming right from work, so he won't change. Besides, you can get to Terry's early and get the best seats."

"Will they really be the best? Remember, I've been there."

"No, but we can pretend." Vladlena tugged my sleeve. "Let's go. We can drop by your cabin on the way. The boys will clean the table."

"Aren't they coming?"

"It's game night," Mateo said. "We have a raid. Maybe we'll be there late."

"After Mateo wrecks us with his bad planning," Tobey said.

"Let's go. They'll be talking like this forever now." Vladlena gave us our cue to leave.

"What sort of games do they play?" I said.

"Anything. Mateo picked up a new civil war-rebellion thing on Gaul. My guild plays Thursday nights. I'll send you an invitation."

Vee didn't need directions to my suite, of course.

"Are you okay with me?" I said. "About Adem?"

"I won't lie. I liked him. But things are different up here. You didn't ask to be married to him. He didn't ask to marry you. There is no reason to resent either of you for it. There are no lies. No secrets. Besides, Adem isn't the only lonely Trader on this boat. So, yeah, we're okay." She linked her arm in mine. "More than. I like you, too."

I tried to concentrate on counting the turns and levels between Adem's quarters and the spine. Vladlena stopped at a door that looked like all the other doors in the corridor. "There you go. If it helps, you can paint it a different color from the other ones. Or you can just count. It's the seventh door on this side of the hallway."

"I'll count. It's still Adem's quarters."

"Oh, he won't mind. Go ahead and paint it something obnoxious. Get Tobey to paint you a mural. He did my door. It's pretty good. I'll show you sometime."

I put my hand over the doorplate. "Do you want to come in?"

"Do you want privacy to change?"

"I might just grab a sweater."

"The less you wear in Terry's the better. It gets hot near the engine room."

"Maybe I'll put on a clean t-shirt then."

Vladlena followed me inside and sat on the bed. "When did Adem move out?"

"This morning. I didn't give him much notice. I haven't seen him since."

"He'll be fine." She looked at the guitars hanging on the walls. "He took the Martin."

"What's so special about the Martin?"

"Made on Earth. One of the wake crew brought it along. Change. We have drinking to do."

I opened the closet door. "I haven't unpacked yet. This might take a minute." I slid open a drawer marked "fun wear" and pulled out one of my old Sandcats t-shirts. I unzipped my coveralls and tied the arms around my waist while I pulled on the t-shirt. I couldn't tell if Vladlena was watching me or not. I'd hooked up with women before and enjoyed it enough to do it again, and Vladlena seemed like someone who could keep it light. But, I reminded myself, I was married now and things were different. I pulled the coverall top back up but left it unzipped.

"Cute T-shirt," Vee said.

"It's from a band I was in."

"You should play something tonight. They open the mic between sets."

"I'm really rusty. It would sound terrible." We were back out in the hallway, and I waited for Vee to pick a direction. I knew we were close, but I couldn't remember if we headed up or down, left or right.

"You haven't heard Dooley, yet." She kissed me on the cheek.

We arrived fashionably late. Adem and his father were into their first set when we walked in. We had reserved seats right in front of the stage. They played a few more songs then Dooley waved to me. "Come on up and play something, darlin'!" He was laying the accent on thick. I tried to beg off, but he kept at it. I gave up when Vee started in, too.

Adem offered me his guitar. "Nice shirt. Did you ever hear them play?"

"I started the band."

Adem opened his mouth to say something, but Dooley cut him off by shoving a mandolin into his hand.

Dooley was all smiles. "I'll stick with the pipes. Something tells me we're going to have to run to keep up."

"It's been such a long time since I played!"

"Just remember that the sound comes out of the hole in the front," Dooley said.

I gave them the key and the time signature for one of the first song I'd ever heard Adem play. It was a dark tune about a man who'd let himself be hanged to death rather than admit he was fucking his best friend's wife. Adem's performance had been fine – sad and lovelorn – but there was more to find in the song. There was anger in there, or should be, because the woman hadn't stepped up and said something to keep her lover alive. He'd died to save her reputation, and she'd let him do it. Did that mean she didn't love him? That she loved herself more? I wasn't sure, and I didn't think the hanged man would know, either. And what did her husband think every time she put on her black veil and hung out in the cemetery?

The Martin felt good in my hands, although the fret board and neck were wider than the electrics I played, and though it wasn't my strength, I sang, too. I tried to put that feeling of anger and doubt into my voice and fingers while Adem and his father kept up the rhythm and filled in behind me. Finding the emotions wasn't hard. It was the same mix I'd been feeling since I first learned I was in an arranged marriage.

The crowd in the bar fell silent as the last notes of the song died away. I wondered if I had done something wrong, ruined their favorite song or maybe played the whole thing with my underwear showing. The urge to check faded when the applause began. The clapping started in the center and spread through the small space.

I handed the guitar back to Adem and fled back to my seat.

"That was amazing! Adem's mouth is still hanging open. You can really play!" Vee was shaking me.

I gulped my drink too fast and started coughing

"I'm glad you were all here to listen to that. It might be the first time that guitar has ever been played." Dooley on stage, upstaging his son. My husband.

Half the audience got the joke and treated the other half to the punch line. The look on Adem's face told me he didn't find it overly funny.

Dooley reclaimed the mandolin. "Here's one from my two favorite Irishmen…" He and Adem started playing a Beatles song that I remembered hearing among the Spaceman recordings. It was a pretty song, but not the best for Adem's voice.

The crowd resumed its chatter, letting Adem and Dooley fill in the background of their conversations.

Mateo slid into the seat beside me. "That was fucking amazing!"

"You're here early?" Vee said.

"We lost a lot of ground and most of our gear to Jackie and her guild. They'll be here once they finish patting themselves on the back."

Vee looked smug. "Trained her myself."

"Where did you learn to play like that?" Mateo said.

"Started taking lessons when I was a kid. I play seven instruments. Seven and a half if you count the saxophone. I was in a couple of bands."

"Played that old guitar better than Adem ever did."

"I'm alright on guitar, but I'm better on violin and cello. When I get settled, I'll give you a real show."

Vee nodded toward the stage. "Looks like the Spaceman was a little staggered by having competition. He hasn't taken his eyes off you since you sat down."

I looked up, catching Adem's eyes. He looked directly at me, then purposefully looked at another part of the audience.

"He's either dazzled…" Vee said.

"Or he hates me for showing him up." I kicked myself for not holding back some. Men's egos could be so damned fragile. "It's his fault. The lessons were part of my contract."

"He gets what he deserves then. Let me get the next round to celebrate."

Adem and his father took a break after an hour or so and invited anyone else who wanted to play up to the stage. Adem didn't offer the Martin to anyone else. Only one of the ad hoc groups showed any promise. They played a couple of songs and sat down to solid applause. Everyone else got a round of polite kudos from anyone sober enough to listen through the sets. Adem and Dooley finished off the night with another five-song set and one encore, and Dooley announced last call.

"We can get some drinks to go to my cabin for a while," Vee said.

"I'm kind of tired after chasing around the ship all day, and I have my first shift in engineering tomorrow." I faked a yawn. "Got to make a good first impression."

"Understood. I keep forgetting you haven't been up here long. Do you need a guide back to your quarters?"

"I think I got it." And if I didn't, the nearsmart did. The night was reminding me way too much of many I'd had back in university. Lots of booze, interesting people, no strings attached… They'd been fun, but revisiting them didn't seem like a good idea in the early days of my marriage. "Have a good time."

"With these guys?" She glanced at Mateo and Tobey, who were still arguing about something that happened in-game. "I really doubt it."

I waved goodnight and left the bar as if I knew exactly where

I was going. I did better than I thought I would have. I only had to ask the nearsmart for help with one turn. When I got to my quarters, the shower cheerfully informed me that I'd used my hot water allocation for the day, so I washed up in the sink and lay down on the bed. The ceiling spun lazily above me to remind me that I'd probably had too much to drink again.

I had passed out too fast the night before to notice the sounds of the ship. The big engines made their presence known as a feeling more than a sound, but the air and water systems gurgled and sighed behind the walls. I expected to hear creaks and groans from the superstructure as it did battle with the enormous forces our acceleration was creating, but the mass-grav systems kept everything quiet.

The bed was soft, and I stretched out trying not to think about how far away I was from home and how much time had gone by there. A week? A month? There were plenty of times I hadn't talked to my mother for that long. The record was five months after I'd moved out of the undergraduate dorms to live with a zoologist I'd met in a campus bar. She had rarely been home, and I held up my end of the relationship mostly by tending to her menagerie of pets and specimens. She'd been the one to tell me about the breathing problems of captive sandcats. Poor Nibbles. Months nearly suffocating with a little kid pawing at him and then a messy end.

The door intercom crackled. "It's me," the voice said. "It's Adem."

ADEM

Adem kept his thumb on the intercom button. "Got a minute?"

Adem had nearly fallen over when Hisako told him she was the founder of the Sandcats. Now he was fighting the urge to gush like a fanboy. Seconds ticked by before the door slid open. He presented a jar of clear liquid. "Drink? I made it myself."

Hisako stepped back into the suite. "How can I refuse that? I'm sure there are glasses in here somewhere."

Adem nodded toward a wall cabinet. "In there. Top shelf." He held the Martin out to her. "Thought you might give me a lesson."

She blushed. "I'm sorry about—"

Adem interrupted, "You were amazing. I downloaded all the Sandcats' recordings when we interfaced with Gaul's worldnet. I had no idea you were—"

"I left the band before it got big."

"I know, but they were better before they got their patron." Adem leaned the guitar against the wall and opened the cabinet to get two glasses. He filled a small glass halfway with his engine room hooch and handed it to Hisako. "This is pretty potent, but it doesn't have any of Dooley's hangover additives."

"Does he really lace the drinks?"

"He never answers that question directly, but probably. If you're careful, it's not so bad. If not, you'll have a terrible next day."

"I learned that this morning."

"Lucy told me about that. She figured you were out long enough to score about a seven on the hangover scale. You don't want a ten."

"I never want that."

"Not twice. Should we toast or something?"

He was thinking a toast to their future, something that suggested she would one day adapt to the idea she was married and now lived on a spaceship.

She held up her glass. "To good music."

Fair enough. He could drink to that and did. The moonshine was cold and smooth. Hisako coughed. "It's very fresh."

"It will make you blink, but you won't go blind." Adem sat on the edge of the bed. "You're a better player than I am. I've been doing that song for years and never made it sound that good."

"It's not about technique." She took another slug of the liquor. "Correction, it's not *all* about technique."

"I'm completely self-taught. Can't even really read music."

"Years of lessons and my music aptitude is very high." Her voice turned brittle. "The kids at school started calling me a splice when I was little, but I didn't know it was true until recently."

"The gene stuff is a lot better than it used to be. Probably one of the only sciences that has advanced."

"The EuroD do love their perfect children." She left the bed to Adem and took a seat in the desk chair. "I think I grew up hating you. I hated your entire family because my mother kept telling me how grateful I should be to you. I even hated my friends because they had everything without having to make a deal with the devil to get it."

"You think I'm the devil?" Adem said.

"Or your mother is."

"I'm really sorry." He started to get up. "I'll go."

She motioned for him to stay. "What's to be sorry for? I grew up with food and a roof. I'm very well educated, and I am a near-genius. Plus, I started one of the best bands on Gaul, and I'm entry-level rich. Life is grand."

"Still." Adem didn't know what to do with his hands.

"Yeah, still." She held the glass out to Adem for a refill. "I met a little girl in *La Merde* a few years ago. If not for you, I could have been her."

She took her fresh drink and stood beside the view screen that passed for the suite's window. Adem had it set to show the starscape outside the ship's hull. The stars weren't all that visible at near *c*, but the nearsmart made some good guesses. "Are you here expecting sex?"

"I don't think that would be right."

"We're married. How could it be more right?" She laughed.

He put his glass on the nightstand "Coming here was a bad idea. I'm sorry."

"Stop apologizing." She picked up the Martin. "You could do a lot more with this. It has beautiful tone."

"We were in for an overhaul about a dozen years ago, and I found it in a storage locker. A member of the wake crew brought it from Earth. I started teaching myself how to play."

Hisako strummed a few bars of the song about the woman with the black veil. "The song's not just about feeling sad. The narrator is feeling all kinds of shit. There's a whole story behind the song. Why was she cheating on her husband? Was it a one-time thing or had they been lovers for years?" When she started singing the first verse, Adem began to understand. "Maybe you need to have hated and loved someone at the same time to really get it. Have you ever done that?"

"Maybe."

"You'd know it if you had."

He stood. "None of this was my idea, Hisako. My family–"

"I know. Lucy told me about the worm-drive. Looks like we're both stuck." She offered the guitar back to him.

"Hang onto it." He plucked a different guitar from the wall. "I'll use this one for a while. Thanks for the lesson."

Adem was halfway down the corridor before he remembered his new quarters were in the opposite direction. He wasn't looking forward to going there. The new digs were small, good for sleeping and not much else. There was barely room to pace.

He squeezed the neck of the guitar. It was the worst of the bunch. Totally synthetic, printed from an old file, and assembled at his engineering station. It had a flat, lifeless sound and barely stayed in tune for an entire song. Smashing it against the wall might actually improve it.

But it wasn't the guitar's fault it was shoddy and getting a better one would require another conversation with Hisako. Adem wasn't ready for that. He turned a corner and went looking for a quiet place to play.

HISAKO

Two days out of Gaul

Miraculously, Adem's homemade hooch countered Dooley's mad-scientist cocktails and I woke up clearheaded. I decided I probably owed Adem an apology – it wasn't his fault he was the face of all that was wrong in my life – but years of bile had found its focus on one person, and redistributing it wasn't going to be easy.

I showered and opted for a solo breakfast, just me and my reader at a quiet table in the cafeteria. Mateo and his friendly grin ruined it by sliding into the seat across from me. "You ready for today?"

Mixing booze and study-drugs would have put me well beyond Dooley's level ten hangover, so I hadn't spared a glance for the engineering manuals. "Not at all. Am I in trouble?"

"Nah. We'll go over everything, and I'll give you access to the simulation stims. You'll know your way around in no time. I was barely toilet-trained when I started."

When I didn't respond immediately, Mateo began to look like he was going to ask me something both vapid and personal like 'how was I getting on?' or 'how are things going with Adem?' For years, I'd relied on 'what are you studying?' to redirect and avoid having to answer vapid, personal questions, but that might not work on the *Hajj*. Fortunately, I was a fast learner. "Why did you come aboard the ship?" I said.

Bingo. Everybody had a story. Mateo started rearranging the condiments on the table. "I grew up on Nov Tero, and my parents were not well-educated. In the poorer sections, they sometimes call Traders 'Immortals' because they don't appear to age." He smiled sadly. "The gifts of relativity. Anyway, my parents bought into the whole thing and indentured themselves so I could live forever. They spent their whole lives mining copper to buy me a share on a Trader ship."

"When did you figure it out?"

"School. I never told them, though. They were so excited the last time I saw them. Twenty-five years had gone by, and I was barely a year older. Mission accomplished."

I shut down my reader and slid it into the thigh pocket of my coveralls. "I'm ready to go if you are."

"We'll have a good day. As long as Rakin stays off the floor, things run pretty smoothly."

Mateo made me lead the way to the engine room. I recognized a junction panel here, a conduit there, and got us there without much trouble. I gave it even odds that I'd be able to find my way back to my suite – Adem's suite – at the end of the shift.

The silent thrum of the fusion drive was much stronger in the engine room. The vibration ran up my feet and… I flushed.

Mateo grinned. "Everyone feels it. Sometimes I think the whole department runs on sexual tension." He pointed. "We'll start over there with the main console. I'll walk you through the–"

Mateo was cut off by a sharp double tap. We both looked up to see Rakin Sadiq behind the glass of an observation window.

"That's his office. Hold on. Let me see what he wants."

Mateo climbed a short ladder to a catwalk and stepped into Rakin's office. I could see them talking through the window. Mateo came back down. "He wants to see you before we get started."

"What about?"

"He's head of the department. He probably just wants to make sure you know it."

I climbed the ladder to Rakin's little throne room and slid open the door. He clutched me to his paunch and kissed both of my cheeks. "You've been to the bridge? Forget it. Welcome to the most important part of the ship!"

I pulled free and bowed the way my teachers had taught me to bow to older, richer people. "I look forward to learning from you and your staff, Uncle."

He waved his hand. "You won't learn anything useful from them. You've been to a real university. You probably learned more in one day there than these idiots will pick up in a lifetime. Can I offer you some refreshment?"

"I just had breakfast."

He put a mug of coffee in my hand anyway and directed me to a small couch. He sat close to me and draped his heavy arm along the couch's back. I could feel its warmth on my shoulders. His knee brushed mine. "I was supposed to have been captain, you know, but I left my poor sister to carry on the family business." He sighed. "I have always felt a little guilty about that."

"You came back."

"I did." He studied my face. "I have a proposition for you."

I was pretty sure I didn't want to hear his idea. No one had said a good word about him to me, and this meeting wasn't doing him any favors either. He wide face seemed set in a permanent leer.

"It's nothing untoward," he said, sensing my discomfort. "I need your help with an engineering project."

"You have an entire team of engineers at your disposal, Uncle."

"None of them can do for me what you can."

"What do you need?"

"Would you like a drink?" He made a long arm and poured himself a glass of something amber from a decanter. He took a sip and smacked his lips. "A family, as I am sure you know, is a complicated organism. Fraught with well-meaning secrets and some not so well-meaning."

I waited. My family had a lot of things it didn't talk about and many problems that went unaddressed, but secrets... The biggest one, maybe the only one, had come out when I was thirteen.

"I'm afraid, dear niece, you will soon learn the motives behind your marriage arrangement were not solely of the heart."

Shocking. "I'm sorry, I don't understand."

"We are much alike, Hisako. You don't want to be on this antique any more than I do. I knew that the moment I saw you. We want control of our own lives. We want to be free." He sipped from his glass. "I can give you freedom and enough money that no one can ever take it away again."

"How?"

"We'll talk more about this later, but I will say this: there are things rarer than UA worm-drives."

Classified information, my ass. "I–"

Rakin put his finger to his lips. "It would be wise not to mention this little chat to anyone. People like you and I value our autonomy, but my sister takes delight in controlling others. She doesn't value thoughts that come from outside her little cabal." He gestured toward the door. "Good day."

He failed to stand and show me out, so I gave up on etiquette and left without bowing. I was a little unsteady on the ladder but recovered by the time I reached the engine room floor.

"You okay?" Mateo said.

"Just a little light-headed." And wildly curious. I didn't like Rakin but Maneera Sadiq had done little to earn my loyalty.

"I can show you the break room first, so you can catch your breath."

"Let's just get to work," I said.

By the end of the shift, I knew there was no way two weeks in engineering was going to teach me enough about the ship to be of any great use. There were people on Mateo's team who could tear many of the systems apart and put them back together. Mateo could probably rebuild a lot of them from scratch. The best I could hope for was to become someone who could tell by the readouts and lights whether they were working right.

"So that's the tour," Mateo concluded after eight hours of leading me around the engineering section and through what felt like miles of conduits and corridors. "Any questions?"

I threw up my hands. "I don't see how anyone expects me to become fluent in these things by the time my rotation is up. It's impossible."

"It is. But everyone aboard does a couple of weeks down here just to get the lay of the land. The captain likes to know she can send anyone she gets her hands on down here and get a reasonably accurate status report back."

That made me feel a little better.

"You'll learn how to do some basic maintenance, too. No one is expecting you to become an expert. That would take years."

"I thought… I guess I don't know what I thought." I'd assumed my genes and my education would make me the smartest person on the ship, but it had only taken Mateo one shift to show me that wasn't true. "There's a lot I don't know."

"Don't feel bad. I'd be lost talking about mass-grav. I'm sure you could work circles around me up there."

"You'd be surprised." No one alive really knew how mass-grav worked. There were plenty of theories and so-called experts, but no one was qualified to do much beyond plugging things in and fiddling with the settings, and even that was asking for trouble. I knew as much about how they worked as anyone, and I wasn't much more than a button pusher. "It's UA tech. Rigged to self-destruct if anyone tries to get a good look at it." Didn't save them and only screwed the rest of us over. "Show me life-support again, and we'll call it a day."

Captain Maneera Sadiq refilled her mug from the coffee decanter at the center of the small dining table in her suite and offered to refill mine. I demurred. I had barely tasted the first serving, and I was a little afraid it would kill me. It was stronger even than the Turkish coffee my mother sometimes treated herself to. "You know I've never actually operated a worm-drive, don't you? I don't know anyone who has."

"But you know how they work."

"I've read a manual. I know the theories. I know how a star works, too, but don't expect me to build one for you. The last person to see the inside of a worm-drive died a thousand standard years ago. The UA tamper-proofed them in a dozen different ways."

"If it isn't functional, there's nothing we can do," the captain said. "We'll put it on the market, sell it to the highest bidder, and let them worry about the tamper-proofing."

I considered the inky darkness inside my coffee cup. Neither cream nor sugar had made an appearance on the table.

"Hisako, can you imagine what it would mean if we were able to measure trade runs in standard months instead of decades?"

"It would make you an awful lot of money."

"You as well. It would also allow you to see your mother again before she is an old woman. Reunite with your friends before they forget you. There could be cultural and educational exchanges between the planets. Tourism. Business opportunities. Scientific advancement. Humanity could be one species again, one giant civilization."

"What makes you think they're going to let you keep it?"

"They who?"

"Anyone. The Nov Tero syndicates. The Gaul military. Freedom." I ticked the names off on my fingers. "Any of those planets could find some use for a working worm-drive."

The captain wiped her mouth with a napkin. "The salvage laws are on our side. What we find, we keep."

"The laws won't matter when something so rare is at stake. Even the Traders' Union will put up a fight."

That amused her. "My family helped create the Union. The other families might mutter and grumble a bit, but the Union is held together by laws my parents and grandparents wrote. The drive is ours."

"I can't promise you I can make it work." I folded my arms.

"If it doesn't work, you'll get your share of the money we make by selling it and the other salvage from the *Hadfield*."

"What else did you take?"

"Everything we could scrape out of the computers. A dozen androids. Some of the personal effects of the crew. Lots and lots of spare parts. We'll make a profit no matter what happens."

"Is that all that matters to you?"

"It's up there." She offered me a plate of pastries, but I declined. "Dooley wants to move an asteroid into orbit around Nov Tero or Gaul and retire there. That sounds better to me every year."

"Everyone says Nov Tero is a snake pit, and there's a revolution brewing on Gaul."

"If there's a war in progress, we can stay aboard another year or two and let it pass beneath us." She folded her napkin onto the table. "If you're finished eating, let me show you what we have."

The captain stopped the lift a quarter-way down the spine and keyed her ID into the door of a cargo pod. It opened onto tightly packed stacks of crates and equipment.

"Is this all from the *Hadfield*?" I said. "I'm surprised you didn't just take the whole ship."

"Its sister killed a planet. I can't think of anyone who would want to fly such a thing, can you?"

"There are people in *La Mur* who use frozen refugees to decorate their homes."

Only her eyes reacted. "Let me amend that. I can't think of anyone I would want to see flying it." She rapped her knuckles on one of the crates. "What do you need to make this work?"

"Time. And access to the *Hadfield*'s records. The United Americas invented the thing; I imagine they have an installation manual. How did you get it off the ship intact?"

"Like all UA tech it's modular. Disconnect it and carry it away. No tampering required." She smiled. "Odessa Romanov and her new android are working to decrypt the records. What else?"

"Three or four good techs."

"I have given you full access to the personnel records. Let me know who you want, and I will have them reassigned. This will be an independent project outside the chain of command. You will report only to me." Her eyes shifted from warm to steel. "Am I clear on that?"

"Lucy already told me the project was classified." And the circle of confidentiality had already sprung a leak. But if Maneera didn't know that, I wasn't going to be the one to tell her.

She laughed. "Classified? It's a very small ship, Hisako. Anyway, I have to present the plan to the shareholders soon. But I do want to keep information leaks to a minimum. At the very least, I want to know what you and your team know first."

A thought dawned. "I suppose you're going to ask me to put Adem on my crew so we can spend more time together."

"That's entirely up to you." Her eyes were cool. "He's the best all-around technician on the ship. The rest…?" She placed her hand on the worm-drive crate. "You're adults in a business arrangement. It's up to you to decide if you want to turn that into something more."

We went back to the lift, and Maneera showed me to a workroom in the belly of the command section. She patted my arm maternally and left me to my thoughts. I contacted Odessa, and she invited me to her suite, which was nearby. A naked man greeted me at her door.

"Good evening," he said. "I believe I may have been taken by pirates or terrorists. Please contact the authorities."

"Um." I was taken aback, but I wasn't sure if his nudity or his speech had done the work.

"Ignore him," said a voice from deeper inside the suite. "That's just Reg. He's an android. Reg, this is Hisako Sasaki."

I got a better look at Reg as I stepped through the door. It was definitely male, well-formed, and missing the back of his skull. There was a mass of electronics and tell-tale lights where his brain should have been.

"Good day, Hisako," it said. "What pronouns do you prefer?"

"It looks so real."

Odessa frowned. "Reg asked you a question. It's not polite to ignore him."

The android's gray eyes were on mine. If it made her happy. "Good evening, Reg. I prefer she, her, hers. How are you?"

The android smiled. "I am fine. I believe I may have been taken by pirates or terrorists. Please contact the authorities." It rattled off a string of numbers.

Odessa patted its shoulder. "There's a good boy. You can ignore us until I call on you."

Reg powered down, becoming as inanimate as furniture.

"Seems a little stiff," I said. "I thought these guys were supposed to have more personality."

"I had to write him a new one. It's just a shell. A lot of his programming is inactive or he wouldn't be helping us."

The android's skin was cool to the touch and a little less pliable than human flesh.

"They almost got it, but not quite," Odessa said. "His mind barely qualifies as a nearsmart – I could change that, of course – but they made the body as human as they could."

"Why?"

"It was made to interact with people. I expect he fits in better like this than if he had tentacles. Besides, humans have needs and fraternization was frowned upon in the UA military."

I felt my eyebrows surge upward. "They had sex with him?"

"He's fully functional. I left that part of his programming active. He's just an over-qualified sex toy if you look at it right."

I suppressed a shudder. "What happens after he gets us the files? Back in the crate and bound for auction?"

"He's all mine," she said. "It was part of the deal with the captain. I get two of them. There's another under the bed. I'm going to reverse engineer them and go into business."

"Who's rich enough to buy an android? I've seen a few serving robots in *La Mur* but nothing nearly as fancy as him."

"I won't be making them as fancy. There's enough platinum in Reg to buy my own planet. But I can make do. My androids won't be as smart, but they'll be good enough for most work. Cheaper and way more reliable than those *La Mur* antiques once I get a factory going."

I'd had enough small talk with the technophile. "How soon can I get into the *Hadfield*'s files?"

"We cracked the encryption a while ago. We've just been waiting for you. The decryption ripped up the nearsmart's organization structure, but I can show you how to build a new index."

With Odessa's help, I hunted up any files pertaining to the worm-drive. "There's the manual, and…" I blinked and swiped to the next page. "Did you look at any of this?"

"No. Once I solved the problem I–"

"You report to me, right?" I asked Odessa. "I'm in charge."

Her eyes narrowed. "Of this project."

"I want to put all this in secure storage. Passcode protected. My eyes only."

ADEM

One month out of Gaul

Rakin Sadiq stared at his sister, his mouth gaping. "This is insanity!" He wasn't the only one around the conference table expressing disbelief, but they were definitely in the minority.

"You said something had to change, brother. This would be a change."

"The *Hajj* is slowing down, Uncle," Lucy said. "We've lost .03 percent off our best speed. If this works, we'll be faster than any other ship in the Traders' Union."

"If it works." Rakin waved his hands. "It won't work. You'll kill us all. Who knows if the drive is even intact, let alone if we can adapt it to our systems? I forbid it."

"This is a democracy, Uncle," Adem said. "That means you can't forbid anything."

Dooley smiled. "If you're afraid, Rakin, I'll be happy to buy you out right now. We can drop you somewhere, and you'll miss the whole thing."

"Kalinda, dear, are you going to let this happen? I mean, fine, salvage and sell the thing, but install it on the ship?" Rakin switched his focus to the crewman beside her. "Don't you see she's going to ruin us?"

Both women squirmed. Kalinda Maynard, the investors'

representative, worked off a set of priorities provided by her employers, and priority one was profit. The crew's elected representative, Jolyon Ong, was fidgety in general, but Adem could imagine the messages she was getting via her reader and comm. Everyone who traveled in space had fantasized about a worm-drive at one point or another, but learning one was aboard had been a swift, sharp shock.

"You've seen the evidence. You know my plan," the captain said.

"Evidence," Rakin sputtered. "I've seen a transcript of a conversation with a crazy wanderer, who our mother never approved of, and a couple of stills of old junk from a derelict battleship. How do you even know you got the whole drive?"

"That's why Adem brought an expert into the family." The captain smiled at Hisako. "Why don't we hear what she has to say?"

"The worm-drive is intact." Hisako's hands and shoulders were relaxed, her voice confident. "Moreover, Odessa Romanov has cracked into the *Christopher Hadfield*'s database and found instructions on installation and operation of the drive. I believe we can do this."

Adem believed it, too. Working alongside Hisako for the past month had convinced him of her intelligence and abilities. If anyone could pull it off, she could.

"What about our safety?" Jolyon said.

"The danger is minimal," Hisako said. "The drive will either function normally, or it won't work at all. We'll install it and test it. If it doesn't put us where we want, we won't go."

The captain looked around the table. "Shall we bring this to a vote?"

"My three percent says no. Hell, no!" Rakin crossed his arms and looked at Kalinda expectantly.

"With no way to consult with my employers, I also say no to the proposal."

"That's another twenty-nine shares," Rakin said. "Crew?"

Jolyon held up her finger. "Tabulating." All over the ship the crew was voting on the proposal via their readers. "We have ten percent against. Twelve percent for."

The captain cleared her throat. "Check my math, Rakin. That's forty-one shares against, twelve for. I'll add my twenty-four shares now, so forty-one to thirty-six. Dooley?"

Rakin snorted. "Of course, he'll vote with you."

"That's never a given," Dooley said. "You know that as well as I do, Rakin. I have a lot of beer on this ship to look out for. However, I vote in favor."

"Forty-seven percent for installing the worm-drive and testing it on the way to Nov Tero," the captain said. "Forty-two against. Lucy? Adem? Hisako?"

"Be reasonable." Rakin put on his best wise-uncle face. "We could end up adrift or worse. Then where will we be?"

"Thank you for your concern, Uncle. You seem so sincere." Lucy grinned. "My five shares are for the plan."

Adem's eyes were tired. "Mine, too. My four shares, I mean." One of his shares and one of his mother's had been spun off for Hisako's wedding present.

"That leaves you," Dooley said to Hisako. "Remember, just because they're family doesn't mean you can't yell at them or vote against them."

"How can I refuse?" Her smile was brittle. "This is literally what I was born for. I vote in favor of the captain's plan."

"That's two more shares in favor, bringing us to fifty-eight shares for and forty-two against. The motion carries."

"You sure you don't want us to buy you out, Rakin?" Dooley said.

Rakin looked as though he might spit. "You don't have the money." He included his sister in his look of distaste. "Neither of you do. You spent too much on useless information and bribes to failing governments. If this doesn't work, you're ruined. I'll make sure of it."

"I can buy your shares, Uncle." Lucy said. "It would be worth it to get you off the ship."

Rakin rose from the table. "You're all so far out on the edge I don't imagine you know what safety looks like. If you're lucky I'll buy your shares out of arrears, and you'll have enough left for a squat in the swamp zone on Freedom." He left without looking back.

Kalinda looked like she was about to chase after Rakin, but Jolyon led her out the opposite door.

"Are they dating or conspiring?" Adem said.

"Dating," Lucy said.

The captain sighed. "I am going to take that as a motion to adjourn. Any seconds?"

Dooley raised his hand. "I second, and move that drinks are on the house for anyone who shows up at Terry's tonight."

"Was what Rakin said true?" Adem said. "Are you in that deep?"

The captain rubbed her eyes. "Let's just say that if this goes bad, we might need to borrow some money from you for that swamp squat."

"Nah," Dooley said. "I still have family in the swamp zone. We'll be alright. But Rakin's not wrong about everything. We're two years overdue for an overhaul and other maintenance. The way we're doing things now won't work much longer."

"I'll run this rig into a star before I let her be a slaver," the captain said. "And damn the lawsuits."

"It's just a ship," Adem said. "If Rakin takes over, none of us will stay. It's not like it will be our home anymore. We'll just have to find something else to do."

The captain smiled. "Maybe the Spaceman needs a manager."

Lucy followed her brother out of the conference room. "You were moodier than usual in there."

"I'm tired." Adem rubbed his face. "My quarters are lousy, I'm a shitty guitar player, and my mother traded two years of my life for a worm-drive. I'm lonely. I'm angry. I'm horny."

"You didn't have to give Hisako your room, you know."

"Didn't have to?" His look of outrage faded. "True, but–"

"But it was the right thing to do, and my little brother always ends up doing the right thing."

Adem stopped walking. "The right thing sucks."

"It does sometimes." She put her hand on his waist. "Vee and I had a bet about whether or not your brain was going to explode like this. Hisako had twenty-four years to get pissed off and work through it. You've only had eleven months."

"I don't even know if I like her as a person. I've been working with her, doing my job, but I feel like she wants me dead. I'm on tiptoes all the damned time."

"You don't have to stay married, either. Once the contract's up you can cut your losses, start dating again, maybe look up Sarat…"

Adem sighed. "Do you realize that it's been more than ten years for him? Even if I wanted to, and I'm not saying I do, he has an entirely different life now, and I'm not part of it." Adem resumed walking. "I don't want to talk about this anymore."

"Which of you won the bet?" Adem added.

Lucy took his hand. "I did."

HISAKO

Bullets twanged off the metal siding above my head. I crouched lower, making myself as small as possible in the lee of an overturned transit capsule. My gun was low on ammo. Another fine mess I'd gotten myself into.

In wake of the shareholders' meeting, I met Vee in the forward stim studio for an evening of mayhem with her gaming guild. It was one of Tobey's games, she said, the revolution thing he'd picked up on Gaul. I stripped down to my underwear and climbed into the stim capsule Vee assigned me. In seconds, I was a EuroD soldier, armed and armored, bent on taking down the guerrillas and turning *La Merde* to rubble. They weren't making it easy.

"I found the mission brief!" Vee announced over our comm gear. "Guerrillas have a big missile they're going to launch at *La Mur*. Lots and lots of pretty EuroD corpses!"

Something exploded overhead, and bits of brick and rusted metal dropped into my hiding place. I felt every piece, thanks to Odessa's work over the years to soup up the *Hajj*'s stim interface. It wouldn't kill me, she said, but it might leave some bruises.

Vee leaned out from cover to fire her grenade launcher toward the bullets' origin. The explosion took down an already battered storefront on the other side of the street. The shooting stopped. "Let's go!" she said. "Double time!"

I uncurled and ran after her, Odessa close behind me. There was an overturned bus on the road ahead. I ignited my jetpack and leapt over it. In the air I was a better target; bullets sang past me again, but I cleared the bus faster than the rest of my team. I knelt behind a toppled construction drone and began to lay down covering fire. The smoke from the drone helped to hide me.

"I need ammo!" I shouted into my comm. "I'm behind the big robot, which shouldn't be here because all the ones that still worked went to *La Mur* years ago!"

There were a number of such anachronisms in the game. Lean-tos and shanties were not rugged enough to take a punch, much less a bullet, so the programmers had taken the sort of buildings that were in midtown, roughed them up, and moved them to *La Merde*. The fighters we'd encountered thus far had been dressed in rags, but underneath they'd been disturbingly fit. Prime specimens, really, with no sign of malnutrition or want. And they were so well-armed!

"Are you complaining about the game's accuracy again?" One of Tina's supply drones buzzed overhead and dropped a case of ammunition for my gun. Tina usually worked in life-support, but at the moment she was our sniper and logistics specialist.

I slammed a fresh clip into my gun and peeked over the robot. Nothing was coming. "This game was made in Versailles City. You'd have thought they would have done a little research."

"Four years have passed down there," Tina said through the drone. "Maybe it changed."

I waved the drone away. The game had already been two years old when Tobey bought it, so I was going to chalk the anachronisms up to plot convenience and lazy writing.

Vee huffed and puffed to my position and squatted behind the robot with me. "Sniper tower up ahead. We need to take it out before we can advance." She held out her hand and a hologram of the target, a thirty-story apartment building, floated over it.

"There's nothing like that down here." I pointed over my shoulder with my thumb. "Anything that tall would be back that-a-way."

"Play the game, not your memory, Sako," Vee spoke into her comm. "Odessa will be with us in a minute. She's clearing out a nest."

I checked my ammo and opened up my HUD to peruse the health stats of my teammates. I was the team healer, ready to spring into action with my trusty medkit, but everyone was in the green. A flurry of bootsteps turned into a dramatic slide as Odessa joined us.

Vee waited for the dust to clear before speaking. "Was it Tobey?"

"Nah." Odessa switched her cigar from the right side of her mouth to the left. "Buncha NPCs. Cannon fodder."

Vee opened the mission map on her hand hologram thing. "I wonder where they are."

I peeked over the robot again. All clear. "We should probably get moving."

"Head to the tower on my mark." Vee put the map away and checked her grenade launcher. She stood. "Mark!"

I followed her at a fast jog. On my left, Odessa's head exploded.

"Sniper!" Vee shouted. "Take cover!"

I bent to grab Odessa's bullet belt or whatever and dragged her along with me to the side of a crashed shuttle. I readied the revival "nanobot" injection. Depending on the game mechanic, waiting too long would make the injection fail or turn Odessa into a hungry zombie, but only a few seconds had passed. Her head reformed.

"Sniper?" she said.

I pulled other tools out of my medkit to rebuild her health and ability stats. My comm crackled, and Vee mumbled a situation report.

"Where did the shot come from?" Odessa said.

"Ahead and up. Probably our target. Vee thinks there are two shooters on the roof of the building." I checked Odessa's stats. She was as close to brand-new as I could get her. "She's going to launch a few grenades toward them. When we hear the first one go off, we're supposed to get up and run toward the tower. Right up close to the building they can't shoot us."

"Vee says that? Okay."

I commed Vee to report Odessa was back on her feet. My racing heart wasn't getting the message that we were only playing a game.

Odessa put her hand on my shoulder. "Wait for the bang."

The whump of Vee's grenade launcher almost sent me into a sprint, but I held back until I heard the explosion. I heard another whump as Vee provided cover for our run. My skin crawled as I imagined the sniper's scope crawling across my back.

"Zigzag!" Odessa yelled. "Don't make it easy for them."

We stopped hard against an apartment building that looked a lot like the one I grew up in. We were met at the door by a heavily bandaged little boy.

"I'm hungry," he said, "and my parents are dead. Do you have some food?"

I had a stash of meal bars I was supposed to use when my stamina levels dropped. "Do you think I should give him something?"

"Try it and see what happens. Maybe he'll reward you."

I knelt in front of the boy and reached into my pack. The boy smiled. Odessa stitched a red line up his chest and neck with her machine pistol. His blood splashed on my helmet visor as he fell.

"What the fuck you do that for?"

She toed the corpse. "He had a grenade behind his back. I saw it in the reflection of the window there." The explosive rolled free of the boy's body. I picked it up.

"This really doesn't make sense," I said. "Kids are precious here. They wouldn't–"

"Come on!"

I kept the rest of the thought to myself and followed Odessa to the stairwell. I remembered the family I'd had to climb through the last time I visited my mother. We encountered more children and a couple of old ladies but didn't stop to chat. Tina shot a crying woman who didn't take our disinterest for an answer. The woman dropped a pistol as she fell.

"This is fucked up," I said. "I've never played a game where you had to watch out for civilians."

"I guess there are no civilians in a revolution."

Our armor creaked as we climbed. Glass and trash crunched under the heavy soles of our boots. The people we'd seen in the building hadn't been wearing shoes, another anachronism. People who lived in *La Merde* were resourceful. If they couldn't buy it, they made it themselves.

"You're thinking again," Odessa said.

"Is this what people really picture when they think about refugees? A bunch of dirty people with one hand out for a donation and the other hand with a bomb in it? I've been to *La Merde*. It's not all like that."

"It's just a game, Hisako."

We made it to the roof without getting killed. The snipers were NPCs, their combat AI so focused on sniping that we barely had to sneak to get behind them and riddle them with bullets. Mission accomplished.

Odessa peered down the building and opened her pack.

"What are you doing?" I said.

"Rappelling down the side. I'm not going back through all those people with you. You're as bad as Adem when he gets back from one of his walks."

Back at street level, we ordered more ammo from Tina and

reunited with Vee. She offered us both high fives.

"I found them." Vee brought up her holographic map again. There was a red smudge on it now.

"I think that's supposed to be the Square," I said. "It's an outdoor market and festival thing down near the space elevator."

"It's also guerrilla HQ and the missile launch site."

"Human shield?" Odessa said.

"Right out of the guerrilla-warfare handbook." Vee's grin was savage. "Let's get this done."

"Don't feed the widows and orphans," Odessa warned. "They have grenades."

The trip to the Square was easy, although we had to stop to give Odessa time to disarm a doorway that was rigged to explode. Vee checked in with Tina who was having a hard time finding a good position.

"No sniper support," Vee reported. "The clock's ticking. We'll have to risk it."

The market stalls inside the Square were empty, but they'd definitely been modeled on the ones I saw when we found Marjani. The programmers probably watched the documentary, too.

"The elevator tower came down on all of this before we left," I said.

"Nostalgia later," Odessa said. "We've got about ten minutes before the missile launches, and I don't want to give Tobey bragging rights."

"You just don't want to have to sleep with him again. You need to stop making that bet."

"You could loan him Reg," I said.

She said she'd think about it, but five seconds later a sniper's bullets streaked out of nowhere, and she was dead again. Vee and I ran full tilt toward the Square's second corner.

"I didn't see that coming!" Vee said.

"Any chance Tina can get a drop on him?"

"Maybe. If we keep moving, we should be all right."

The missile launchpad was in the Children's Village which, for the game's convenience, was not deserted. Maybe the kids had nowhere else to go.

"Keep an eye out. Mateo likes to pop out and–" The bullets cut her off. Vee fell, nearly out of health, and I dragged her behind one of the low huts and slapped a bandage on her chest.

"Go." She gritted her teeth. The neural feedback was making her pretty uncomfortable. "There's no time for anything else. Shut down the missile."

"I don't have any tech skills."

"Shoot it then. Or blow it up."

I left her bleeding and crept around the other side of the hut. Tobey was guarding the missile emplacement, and I emptied my gun at him. I hit him, but not enough to take him out. He dove for cover. "You're almost out of time, Hisako!"

He had set the missile up in the thickest part of the Children's Village, so he could use the kids and their ratty huts as shields. I slid the grenade I took from the orphan out of my bag and pulled the ring, keeping my fist tight around the handle.

"Do you have any food?" A little girl with matted hair stared at me from out of the crowd of children. Her face was dirty. Another could-have-been little sister.

"What are you waiting for, Sako?" Vee shouted. "Save *La Mur*!"

"I'm really hungry," the girl said. "I haven't eaten in days."

I threw the grenade. Any good EuroD would.

ADEM

Adem slid open the stim capsule. Yet another play-through without getting so much as a scratch. He'd found the perfect hiding place atop the wall surrounding the Square and had taken down Odessa, wounded Vee, and had been about to shoot Hisako when–

Tobey was still laughing his ass off at her bobbled grenade throw. The explosive had bounced back and landed at Hisako's feet, obliterating both her and Vee. Tina showed up in time to finish what Hisako had started with Tobey, but it had been too late. The missile launched on schedule, blowing apart maybe a sixteenth of *La Mur*. Score a small win for the common man, subtract all the kids who died serving as a shield. A rare victory over Vee's Furies. Tobey would be bragging about it for months.

Drinks at Terry's Place were the post-game ritual. The players would razz each other's strategies and argue over who'd made the best kill. Adem's narrow bed was calling loudly, but beer promised a muzzy end to the long day. He finger-combed his hair and followed Tobey and the rest of the team down to the bar.

Adem ordered a beer and helped push several mismatched tables together to form a single big one. He took a seat on the boys' side and saluted Tobey with his beer. "This is, what, the second time in history you've beaten the Furies?"

"Third, if you count the time that nuke went off and wiped out everyone on the map." Tobey scrubbed his mouth with the back of his hand. He was drinking Dooley's latest concoction, and it looked like a fast worker.

"You can't count that one," Mateo said. "Both sides wiped, and we failed the mission."

"They failed, too, but we're the ones who set the bomb off," Tobey said.

The door slid open. Enter the Furies.

Tobey waved. "Hey, remember that time with the nuke…?" He was already getting mush-mouthed. Adem resolved to stick with the beer.

"You're not still claiming that as a win, are you?" Vee said.

"At worst it was a draw," Tobey said.

"How can it be a draw when it was a complete fuck up?" Odessa snorted. "We need to pull that game out of the archives and play it again or put this to rest."

Vee ordered drinks for her team and sat with them on the other side of the long table. "I can't believe you went for a human shield, Tob. Kids! That way leads to the dark side, pal." She sounded unimpressed.

Tobey put his glass down too carefully. "That's what terrorists do."

"If it wasn't for that sniper, we would have stopped you cold." Vee squinted at Adem. "I didn't even know you were playing."

"Tobey caught me on the way back to my suite."

Odessa was arguing with Mateo. "If we'd had another couple of minutes, Tina could have come around and nailed you both."

"I had you in my sights when Sako's grenade went off." Tina had set the elaborate cocktail aside and, like Adem, was sticking to beer.

Hisako put her head in her hands. "I'm never going to live that down, am I?"

"A healer against a human shield?" Tobey hooted. "Your accuracy was absolutely blown. I'm surprised you were able to throw."

"A lot of games don't have the human shield option," Vee said.

"You can only use it in this one if you play the terrorist side."

"They're not terrorists," Adem and Hiasko spoke simultaneously. Their eyes met for an instant, and they shared a smile.

"That's not what the game says." Vee ordered another round of drinks for her side.

"Forget that," Hisako said. "If the guerrillas – still not terrorists – were really fighting for a better life in *La Merde*, there's no way they'd put their kids in danger. However, I could see the EuroD side threatening the Children's Village as a deterrent."

Adem nodded agreement.

"Where'd the guerillas even get that missile?" Hisako continued. "I could see guns, maybe, although I'm not sure where those would come from either, but a high-tech missile? No way."

"They must have bought it," Vee said.

"With what money? From whom?" Hisako brandished her cocktail. "Someone else had to be involved."

"The scenario didn't make a lot of sense," Adem said. "Arming old ladies and kids and putting them in stairwells? That's not an attack. That's a last-ditch defensive measure. The EuroD had to be the aggressor."

"Ooh, listen to Mr Earth History." Tobey's eyelids were drooping. "It's a game. We played by the rules, and we won."

"The rules are stupid, then," Hisako said.

"Stupid or no, Tobey's right," Vee said. "They won fair and square. Next time, it will be different."

"For now though," Mateo's smile said it all, "I understand there was a bet made."

Tobey blushed. "You don't have to. I mean just because we…"

"I never welsh on a bet. Sets a bad precedent," Odessa said. "I'll send Reg over later tonight. Hisako's idea. It's very gentle."

Tobey paled.

Adem risked another smile at Hisako, hoping that she'd appreciated the fact that he saw things her way. "I talked to folks in *La Merde* when the tower came down. They think the EuroDs did it or paid to have it done."

Hisako frowned. "How does that make sense? *La Mur* depends on the elevator."

"*La Mur* wasn't underneath the tower when it fell, though. Only the refugee community lost homes and lives. The elevator was probably back up, business as usual, in a few weeks."

"My father was part…" She looked down at her drink. "Let's say he knew some of the angrier people in *La Merde*. They were always talking about doing something like that."

"Maybe. But talking is one thing. Makes no sense that they'd bring the tower down on their own people, barely affecting the EuroD, yet giving them the excuse for a crackdown." He twisted his wedding ring absentmindedly. "I just don't see it."

"Bad planning?"

He raised his glass. "To not making bad plans."

They clinked glasses. Further down the play-by-play continued. Tobey's head was on the table, and he appeared to be asleep. Odessa was re-enacting the battle in the Square using silverware and salt-and-pepper shakers. Vee was challenging Mateo to an arm wrestle.

Adem drained his beer. "I'm going to turn in."

"I won't be far behind you. This project is kicking my ass." Hisako rested her forehead in the palms of her hands. "Before you go…"

"Yeah?" Adem froze, half-out of his seat.

"I want to apologize." Hisako lowered her hands. "It's not your fault I'm here, and I'm going to try acting like I know it."

"That would be nice. Being married doesn't mean we can't be friends."

HISAKO

Three months out of Gaul

"My sources tell me things are going well." Rakin waggled a bottle of vodka at me. "I am here to help you celebrate."

Sources, plural. It wasn't a big surprise. The crew was small and tightly quartered, and the most innocent slip made loud echoes. We'd told no one but the captain about our testing schedule, but everyone aboard seemed to know the first worm-drive trial was only a few weeks away. There was even a trial-date pool filling up one whole wall at Terry's.

"It's late, Uncle." I leaned against the doorway. It felt like the conversation might take a while. "Does your source list include the blond guy, the bald gaming addict, or the woman who sleeps with robots?"

"I won't waste time trying to convince you it's my niece, but what makes you think it's not your husband? How is he, by the way? Are you two settling in well together?"

Rakin's smile made me feel like he was imagining me naked and dead at the same time. It reminded me of some of the EuroD fathers I'd met. "I'm sure your sources have filled you in on that, too."

"My sympathies. I was married once."

"You must have gotten on well."

"Much better after she died." He lowered his voice. "You should let me in. I assure you, Nov Tero vodka is an opportunity," he stressed the word, "not to be missed."

Four months is a long time to form relationships. Vee and Lucy were great. Mateo was fun. Odessa was charmingly quirky. Even Adem was starting to grow on me. Maneera, though… The thought of making her life more difficult had its appeal.

Rakin followed me inside and twisted the stopper off the bottle. I pointed out the shelf of glasses. He poured two then relaxed his bulk into my desk chair. "Nov Tero gravity is a few points lower than my sister likes to keep on the ship. I miss it."

The ship's gravity suited me just fine. It was a little less than the pull I'd grown up with and made waking up with a hangover more bearable. I sat on the edge of the bed before Rakin had the audacity to ask me to take a seat in my own place.

"Where did we leave off?" he said.

"Either with a nebulous proposition or histrionics about why the worm drive won't work."

"Even if it does, we'll still be delivering groceries for a living. No great improvement."

"It could make the family a lot of money."

"Money is just a way to keep score." He edged the second glass toward me.

I ignored it. "What the fuck do you want, Rakin?"

His face darkened, either at my failure to use an honorific or the fact that I, a mere woman, used foul language in front of him but, with an effort, he redonned his composure. "I have friends who are interested in protecting themselves. You are in possession of something that can help."

"There's only one worm-drive."

"And little protection it will be, as my sister will discover in time. I'm looking for something more immediate." He made a pistol shape with his hand and pretended to shoot me with it.

The back of my neck prickled. "You want weapons."

"And my sister foolishly left all of them behind on the warship. However, you can help me get something nearly as useful. I'm told the files we downloaded from the *Hadfield's* computers are full of–" Rakin snickered, "–interesting things."

I tried to keep the panic and anger off my face. Odessa must have hacked me. It was the only way Rakin could know about the UA files. If I had a better computer tech, I'd fire her.

"Operating manuals for ship systems mostly." I bit my tongue to fight off the sudden attack of dry mouth.

"Perfect. I'm interested in one of the manuals. For a weapon."

There was a roaring in my ears. I was surprised Rakin couldn't hear it. If all he wanted was one of the operating manuals, maybe he didn't know everything. "You said yourself there are no weapons."

Rakin poured himself another glass of the icy vodka. "It's a charade, a bluff. If one side can make the other believe they possess something very frightening, it's possible to win on the threat alone."

"How frightening?" Missiles were frightening. Bombs were scary, too. Rakin wouldn't need manuals for guns, and those were probably the least scary. The only UA weapons system terrifying enough to make a good bluff was… Shit.

"Frightening enough to destroy a planet. You've heard of Makkah, I hazard? I don't need such a threat myself, but I would be happy to supply it to others who do."

The MCD. The United America's mass-compression device. The beauty of mass-grav control perverted into a weapon. The planet crusher. The squeezer. Used only once in a war a millennium ago, it destroyed an entire civilization. I felt sick. "Who would possibly want that?"

"I could sell it easily on Nov Tero, and I have connections elsewhere.

Most want weapons more than they want the threat of weaponry, but I'm sure they could be made to see the practicality." He held up his hand. "I don't have to offer it on Gaul, of course, but in the right hands it could bring about a world order better suited to people like your charming, overworked mother. I suspect your father might have approved."

Too close. "You don't know anything about what my father would have wanted."

"This is really fine. Don't let it go to waste." He clinked his glass against the one I hadn't touched. "I researched your family, and I can make some good guesses about your father and his time in prison."

"That was a mistake. He wasn't involved in anything."

"But the EuroD didn't care about that. He was just a worker from *La Merde*. It wasn't even worth trying his case properly." He drummed his fingers on the desk. "Once word gets around about our salvage trip to the *Hadfield*, the manual for the squeezer would give pause to the powerful. They don't know my sister is a fool. I think they would be very hesitant to call that particular bluff."

"I can't believe you're asking me this."

"I'll pay you, of course. Enough to buy yourself out of your contract and set yourself up in style on any planet you want. Your mother, too. She won't have to live in that shabby apartment with *La Merde* creeping up around her ears."

The glass on the desk beckoned. I'd not planned to give him the satisfaction of sharing a drink with him, but I suddenly needed one more than I'd ever needed anything in my life.

"There are others on your team I could ask, but I prefer to work with family. Plus, Dr Sasaki, you have a certain credibility in the field that could help me sell it." He heaved himself to his feet. "Again, you'd be wise to keep my sister out of this. If she starts watching you, I will be forced to turn to my other sources."

My head was swimming. The captain, my mother, a possible revolution on Gaul... "I'll think about it."

Rakin had been about to reclaim his bottle, but my words caught him short, maybe even surprised him. He withdrew his hand. "I'll just leave that with you."

ADEM

Four months out of Gaul

The *Hajj* hung motionless in space. When in motion, inertia was on the crew's side. If the engines cut out, the ship would stay on course. Headed toward some human civilization, rescue might be possible. But being frozen there at zero velocity had Adem's teeth on edge.

Sometimes the engines built by the United Americas just stopped, without reason or warning, and never came on again. It had happened on other Trader ships. If it happened now, leaving the *Hajj* a fixed point in space until the Big Crunch... Adem shuddered. In all his years on board, unless it was docked, the *Hajj* had never been so still.

But that's what Hisako needed for her tests.

"That is going to work," she said.

"I won't argue." Adem stuck his multi-tool back in his pocket and stepped away from the probe. Cameras, sensors, and a computer wrapped around some spare thrusters. It was ugly, ungainly, and unique. Adem's first attempt at building something capable of powered flight. The little spacecraft's job was not overly complicated: go forward twenty-nine klicks, take some pictures, and return. The fact that its course would take the probe through an artificially created wormhole changed little, at least in theory. "Let's go up to the bridge and make sure."

Adem had built the probe in the forward airlock. Upon reaching the bridge, he launched it by removing the air, opening the outer door, and applying the forward thrusters by remote control. The probe floated free until he brought it to heel to the left of the bridge. "Hisako, look out the port window and wave." The photo came up on the primary view screen, a portrait of starship and scientist. "I think we're ready to go."

Hisako woke the newly installed console. Worm-drive control. "We're fully charged," she said. "I'm doing it."

With an invisible hand, the *Hajj* reached out to the space-time ahead of it and squeezed. Even after four months on the project, Adem didn't understand all the physics behind it. The drive's technology was related to the ship's mass-grav system, and gravity-wave manipulation, dark-matter injections, magnetism, negative energy, and quantum entanglement all played a part. The important bit, he'd decided, was that it worked.

"We've got a stable wormhole!" Hisako said. "Send the probe through!"

Adem activated the program he'd coded for the probe. He could not see the wormhole, but sensors on the ship and probe said it was there. His tiny spacecraft – he should have named it! – sped away from the *Hajj*, diminished in the bow camera's view, and disappeared.

"It should only take a minute." Adem kept an eye on the clock. "How's the hole?"

"Holding," Hisako said.

"I just decided to name the probe. *The Midnight Special.* Any objections?" Seeing none, he told the nearsmart to put it in the ship's record.

"How much longer?" the captain said. Her voice was tense, her face shiny. She sat forward in her chair like she might need to leap out at any moment.

"It's back." The probe sped back into the camera's range. "And it's transmitting." Adem sent the pictures to the view screen.

"That looks like Nov Tero to me," Lucy said. "Nice work!"

Hisako's shoulders relaxed. "I'm closing the wormhole." The *Hajj* released its grip. "It's closed. No sign of a tear."

"Get *The Special* back inside and pull it apart. I want to know how it held up." The captain leaned back in her chair. "When can we try it again?"

Adem and Hisako exchanged glances. "Give me a couple of days," she said. "If the probe checks out, we can reuse it. If not, Adem can—"

"If the probe's damaged, I'm not risking the ship," the captain said. "You have two days. Being parked like this makes me tense. I keep thinking someone is going to plow into us."

Collision with another ship was near impossible, even more so because of the course change Lucy had made when they left Gaul, but the very idea made Adem's skin crawl.

"Two days," Hisako said. "Adem, can you handle the autopsy on the probe by yourself? I want to run a diagnostic on the drive."

Adem steered *The Midnight Special* back into the airlock. Maiden voyage complete, trial one successful.

HISAKO

Four and a half months out of Gaul

Lucy wasn't showing the proper amount of tension. Nobody was, so I opted to carry it all myself.

"Hit the right place at the right speed, and we'll go right through," I said. "The hole will close up behind us and – Bam! – Nov Tero!"

I couldn't shut up. Lucy knew the procedure as well as I did, and "bam" was not a word I wanted to associate with our first space-time shortcut. Eight successful trials with *The Midnight Special* notwithstanding, there was a lot riding on the next ten minutes. I cleared my throat. "If you're worried, we could let the nearsmart do it."

That's how the UA military traveled through wormholes, but, no, not Lucy Sadiq.

"No one flies the *Hajj* but me," she said. "Time to let it go."

"How long?" Maneera asked. She had worked off her stress in advance by beating the crap out of all comers in the gym that morning. Dooley was still dealing with all the strains and sprains.

"Nine minutes thirty," I said.

"Check the numbers again. Be sure."

I had lost track of how many times she'd said that since we told her we were ready to go. It made me wonder if she would have been happier if the drive had something wrong with it, or I'd been unable to install it on the *Hajj*. She'd be in the black from selling off *Hadfield* salvage anyway and someone else could take the giant leap into civilian faster-than-light travel.

I ran my calculations through the nearsmart and checked them against an independent set I gave Odessa's android pal, Reg. They matched again. "We're ready to go."

"Five minutes," Lucy said.

The worm-drive triggered at two minutes, the field it projected extending ahead of the ship and collapsing space-time as we accelerated.

"One minute."

The captain punched her intercom button. "Brace for impact. We're going through."

"I see it. It's big, bad, and beautiful," Lucy said, "and we'll be at the front door in twenty seconds."

I held my breath.

The ship lurched, tossing me and anyone else standing to the deck. The lights went out. My head hit something, and I saw stars. Dimly, I heard the captain yelling. "Mass-grav is out. Micro-g protocols everyone. Adem, check your sister!"

"She's breathing. Pulse is good. But she's out."

"Get us some light! I don't care how you do it."

"The nearsmart is down," that was someone else, "power and comms are out."

White light flared as Adem held up his multi-tool. He did something to the unlit end and pressed it to the ceiling where it stuck. "That will last about an hour. Let me see if I can do something more permanent."

"Is anyone hurt?" the captain addressed the room.

There were groans as the bridge crew reported in. I tried to stand

and ended up on the ceiling. Micro-g protocols. I found something to hang onto. My stomach hurt. I was in charge of the worm-drive project, and whatever had gone wrong was on me.

"Where are we?"

"Captain, everything's down," the astrogator said. "I can't get a position."

"Look out the damned windows!"

The astrogator, I couldn't remember his name, flew below me to the port-side viewing window and consulted his reader.

"Hisako, what happened?" Maneera's attention was on me, and it burned.

"No idea. Everything was going like fine until–"

"Find out."

"The stars look right." The astrogator finished his surveys. "We're where we're supposed to be."

The bridge lights stuttered on at about eighty percent. Adem sailed up and reclaimed his multi-tool. "Emergency power. I bypassed the nearsmart. Ventilation fans are coming on, too. That will give us about six hours to figure things out before it gets stuffy. I'll take the crawlspace to engineering and get it sorted."

"Put on a suit and go up top first," the captain overruled. "With communications down, we don't even know if the engineering section is still there. If the timing was wrong, the wormhole could have pinched us in half."

"If everything looks okay up top, we might as well walk to engineering on the outside. Be quicker than coming back in and crawling through the spine."

"Approved. Just don't do anything stupid. Hisako, go with him."

"I've never space-walked!"

"Just do what Adem does. You'll be fine."

Adem hung upside down from the ceiling and kissed the captain on the cheek. He nodded to me. "You good?"

"I'm going to get us both killed."

"Nah. This is the easy part. Come on." He grabbed my arm and towed me toward the emergency airlock.

I followed the instructions the nearsmart had drummed into my brain. I'd never gotten round to the test, but getting into the suit wasn't much harder than putting on a pair of coveralls. Adem swore. "Forgot that the nearsmart is out. The suits have radios in them. Make sure yours is on before you seal the helmet."

We tested the radios and squeezed into the emergency airlock.

"What did we do wrong?" I said.

"If we'd had a systems failure, we'd be dead already. Gutierrez says we're in the right place."

Gutierrez. That was the navigator's name. "Based on a look out the window!"

"He knows what he's doing. Provided we're intact and can get everything restarted, I'd say we won. We just took the *Hajj* through a wormhole."

When the pressure equalized, we floated up the ladder to the outer door and emerged on top of the command module. My stomach swooped.

"Keep your eyes on the hull if you have to," Adam buzzed at me over the suit radio. "Safety-wise, it's not a bad idea anyway."

I fought the vertigo to get a look at the stars. "There are so many of them." I flushed. It was a stupid thing to say, but I had no other words.

"Keep your breathing under control. Match the duration of your exhales to your inhales, and you'll mitigate your adrenaline response. Wait here for a second." He pulled a line from my belt and attached it to a ring mounted outside the airlock.

I crouched like an insect on the ship's hull, holding on for dear life against the eternal drop we were hanging over. I had an insane urge to unclip my tether and fly. I settled for lifting my arms above my head. There were tears on my cheeks, but I didn't care. No one could see me through the faceplate of the helmet, and it was just so beautiful, so… regal. The radio crackled. "The engineering section is still there," Adem said. "Come on. Stay on the blue stripe. Your boots are magnetized, but not all of the hull is ferrous."

I forced myself to look down. The blue stripe was about twice as wide as an uptown sidewalk. I put both boots on it carefully. "What about the tether?"

"You'll see another ring in about seven meters. There's another tether on the other side of your belt. Clip it into the ring and hit the button. The one near the airlock will release and wind back into your belt. There are rings all down the stripe."

I lifted my right foot.

"Keep one foot on the ship at all times. Shuffle if you need to."

The universe beckoned, but I kept my eyes on my feet as I followed the blue stripe to where Adem stood waiting for me. He pointed. "The path goes along the spine. It will take us about half an hour to get there in these things."

The suits were good for eight hours. I nodded.

"If you're nodding, I can't see it. You actually have to speak to me."

"I'm ready." I tried to keep the shaking out of my voice.

"We got this."

I mimicked his slow steady gait, making sure my off foot was firmly planted before I took a step. My breathing tried to get away from me, but I chased it down and forced it under control.

"What happens if we can't get everything restarted?" I said.

"We're close enough for a rescue at this point. Maybe even a tow. Hopefully it won't come to that." He twisted around and pointed to a point of light. "That's Nov Tero. If we can open another wormhole, we might make it back to Gaul eleven standard years after we left. Crazy to think about."

My mother would still be in her fifties. If there was a war going on, I could use Rakin's money to get her off the planet, maybe to Freedom. I could easily get work at a university there if I showed up with the schematics for the worm-drive, not to mention the rest of the decrypted files from the *Hadfield*. Then I'd get rich by "re-inventing" all the missing tech. "How much do you think your mother would charge if I wanted out of our contract?"

He was slow to answer. "Legally, she wouldn't have to release you, but my guess is expenses plus time and pain in the ass. Less if you trained someone up on the worm-drive. How long do you think that would take?"

The manuals had been written for soldiers not scientists. The crew needed to be able to service the thing and make it run, not build a new one from scratch. "I don't know. I'll talk to Mateo about it."

"Be a good idea to train him anyway. You could fall over dead any minute."

It almost sounded like he wished I would do just that.

"I can teach him the basics in a few months."

"Do you think you know enough now to build another one?"

"I can install one, sure. Tune it, make it work. But I wouldn't know where to begin to make one. The processes, the parts, the materials... Odessa is having the same problem with her android. They made the brains out of a platinum-iridium alloy, and there's not much of either out here."

"There was plenty on Earth. Now that we have a worm-drive, we could go back and see what's left." Adem held up his hand. "We're here."

The blue stripe was interrupted by another hatch. Adem flipped open a panel and studied the small screen under it. "I can't tell if the lock is working. Stand back a little."

I shuffled back a few feet, careful to stay on the stripe. Adem opened a smaller hatch and reached in to pump the emergency release handle. The door opened slowly.

"You go through first. I'll reseal the door."

I crawled down the ladder backward. There was no way to get my helmet lamp pointed in the right direction, so I had to feel along with my feet for each rung. Adem came behind me, pausing to pump the door closed.

"Stop there." Adem squeezed past me. "Hold onto the ladder. If we're lucky, there's going to be some wind."

He opened the door slowly to allow the pressure to equalize. We came through a hatch in the ceiling of Rakin's office. Adem unsealed his helmet. "We'll work faster without the suits, but remember where we put them."

A light flashed in my face, and I flinched. The light holder realized his mistake and directed his beam toward my feet. "Hisako?"

It was Mateo.

"And Adem," I said.

"Thank God," Mateo said. "We weren't sure the command section made it. What happened?"

"We'll figure that out later," Adem said. "For now, we get the power back on."

"That's easy enough. The nearsmart shut everything down to divert more power to mass-grav. If we restore power to the computer, it can do the rest."

"Anyone hurt down here?"

"Bumps and bruises. Tobey got a pretty good sprain when he caught himself wrong against the deck. I splinted it."

"Let's get the lights back on."

We restored power to the nearsmart, and the computer did the same for the rest of the ship. In an hour everything was running normally again.

"So, what happened?" Even over the comm Maneera was terrifying.

"The worm-drive draws a lot of power," Adem said. "When we took the *Hajj* through, the nearsmart had to divert power to mass-grav to deal with our acceleration, and there wasn't enough to go around. The nearsmart cut everything else to power the mass-grav. Probably saved our lives."

"Does that mean we can't use the worm-drive again?"

Adem looked at me.

"The *Hadfield* had a military-grade power system. The *Hajj* is a civilian vessel, but if we reduce the power load before we go through, we should be okay," I said. "We could put everything but mass-grav and the drive on backup power and zip through just as you please."

"Good news. By the way, we're right on target. We shaved about nine months relative off the trip."

"That's incredible." Adem's eyes were wide.

"Run a full diagnostic. Make sure we didn't break anything."

Adem returned to our workspace with his arms full of parts and tools about thirteen hours later. 01:37, to be exact. "You have carbon on your face," he said.

I rubbed my cheek. Adem dumped the tools at his workstation and pointed to his chin to show me the right spot.

"Everything checked out," he said. "I even threw an x-ray emitter on the probe out to look for material fatigue. Where is everyone?"

"Gone. Something about drinks and celebration. And sleep."

"Are you hungry? I know a place."

The place was closed for another five and half hours, but Adem had a key. I followed him into the cafeteria's small kitchen. He opened the chiller and peered inside.

"I didn't know you could cook," I said.

"I'm a whiz at reheating Chef's potstickers." He cracked four eggs into a bowl and pulled a whisk out of a drawer. "You must be feeling pretty good about today."

"I feel great about proving Francis wrong. When I write this up, he's going to lose tenure."

Adem pointed at the bowl of eggs with the whisk. "This is going to be something like fried rice. Is that okay?"

"I'll cut up the vegetables."

Adem got the rice started and put the potstickers in the oven to reheat.

"I can't imagine your mother taught you how to do this," I said.

He laughed. "No. Dooley all the way. I have five meals I do pretty well, but Dooley could put Chef out of a job. I used to cook for Lucy and Hafgan a lot when we were kids."

"Dooley told me about Hafgan."

"Died of old age while I was out here skipping around." Adem turned off the burner under the wok. "Plates."

We took the food to a table in the empty cafeteria.

"You seem better," he said. "Maybe you're getting used to the place."

"The work has helped." I pointed at him with a fork. "You know, in a perfect world your mother could have just shown up with this crazy plan and hired me. It wasn't like I had a lot of prospects."

"University gig. Little flat in *La Mur*. Couple of vacations a year to New Berlin or Versailles Station. Doesn't sound so bad."

"You're forgetting the revolution. With a useless degree and rich-but-not-rich enough money, I'd be lucky not to have my head chopped off in the Square."

"Decapitation would be a downside." He nodded slowly. "But, if she waited until this year to make the offer, you might not have been qualified for the job."

"I might have." I separated the pile of rice and vegetables into half then into quarters to avoid looking at him. "Why did your mother pick us? There had to be a dozen families looking for an arrangement."

Adem lay his fork across his empty plate and wiped his mouth with a paper napkin. "Two hundred and thirteen families. I read through the profiles and picked your mother and father myself."

"So why did you? There had to be better prospects."

"I liked your parents. Respected the way they presented themselves. A lot of the other applicants were middle-rich EuroDs looking to trade their offspring for business connections. Some of them had conceived just so they could put a profile up and froze the embryos until they could find the right deal. I nixed them immediately. There weren't a lot of applicants from *La Merde*. Your parents stood out."

"Most families from *La Merde* couldn't afford the application fee."

"How did your parents do it?"

"Probably a loan. That could explain why my mother and father never stopped working even…"

"Even though they could have lived off their daughter?" Adem smiled. "Your parents were desperate to give you a good life, Sako. I think they saw this…" he gestured, "marrying into my family as a gift. It wasn't like we were buying something out of a catalog. Both parties had to agree to it. They had options, too, and they picked us."

"And I'm supposed to be grateful for that?"

"Grateful to us? Hell, no. Mom's getting what she paid for. You're giving her family a giant leg up on the competition. If you're going to thank anyone, thank your parents."

I sort of hated that he was right. "What are you grateful for in all of this?"

"This wasn't my idea, and I'd be lying if I said I wasn't more than a little pissed at the captain for getting me into this. But it worked." He chuckled. "It really did. I suppose I'm grateful for you, Hisako. I'm glad you're here."

ADEM

Eight days from Nov Tero

Adem whistled as he wiped down the table and cleaned up what little mess he had made in the kitchen. He felt good. The adrenaline rush of the emergency, followed by the long cool down of the ship-wide diagnostic and the cooking, had left him tired but strangely chipper. The conversation with Hisako hadn't hurt, either.

He locked the kitchen door and smothered a yawn. It had been nice putting his aerospace design skills to use, too. Adding the x-ray emitter to the probe had saved him from spending hours in a vacuum suit, and he had several other improvements to *The Midnight Special* in mind. Adem checked his pocket for his reader and headed for his–

Adem cursed and patted down his other pockets. He'd used the reader during the diagnostic, and he remembered carrying it up to the workspace, amongst an armload of tools. He had dumped them on his workstation before coming to the kitchen with Hisako.

Chipper took a beating as Adem retraced his steps. He shaded his eyes as he approached the door of the workspace. The *Hajj* corridors were comfortably dim, but Hisako had set the lighting in the workspace several degrees higher. Adem had lost track of the number of times he'd gone from dim hallway to dark, unoccupied workspace only to be blinded when the automatic lights came on.

The precaution was unnecessary. The workspace was already occupied.

"What's up?" Mateo said. He was sweating and elbow deep in a damaged power converter.

"I've left my reader. What are you doing?"

Mateo swabbed his forehead with his sleeve. "Eh, couldn't sleep so I figured I'd try to get a little ahead."

Everyone on the drive team was going to be cranky-tired come morning. Adem made a mental note to ask his mother for a donation from her special coffee stash. The team deserved the treat and might need the additional caffeine. He stepped to his workstation and searched the day's detritus. The reader was there, half-buried under a scanning unit and a set of sockets. He slipped it into his pocket.

Mateo was still busy with the converter. It was probably just busy work, but Hisako had said something about rigging up some power buffer before the next jump. Adem woke the screen on her workstation, curious in spite of his fatigue. An index of files came up, but he didn't recognize it. It wasn't the one Hisako had prepared for the drive team. Adem scanned the names of the files, rubbed his eyes, and read them more closely. He opened one of them. "Holy sh…" He caught himself before he drew Mateo's attention.

The index had everything, from the procedures for deactivating UA tamper protection to full schematics and repair instructions for their tech. Every piece of technology the United Americas had taken to their graves was there. Adem's hands were shaking. He inspected another file. Mass-grav trouble-shooting and repair! A parts list for the fusion engines! A how-to for food assemblers!

Adem's exhaustion vanished, overwhelmed by a mixture of hope and grief. A thousand years in survival mode had left humanity scratching amongst the ruins of technology it didn't have time or resources to rediscover. The knowledge in the database could change life on all the worlds. Why hadn't Hisako shared it? Did she not understand what it meant?

He took it all, copying the decrypted files to his reader and, when that filled up, uploading them to his password-protected corner of the *Hajj* computers. When he was finished, he returned to the index. The date and time of access were listed alongside the files. He ran his finger down the list to see which ones Hisako had been looking at last.

Adem's hand floated to his mouth. What did Hisako want with the operations manual for the most powerful weapon in human history?

HISAKO

Eight days from Nov Tero

I wasn't sure Vee would get up for anything short of a medical emergency or a wild party, but she opened the door to her suite seconds after I triggered her intercom. She was dressed in workout clothes.

"Were you sleeping?" I said.

"I'm on second shift for the next couple of days. Soon though."

"I need your advice about something."

Her suite was bigger than Adem's, enough space for a sitting area. In minutes, she had installed me on a small couch, feet up, drink in hand. She sat beside me. "Tell Auntie Vee all about it. No. Let me guess," she said. "Adem?"

"Nothing like that. But I really, really need you to keep this to yourself."

"As long as you're not planning to kill someone or blow up the ship, I will stay mum." She tapped her chin. "And it might depend on who you were planning to kill."

I was exhausted, sinking into the couch, almost too comfortable, but what I needed to talk about was anything but laid back. I put my feet on the floor, sat up straight, and told her everything about Rakin's offer and the technical records from the *Hadfield*.

She rubbed her face with both hands. "I should have put more caveats in my vow of silence. You need to tell the captain. This is a ridiculously big deal." The breeziness she'd greeted me with was a thing of the past. "Rakin is slime. You don't need me to tell you that. Nothing he does is good for anyone but Rakin."

"He could do some good for me and my mother."

"Unless you end up living somewhere he's trying to pull this scam. He's not going to stop at one payday. He'll sell to anyone who has the money."

"He's not selling the real weapon," I countered, "just the appearance of it. It's only a few technical documents."

"Those documents are salvage." Vee picked up a throw pillow and held it in her arms. "Okay, let's put aside the fact that helping Rakin would mean stealing from everyone who owns shares in the *Hajj,* myself included... I haven't seen your contract, but I know mine has a bunch of language in it that would wreck my life if I did something like that. Ignoring that, could someone build a working weapon from the documents Rakin asked you for?"

"Absolutely not. There's enough detail in there to build a mockup, maybe, but nothing that works."

"What if they had all of the files on the squeezer? Tech spec, parts list, access codes, the works."

"Maybe. If they had a United Americas tech expert on hand, they could get started. But it would take years to figure out all the substitutions and workarounds, and I doubt there's fabricating equipment in existence that's sophisticated enough to make most of the parts they'd need."

"So, to get a real weapon, Rakin would need all the documentation and someone like you. And we're about to dock at Nov Tero, where he has all kinds of criminal connections." Her eyes widened. "You've heard of kidnapping, right?"

I hadn't thought of that. "He- He said all he wants is the operating manual."

"And he said he could get it from someone else if you didn't help." She cupped her forehead. "Sako, you're supposed to be a fucking genius!"

"But…" I was out of excuses. "Maybe the UA was right to keep this shit locked up where we couldn't get it." Vee got up to pace. I was a little jealous. She had plenty of room for it. "You can't give Rakin what he wants."

"Where does that leave me?"

"Not in a TU prison awaiting trial on a breach of contract charge or chained to a workstation on Nov Tero!" She grabbed my shoulder. "You're part-owner of the fastest Trader ship in the worlds. That's enough to get your mother out of *La Merde*. It should be enough for anyone."

I wasn't convinced, and it must have shown on my face.

"Rakin's not going to sell to the good guys. He doesn't know any. Good guys don't buy weapons of mass destruction. Trust me, Rakin Sadiq is not someone you want to turn into a kingmaker."

What did they say about advice? The advisee only takes it if it jibes with what they were already thinking? "Okay, I won't give him the manual."

"Really?" She sounded almost surprised.

"You give good advice."

Her eyes narrowed. "Here's some more. Go to the captain tomorrow and tell her everything."

I winced.

"You have control issues. I get that. You've never had much. But you can't keep those files a secret, if they even are anymore. If there's half as much in there as you say there is, we're talking worlds changing."

"I know. I'll tell her in the morning." The exhaustion was back. I looked at the clock. Morning was only a couple of hours away.

"That's good, because if you hadn't agreed, I would have had to tell her myself. Vow of silence or not."

"Really?"

"Probably. I'll go with you when you see the captain." She smiled. "For support, not for checking up."

I covered a yawn. "I would appreciate that."

"We should get some sleep." She smiled. "Which side of the bed do you want?"

Adem put two coffees in the middle of my breakfast table. "Cream and sugar, right?" He didn't wait for me to respond and took the seat across from me. I was tired, but he looked borderline exhausted, almost crazed with it. Maybe cooking took a lot out of him. Maybe he'd been up tossing and turning with unspent passion. I had not.

"I talked to Lucy about this, and she agreed that I should talk to you first," he said.

I had no idea what was coming next. Spending time with him over fried rice and potstickers had been nice, even a little date-like, but unless he had really misread it—

"I know about the technical files from the *Hadfield*. You left them up on your workstation last night."

A momentary pang of guilt burned to a crisp. "I logged off when we left for the cafeteria. If you saw anything at my workstation, it was because you were spying on—"

"Hisako, it doesn't matter how I saw it. What matters is…" He took a deliberate breath. "Lucy and I think you're working with Rakin on something that involves," he dropped his voice to a whisper, "that involves the squeezer."

Adem's face told me he didn't want it to be true. I almost felt bad disappointing him. Almost. "Good work, detective. You caught me.

Divorce me and throw me off the ship."

Vee slipped into the chair next to him. "Who are we throwing off the ship?"

"I have a few candidates," I said. "Did you get us an appointment?"

"The captain will meet us in her suite in twenty minutes." She looked at Adem. "Are you coming?"

ADEM

Seven days from Nov Tero

Adem had never been able to read his mother's moods as well as he could his father's. Her face betrayed little, and her body, long disciplined by her martial arts, always looked at peace. If he'd had to guess now, though, he'd say she was furious.

"We never should have let him back on the *Hajj*."

"He's family," Dooley said. "Sometimes you make allowances."

The captain's poker face broke, and she stared incredulously at her husband. "Allowances? I grew up with that man, Abdul. You give him a centimeter, and he'll–!"

Adem watched them spar for a few more minutes before clearing his throat. "What do we do about this?"

"What does your sister know?" Dooley asked.

"Most of it. I talked to her last night. She'd be here if she weren't on watch." Adem held his hand up to forestall the next question. "She's already keeping track of outgoing transmissions. If Uncle Rakin tries to send anything out, we'll know about it."

The captain rounded on Hisako. "We had a deal. You said you'd make sure I heard everything first. Now, I find out you've been hiding things from me and conspiring with my brother."

"You got what you paid for, Maneera. Anything else I gave you was a gift." Hisako turned to Vee. "Remember, coming here was your idea."

"What is she even doing here?" The captain glared daggers at Hisako. "This is a family meeting!"

"She's the one who convinced me to talk to you!"

"You shouldn't have needed convincing! The biggest piece of salvage in a thousand years, and you tried to keep it for yourself." She threw up her hands. "Breach of contract. I wrote the damned thing, I should know."

"That's not why I kept the files! You come into my life with–!"

Adem took a deep breath. "Pipe down!"

Silence fell, and shock appeared on the faces of all present. Adem speaking up was rare enough, yelling...

He paled. "Mother, forgive me. He turned to Vee. "Do you have anything else to add to this?"

She shook her head.

"Head down to the medical center or back to bed or whatever, and please don't talk to anyone about this. I'll make sure Hisako isn't hounded, I promise. Thank you."

Adem waited until she'd gone through the door.

"Now it's just family," he said. "Enough with the breach of contract shit, and no more pointing fingers. Hisako didn't give Rakin what he wanted."

"He said he had a backup," Hisako said. "He said he came to me first because my expertise in UA tech would make his plan easier to sell."

"So, who's the backup?" Dooley said. "It could be anyone working on the worm-drive. Who has access to the files?"

Hisako knuckled the sides of her head. "I had Odessa put a lock on them. No one should have been able to see them but me."

"She could have put in a backdoor," Dooley said.

The captain frowned. "Or made a copy before she locked them."

"I don't think it's Odessa," Adem said. "She's been on the ship for years, and she has no love for the syndicates."

"Who then?" Hisako said. "Mateo? Tobey? Could either of them hack through Odessa's security?"

"It may not be anyone." The captain sighed. "Rakin was an information broker on Nov Tero. A spy. He may have bugged and hacked the whole ship for all we know. I was a fool to let him back."

Dooley took her hand. "We let him back. We took a vote, remember, just like always. The question is what to do about it. Once we're in range of the Nov Tero worldnet there's no controlling what gets cut."

"That's less than four days from now. If Mom accuses him of trying to steal from the shareholders and can't prove it…"

"He can file suit and take my shares," she finished. "I know TU law better than you do."

"It's worse than that." Dooley sucked his teeth. "We have valuable salvage on board that we haven't told the other shareholders about. Rakin could make the case that we were the ones stealing it, and he was just trying to stop us."

Hisako blanched.

"Didn't think about that, did you? Neither did I." The captain massaged the bridge of her nose with two fingers. "So, at worst, he's stealing undeclared shareholder assets, and he hasn't even done that, yet."

"He'll do something, though," Adem said.

"Of course he'll do something!" The frustration was back in her voice. "We're talking about Rakin. I've known him longer than both of you. He's always doing something. That's why my mother chose me as captain." She got up and paced the small stretch of carpet on her side of the table.

"What if we take it to a vote? We can't keep the information from the *Hadfield* to ourselves anyway," Dooley said. "Tell the shareholders we just found the mother lode of tech files and let them decide what to do with it. Once we declare it as an asset, we can keep Rakin from selling it off."

"He might do it anyway," Adem said. "He knows a lot of people on Nov Tero."

"A lot of them want to kill him." The captain sat back down and tented her fingers on the table. "Declaring the files as assets means we need a plan for them. Dooley, I suppose it's too much to assume that you'll agree with me about what to do with the information. I can already see the waves of populism running through your head."

Dooley smiled. "We could make a few rich people richer or we could help a lot of people by giving the information away for free. I know what I'd prefer."

"What do you think we should do with it, Adem?"

Adem had been trying to make up his mind about that since he'd peeked into Hisako's directory. The food assembler alone could change life on any of the worlds. "I don't know. I feel like there are pitfalls everywhere."

"Hisako?"

"We should destroy anything in there about the squeezer. The UA discovered it by accident en route to the worm-drive. Someone will rediscover it eventually, but we shouldn't help them out."

Adem and Dooley nodded in agreement.

"If you destroy the files, I don't want to know about it. Check with Lucy, and see what she thinks. If we're not on the same page by the time we go to the shareholders, I want to at least make sure we're all reading from the same book." The captain gripped the edge of the table like she was trying to bend it to her will. "I'll call a meeting in two days."

The team's workspace was empty when Adem returned to it later that night. He'd filled in Lucy and Vee. Hisako was to talk with Odessa.

Adem worked with the nearsmart to locate all the fabrication and maintenance files for squeezer tech. The search also turned up a batch of video messages, readied but never sent. Adem played one. A member of the weapons crew, a young woman – the name on the message was Maria Alvarez – smiled and joked for her two daughters, Cissy and Raquel. She signed off with, "I'll be home soon. I love you." The two girls most likely had died with the United Americas settlement on Freedom. Adem put the cache of messages in a separate directory and searched on. A broader search turned up a few more tech files, nothing important, nothing that hadn't already been reverse-engineered or replaced by modern inventions, along with a roster of the *Hadfield*'s crew at the time of the Two-Day War. He searched out the captain, Neleh Martin, and found her logbook. He played the final entry. The recorded voice was weary. "The mission was… successful. The *Constitution* scored a direct hit on the planet with the mass-compression field. Makkah compressed by approximately fifteen percent and rebounded into rubble. No survivors are expected. The *Constitution* was also lost. The war is won." The recording ran in silence for fifteen seconds before the captain cleared her throat. "Our weapons are fully functional, however, we've sustained severe damage to our engines and heavy casualties. I've activated the distress beacon, but there is likely no one left to answer. The war is won, but the United Americas has fallen."

The salvage crew from the *Hajj* had found Martin's body on the bridge of her ship. She appeared to have died of a single gunshot wound to the head, presumably self-inflicted. Adem scanned the first log entry of the war and skipped ahead to the third. This time Martin's voice was crisp and professional. "The Queensland settlement on Freedom reported that a single scout ship, presumably manned, slammed into New Washington at 0930 this morning. Destruction was total. The ship's trajectory has been traced back to Makkah. My senior officer, Captain Mark O'Neill of the *Constitution*, has ordered us to counter strike with all possible force. We are en route to Makkah at fastest possible speed. ETA is six months relative."

That recording alone was probably worth the trip out to the derelict. Historians and politicians had debated the cause of the war for years afterward, using it as a scare tactic to push policy and manipulate the citizenry. Adem's great-grandmother had been forced to rename her ship and spend as much time as possible at near *c*.

A Caliphate survivor had started the war. It was possible he'd been some kind of religious radical, but the distance between the settled planets had put an end to most of that tension. More likely it had been personal. The freezer pods assigned to the Caliphate had been shoddily made, with far higher death rates than the ones the UA fashioned for its friends. Maybe the pilot of the attack ship, after spending months alone at near light speed, had arrived at his new home to learn that a loved one, maybe all of his loved ones, had died on the way. The settlement on Makkah would have been ignorant of the attack, with no idea why the UA warships suddenly appeared in orbit.

Adem looked over his work. The squeezer index was complete. Uncle Rakin was right about one thing, certain people would love to get their hands on the information. A resolution to any debate, not to mention a quick fix to the growing refugee crisis. The *Hajj* shareholders – including the crew – could make a killing on top of the bonanza already headed their way. He rubbed his face. Destroying the files was theft, taking money out of the pockets of people he worked with every day. He ordered the nearsmart to overwrite the lot.

HISAKO

Five days from Nov Tero

I took a seat at the table between Adem and Lucy. Maneera had apologized for threatening to bring me up on a breach of contract charge, but we weren't ready to be side by side meeting buddies just yet. Dooley slid a plate of cookies across the table to me.

"What's this all about?" Rakin said, preempting his sister's attempt to call the meeting to order. "We're not close enough to get any news from Nov Tero, so unless you've called us here to crow about not killing us with your second-hand worm-drive, I don't see the point."

The captain smiled. "We won't start seeing the financial advantage of having a worm-drive until we're back on Gaul in a few months – I have a pretty specific shopping list for our partners there – so I'll wait until then to pat myself on the back."

"Then what are we doing here?" said Kalinda. "I'm not interested in making more blind decisions for the investors."

"We had to do this before we interfaced with the Nov Tero network." Maneera signaled to Adem. "And you'll shortly understand why."

Adem woke his reader and a copy of the new directory Odessa made for me appeared on the main screen and on all the other readers around the table. He cleared his throat. "Looks like we got a lot more than we expected when we downloaded the *Hadfield*'s database." He gave them a few seconds to scan the list of files. "We thought we'd get the logs, maybe some messages home. We ended up with the specs for every piece of United Americas technology worth wishing for. We got mass-grav, the worm-drive, the cancer cure, the works. It's all there for adapting, copying, and recreating."

"How long have you known about this?" Kalinda demanded. She hadn't been smiling much since she and Jolyon Ong stopped dating. They were sitting on opposite sides of the table now. Rumor had it Tobey had something to do with it.

"Two days," the captain answered. "I called this meeting as soon as I was made aware. Adem discovered the records while working on the worm-drive."

"It took me a few days to create the directory." Odessa had helped him to mask the time-date stamps on the files in exchange for deleting everything about the UA androids. "I told the captain as soon as I was sure what we had."

Dooley cleared his throat. "I don't need to tell anyone how important this is. Everything the United Americas kept from us is right there."

Rakin flicked his finger to scroll up and down the directory. His face was impassive. "I suppose you want an apology, Maneera. Your gamble paid off."

Rakin was either the best liar I'd ever seen, or he really hadn't known the extent of the *Hadfield* records.

"An apology would be nice, Rakin, but I don't expect it. What I would like is a motion and a vote to proceed."

Dooley raised his hand. "I motion we give it away. Dump all the files into the Nov Tero worldnet when we sync and do the same for every planet we visit. It's not ours to keep."

Rakin cursed. "Give up what is yours all you want! Three percent of that data's value is mine, and I'm not letting it go to anyone for free!"

A noisy debate spread around and over the table in seconds. Maneera used her gavel to get things back under control. "There's a motion on the floor," she said. "Does it have a second?"

Adem seconded it. "There are a lot of people who need help out there. The highest bidder isn't necessarily going to give it to them."

"We risked lives and resources to get this information." Rakin glared at Dooley. "Are your children's lives worth so little to you?"

"We risked our lives to get the worm-drive, Uncle," Adem reminded him. "The tech specs were an accident."

"Accident or not, the data belongs to all of us," Jolyon said. "None of us signed on to the *Hajj* to do charity work."

The argument started again. I imagined it was even worse across the ship and hoped Vee had a handle on it. The captain requested order. "We'll vote on it. Those in favor of distributing the UA files, for free, to all worlds, vote 'aye.' Those opposed, vote 'nay.'"

Dooley and Adem stood alone on the 'aye' side for long moments as the vote trickled in. Two percent of the crew vote joined them, with the rest joining Rakin, Lucy, Maneera, me, and Kalinda in the 'nay' column.

"The motion does not carry."

"Had to try," Dooley said.

Lucy raised her hand. "I motion we bring this conversation to the Traders' Union. If we start selling this stuff willy-nilly, we're going to lose control of it. Say we sell it on Nov Tero tomorrow, then take it to Gaul. What's to keep someone here from taking it to Freedom or Guatama and selling it before we get there?"

That was my cue. I seconded her motion.

Rakin sputtered. "You said yourself we have the fastest ship in the worlds. Who's going to beat us to Guatama? Who's going to even try to sell there? They're broke! The colonies are dying!"

I smiled at him. "It could happen, Uncle, and, if so, there's a big chunk of money we won't get. If we take it to the Union, we can get our claim to it validated. Then anyone who sells it will owe us plus damages."

"I'd like to amend your motion to make it ship policy that we keep the information under wraps until we can call up a full meeting of the Traders' Union. Anyone who leaks will open himself up to heavy litigation," Maneera added.

I resisted looking at Rakin's face. "I second that."

"It will take years to summon the full Union!" Rakin fumed. "We'll have to get messages to every station, every ship!"

"Fastest ship in the worlds, Uncle," Lucy grinned.

"Dooley, you'll get another chance to pitch your free-for-all plan to the Traders' Union." The captain picked up her gavel. "If there is no further discussion, we'll vote on the amendment first."

To: Prof. Manon Toulouse, Université de la Sorbonne
Nouvelle, Versailles City, Gaul
From: Adem Sadiq, PhD, NSU extension

Madam:

I hold a doctorate in Earth History courtesy
of an NSU-accredited nearsmart program. My
dissertation, "The Jeremiad: An Examination
of Themes in United Americas Folk Music,
1940 to 2207," is no doubt floating somewhere
in the NSU archives.

I write to you with greetings and an
opportunity for scholarship. In months or
perhaps years to come, you will, if tuned
into current happenings, learn that the
crew of my vessel, the *Hajj*, has salvaged
many of the artifacts and records of the
United America's battleship, the *Christopher
Hadfield*. The *Hadfield*, as you no doubt recall,
was part of the force assigned to the attack
on the planet Makkah during the Two-Day War.

I would like to bring one artifact in
particular to your attention, an electronic
reader owned by UAMC Cpl. Ryan Thomas, who
was assigned to the *Hadfield* as part of a
rifle squad.

The *Christopher Hadfield* took heavy damage
in the attack, but contrary to accepted
history, it was not destroyed. Cpl. Thomas

and his squad were secured within their rapid-deployment pods at the time of the attack and thus survived. The Marines lived for nearly sixteen months aboard the failing *Hadfield* as it orbited within the Makkah debris cloud.

Unable to effect repairs, Thomas and the other castaways took extreme measures, including cannibalism of the dead, to survive. Thomas died of a self-inflicted gunshot wound after the death of the penultimate survivor, UAMC Pvt. First Class Ellen Goodman.

The aforementioned electronic reader was secured in our recent expedition to the *Christopher Hadfield* and remains in my possession. It contains, among other things, Cpl. Thomas's personal journal.

I expect to be in Versailles City sometime in the spring of 3260. Knowing your interest in the military history of the United Americas, I thought to offer you access to Cpl. Thomas's reader and the data it contains.

If you are interested, please reply by the usual means.

I remain your humble servant,
Adem Sadiq

HISAKO

Nov Tero Station, Nov 15, 3269

The air was thick with pheromones, some of them natural, most of them coming off Dooley's newest concoction. He called it Chill and swore there wasn't a single drop of alcohol in it. Everyone had one in hand. It smelled like sandcat shit.

Vee beckoned me to a corner of Terry's Place that I was developing territorial feelings about. It was just far enough away from the bar to have an intimate conversation. It was our spot.

"You want one?" She tapped the tumbler in front of her. It looked worse than it smelled.

"I'll just get a beer." I elbowed my way back through the artificially mellow crowd. By the time I returned to the table, Vee was consulting her reader.

"Project?" I said.

"Itinerary. We only have a couple of free days once we finish unloading. I want to get in as much as I can."

"Are you going to see your family?"

"They'll try to convince me to stay, but their hearts won't be in it." She rubbed the side of her neck. "I'll be happier and make more money on the *Hajj*."

I scanned her to-do list. "You can really do all that here?"

"It won't be cheap, but we can get a deal if we both go in on it."

I lost interest in follow up questions when Adem stepped up and slid his reader toward me. "We got trouble," he said. "Take a look."

The picture's resolution was fuzzy, like I was seeing the subject through a veil. "Looks like a worm-drive projector."

"Try again." He pointed. "Look at the power transfer and output. Based on what I saw before I erased everything, I think it's a squeezer."

Uh oh. "Where did you get this?"

"Primary airlock scanner. Rakin just went through it with a crate he pulled out of that pod of his."

"He built a squeezer?" My head was swimming. I'd studied the worm-drive for months and was still years away from being able to build one. How had Rakin gotten ahead of me?

"He didn't build anything." Adem's face was pale. "Someone pulled it off the *Hadfield* for him."

"While you were– How?"

"Mateo. He had the time and access. He was in the workspace the night I found out about the files. I bet he gave Rakin access to them, too."

"But how did Rakin know–"

"I called the captain, but she's in a meeting with the partners. No interruptions."

"What's going on?" The alarm in our voices finally got through Vee's artificial mellow. She was struggling to focus.

"Bad things. Sober up." I grabbed Vee's reader. "The next elevator car to the surface closes up in fifteen minutes. Can we make it?"

"You should stay here," he said. "If Rakin grabs you, he'll have the whole package."

He might have said more, but I was moving too fast to hear it. I pushed through the place harder than was polite, relying on

Dooley's cocktail to keep anyone from protesting. Adem followed me out the door.

"Do you know your way around the station?" I said.

"Well enough."

We jogged to the primary airlock and waited impatiently to be cycled through. Once we were in the station proper, we broke into a run, ignoring the questions launched by the members of the crew on guard outside.

"It's not far!" Adem said.

His breath was slow and steady. Mine was not. My heart hammered and before we had gone more than one hundred meters I had a stitch in my side. I began to wish I'd made exercise more of a priority.

"Are you alright?" Adem said.

I waved him on. "Go. I'll catch up."

I lost sight of him around the next corner.

I was sucking air and down to a fast stumble by the time I caught up. Adem had his hands raised to chest level, facing Rakin and two armed men. The gunsels switched their focus to me, then back to Adem before making an unspoken agreement to divide their efforts.

Rakin beckoned me closer. "Perfect timing! We can all go down to the surface together."

"I'm not going anywhere with you," I said, gasping for air.

"You have everything you need already, Uncle," Adem said. "You can let us go back to the ship."

"You underestimate your value." He spread his hands. "One weapons expert and one guarantee of Maneera Sadiq's good behavior. Dr. Sasaki and the device will disappear into the black market in a couple of days, and you and my sister can go back to playing peddler."

Adem slid his right foot forward. "It's going to be difficult to make deals after we report you to the Traders' Union. They aren't partial to thieves."

Rakin laughed. "The Union is doomed. It can only last as long as their ships do, and we both know that won't be long. Then it will be every planet for itself, and I plan to be comfortable on mine." He nodded to the thug on his right, a tall man with a scarred face. "Shall we?"

There was a popping sound, and the other gunsel fell screaming, a flechette embedded in his chest and a surge of electricity overpowering his nervous system. Adem lunged, twisting the pistol out of the other man's hand and bringing him to the deck in a brutal arm lock.

There was a rush of footsteps behind us. Vee picked up the stunned thug's weapon and pointed it at the man Adem was grappling with. "That's enough!"

Adem released his hold and rolled to his feet. The gunsel stayed where he was. His shoulder didn't look right.

"What are you doing?" Rakin's cheeks shook with rage. "You have no authority!"

Odessa put her arm around her android's waist. "Reg, if he moves, zap him, too." She raised her voice. "I did as your mother said and scanned the ship. Rakin has listening devices and cameras everywhere."

Adem woke the comm on his collar. "Rakin Sadiq, I formally accuse you of illegal trading practices and misappropriating assets of *Hajj* shareholders. In accordance with the Traders' Union Bylaws, your property and accounts will be locked down until a hearing is held." He paused. "The nearsmart confirms. It's registered the complaint with the station." He smiled. "Now we have the authority."

Rakin reached toward his jacket pocket.

"Don't do it, Rakin," Vee said. "I grew up here. You don't want to find out how good I am with one of these."

Rakin's hand froze. "My heart. The shock. I just need my medicine."

"Bullshit. Keep your hands where I can see them."

Adem picked the second pistol up off the ground and handed it to me. "Do you know how to use this?" he whispered.

"Not at all." My breath was coming easier now, and the pistol didn't wobble too much as I pointed it at the ground near Rakin's feet.

Adem moved away a few steps and used his comm again. His face was grim when he returned.

"Station security is on the way, and I just spoke to the captain." He looked steadily at Rakin. "You're bound, Uncle. Assets frozen. It doesn't look good. Mom's sending some people to pick up the crate and anything else you might have on you. Don't expect them to be gentle."

"Then what?" I said.

"If he doesn't contest the charges, we let him go here, minus his shares, anything he's taken, and any property he might have on the ship."

"I can't go to Nov Tero," Rakin growled. "Not now."

"You could ask for asylum on the station," Vee said. "Get protective custody in return for giving up some of your old friends to the authorities."

Rakin's fists purpled at his side.

"Option three, then," Adem said. "Uncle, I am authorized to escort you back aboard to await a hearing before the Traders' Union Board of Directors, held at that body's earliest convenience. Is that acceptable?"

"Yes, damn it."

"One more thing," Adem said. "If you're coming back aboard, Mom says you'll be staying in the freezer."

ADEM

Eight days from Gaul

Adem unlinked his reader from the nearsmart. The *Hajj*'s second trip through a wormhole had resulted in zero damage and revealed the location of the plumbing leak he'd been tracking for so long. It would take a while for his quarters to dry completely, but that pipe would never drip again.

He rubbed his face, and his fingers rasped over stubble. It had been a far longer day than he had planned, and he had a decision to make. Hisako came through the door behind him.

"You're still working," she said.

"Wanted to make sure everything was right before I turned in. I'm done now." Adem slid his reader into the pocket of his utilisuit.

"I don't get what you're trying to prove. Everyone else on your shift is asleep or drunk."

"Ordinarily I might be, too. But…" He shrugged. "Things have changed." You changed it, he might have added. Adem turned his back on her and made a show of shutting down the console. "You're not sleeping, so I guess you picked the drinking option."

"It seems to be the thing to do here. Your father is the only one I know aboard who doesn't."

"He says it's haram." He laughed. "Dooley's parents changed his name from Brian O'Dool to Abdul O'Dool and enrolled him in a madrasa as soon as they realized who they'd married him off to. He knows more about Islam than my mother."

"He doesn't seem very devout."

"He's not. He doesn't drink because most of his extended family and friends were drunks."

She stretched her hand out to him. "Come back to your suite with me. I want to show you something."

Adem looked at her askance. "What are you doing, Hisako?"

"Talking," she said. "Come on."

Adem followed her to the suite and waited as she fumbled the door open. She gestured toward the bar. "Pour us some of that fancy vodka. Beats the hell out of the shit you make."

He looked at the label. "This is from Uncle Rakin's stock."

"Wedding present," she said. "It's good. Try it."

Adem poured two glasses.

Hisako sat down and swung her legs up onto the bed. "Play me something."

"I haven't played in a while."

"I haven't, either. We'll swap some songs." She leaned over to pull the Martin off the wall. "I think it misses you."

The old guitar had a habit of going out of tune when the nearsmart dropped the temperature for the night cycle. Adem tuned it by ear and tested his work with a couple of chord progressions.

"What do you want out of life?" Her voice was louder than normal, and the question sounded almost like an accusation.

Adem wasn't sure how to answer. "Family, friends, work, a purpose," he patted the guitar, "music, I guess."

"You know people collect your videos, right? Does that matter to you?"

He used his sleeve to wipe dust off the Martin's body. "I like that they like my work."

"Do you want more of that… fans and applause?" She lay back on the bed and balanced the glass on her stomach. "Living on this ship isn't the way to make that happen."

The ghost of a song trembled in the air as he played with the strings.

"So, there's really nothing you want that you don't have," she said.

"I want Mom and Dad to have their asteroid. I want Lucy to be ship's captain. I want the *Hajj* to keep going." He was getting tired of the question. "I don't know… Enough peace and goodwill to go around?"

"What do you want for me?"

Adem noodled on the strings for a moment or two before replying. "I guess I want what I've always wanted for you. I want you to be happy here and feel like it's your home."

"What does that even mean, Adem? I eat. I drink. I shit. I have friends and a roof over my head. I'm potentially rich. What more is there?"

Adem lifted his hands in surrender. "More. I don't know. Love. The sky, maybe. People say they miss it. Fresh air."

"The sky we evolved under was blue not greenish brown, and the fresh air wasn't made by crushing rocks." She listened to Adem play for a minute. "Do you know anyone who's happy?"

"No one's happy all the time, but I think that's the way it's supposed to be."

"Just live and be content with being happy sometimes. That's life?"

"It beats worrying about it. You've looked pretty happy working on the worm-drive. Maybe it's about being useful to someone."

"That wasn't happiness. That was—" She paused. "That was discovery."

"What's the difference?" He set the guitar aside, leaning it carefully against the wall. "There's joy in learning something new or figuring something out."

"What if it's not enough?"

"Then that's what people are for. We make each other happy."

"Let's try," she moved over. "Get into this bed with me. Make me happy. Take tomorrow off. Take the whole week off. We'll spend it here playing music and having sex."

"Let me get you some water."

"I don't want water." She pulled the covers up to her chin. "Hold on." She struggled under the comforter for nearly a minute before she poked an arm out and dropped her coveralls on the floor. It was soon joined by her bra and t-shirt.

Adem picked up the Martin again. "You should sleep. Let me play you something."

It was a short piece, a simple G-chord progression, with lyrics that were either about losing a loved one or leaving home, Adem had never been sure.

Hisako listened with her eyes closed. "Who wrote that?"

"I found it with the guitar. I imagine the original owner wrote it."

She shivered. "I can't get warm tonight. Take your clothes off and get in here."

"Are you sure you want to do this?"

"No," she said. "But I know I don't want to be alone tonight. Will you stay?"

HISAKO

Seven days from Gaul

I knew if I moved, he'd wake up and start apologizing. So I stayed perfectly still, barely breathing.

My husband – there was that word again – smelled like machinery and conduit dust, but he didn't snore. He was the bogeyman who had haunted my entire life, and he smiled in his sleep.

My head throbbed. I'd had far too many of Dooley's new concoctions with Vee. He called them Forget-Me-Nots, and they smelled like flowers and tasted like fruit-infused water. As advertised, they lowered your inhibitions without any of the other symptoms of drunkenness – no stumbling or slurring – and no matter how many you drank you remembered everything you did.

Adem shifted. I held my breath, hoping it wasn't a sign of consciousness. I counted to thirty, with not a sound in the room other than my pounding head, then let myself breathe.

He was a bed hog, although that might have been the result of the spooning I had insisted on rather than a personal habit.

My tongue was like leather, and the bathroom was all the way across the room. While I wished desperately for latent telekinesis to kick in, Adem slept on his side breathing gently into the pillow. He needed to shave. He always needed to shave, and it lent him a look of danger that didn't fit what I knew of his personality. If we'd had sex instead of falling asleep, I probably would have been wishing for something to put on my beard burn. He had hair on his chest, too, and I resisted the urge to touch it to see if it was scratchy or soft. On Gaul, the men, at least the ones I knew, depilated all the body hair that grew below the neck. A lot of them did their faces, too.

If I woke Adem up, he would get me some water, which might give me time to put some clothes on. I'd kicked my underwear off in the night. I've never liked wearing anything while sleeping. It drove my mother crazy.

Adem was down to his shorts, at least he had been while we were spooning. He might have stripped down in the night, too. I didn't know his habits. We'd been married nearly five months, and this was the longest I'd spent alone with him. I moved centimeters to the edge of the bed and rolled to my feet, scooping last night's outfit off the floor on the way to the bathroom. While I guzzled water, I tried to figure out what to do.

Vee and I had spent the whole night discussing her future, with me doing the lion's share of the advice giving, which was ridiculous all things considered. If she sold her shares off now, she'd have a good bit of money to build a life planetside. If she stayed on the ship, she could take Dooley's place in the medical center when he finally retired and bought that asteroid.

Then last call arrived, and we'd had the brilliant idea that I should sleep with Adem to gain clarity. Now, I was trapped in the bathroom.

I took some painkillers and a long shower. All I had to wear was last night's clothes, and my nose wrinkled at the combination of stale sweat and near toxic alcohol that drifted from them anytime I moved.

I had another glass of water and opened the bathroom door.

Adem was gone, and, in spite of my fervent wishing of a few minutes before, I was almost disappointed. If nothing else, he might have been happy to see me, and he had a great smile. Instead, there was a message flashing on my reader: "Checked my to-do list and decided to go in after all. I feel pretty good after a full night's sleep. Thanks. Maybe we can talk later."

A question mark at the end of that last sentence could have meant that he was hoping for a talk or even asking for one. An exclamation point would have meant he was twelve. The period might mean a talk was a possibility, but one he wasn't much worried about. Or maybe I was reading too much into his punctuation.

My reader lit up with another message, but it wasn't from Adem. It was from his mother.

The invitation led me to the exercise deck. Maneera was waiting for me in a well-padded corner, barefoot and wearing what appeared to be pajamas.

"Tea?" She bent to a small table and tea tray set up at the edge of the floor mat. She handed me an over-sized shot glass of dark, sweet tea. "We have some things to say to each other."

"I can't think of a single thing."

She crossed her ankles and lowered herself to the floor mat. After a moment of awkwardness, me looking down and her looking up at me expectantly, I did, too, albeit with less grace. The mat smelled musty.

"I've apologized for losing my temper and threatening you," she said.

"We were all having a bad day. I don't blame you for that."

"But you blame me for something."

It wasn't a question, but she'd come to the wrong conclusion. "That's not the word I'd use anymore."

The corner of her mouth turned up. "The *Hajj* hasn't been as bad as you feared."

"No." I'd been challenged mentally, given responsibility and agency, improved my skills, made friends and money, maybe even changed the course of human history. "But being here wasn't my idea." Saying it out loud made it seem petty, but there it was.

"Ah, the word you're using now is 'resent.' Where would your own ideas have taken you, I wonder."

"I guess we'll never know."

"You have plenty of time for your own ideas. A lifetime of choices to make." Maneera sipped her tea and made a face. "Too sweet, but that's how my mother taught me to make it."

The tea tasted fine to me. I'd had similar in the cafeteria and delivered to me in the workspace. Without the sugar, black tea was too bitter.

"You created me, Maneera. Without you I might not have been born." I laughed. "I certainly wouldn't have lived as well as I did or gone to fancy schools. I guess I'm grateful for that, but you didn't do it for me."

"I spent the first year of my life traveling so close to the speed of light that I vanished from the calendar," Maneera said. "When I was six, I had to ask the nearsmart to calculate my birthday. It's in March. I forget the day. Adem was born in June."

It sounded almost like she wanted me to feel bad because I knew my birthday down to the standard hour, but I didn't bite. "People who live on the ground aren't real to you. That's how you can be so blithe about manipulating them to fit your plan. If it doesn't happen on the ship, it doesn't count."

"That's a good theory. You can see how living this way might lend itself to that outlook."

"So, you thought nothing of reaching down and changing my life?"

"Not much. Not deeply. I wasn't kidnapping or enslaving you. I needed a worm-drive expert, relatively unattached and ready to go when I needed her."

"Here I am."

"Yes."

"I mean absolutely nothing to you beyond what I can do for you."

"Hardly. You said it yourself. You're on my ship now. You count." Her lips tightened. "I didn't ask to be born into this, either."

"You stayed."

"So far. I can always change my mind. So can you. Take control. Make choices." She rolled to her feet without spilling her tea. "In the meantime, what do you know about jiu-jitsu?"

ADEM

Six days from Gaul

Lucy forwent the door's intercom and barged into Adem's suite. The complicated finger-picking pattern he was attempting with his right hand dissolved into discordance.

"I got your message." She threw herself onto Adem's bed, violently rocking them both. "Have you talked to the captain about this?"

"We talked in the vicinity of it. I was straighter with Dooley." He played the melody line of "The Kesh" – his father's favorite jig. "Makes better sense now than it ever did. His words."

"What will you do?"

"Help out if I can." He smiled. "I'd be lying if I said I wasn't terrified. Probably wouldn't be doing it at all if it weren't for the worm-drive."

"And if that blows up on us?"

"With the best pilot in the worlds and a gene-spliced near-genius running the show? It wouldn't dare."

Lucy pulled herself up to sit next to her brother. "Are two shares going to be enough?"

"No idea. I'll put the other two under you as proxy. Hey, listen to this." Adem played his new arrangement of the "Crawdad Song."

"Nice. I liked it better before I knew it was about eating bugs, but your playing has improved."

"It's called Travis picking. I found a bunch of videos in the *Hadfield* archives." Adem passed the guitar to Lucy. "Give it a shot."

He coached her on the technique and watched her try for a few minutes. "Do you think Mom really expected Hisako and I to fall in love?"

"Little brother, you fall in love with just about everybody you meet. That's your biggest problem."

HISAKO

Gaul, Mar 29, 3270

The taxi refused to take me to my mother's apartment building, so I threaded my way through half a city block of ragged neighborhood before I got within the shadow of the building. I ignored the pleas for help the best I could and tightened my grip on my new stunner in response to the threats.

Taking the lift up to my mother's floor was no longer an option, no matter how much money I offered it. I forged up the stairs, passing through a bivouac on every landing and grateful for the improvements nine weeks in the gym had made to my cardiovascular health. I arrived with hardly a wheeze and rang the bell.

Her door slid open, and we stood, blinking at each other for what seemed like forever. My father's makeshift club was in her hand.

She broke the spell. "You're back early."

"You look the same." Her hair was maybe a little grayer, but the years hadn't changed her much.

"So do you."

"It hasn't even been a year for me."

"You cut your hair."

I'd cut it short, like Vee's, and I still wasn't used to how it felt. It was easier to manage and kept it out of my face during sparring and training. Maneera said I had promise. "How are you?"

"Things are worse." She stepped away from the door to let me come in. "Are you hungry?"

"Not really. Is this a bad time?"

"I work the night shift a couple of times a week now. I was getting ready to leave, but I can call in. I have seniority now."

We took seats in the small living room. I took the couch, and she sat across from me in her own chair. My father's armchair was empty. I patted it. "I'm surprised you kept it."

"It's not in the way." She studied my face. "You look good."

"I am. I really am."

"How is married life?"

"Interesting." I had left Adem and Vee tangled in the sheets of my oversized bed when I'd headed for the elevator two days before. I wasn't sure whether Vee or Dooley's cocktails bore more of the blame, but since there was no chance of it leading to anything… "Mostly good," I said.

"I'm glad." Her face changed. "You left something here." She crossed the floor and stepped into the bedroom she'd shared with my father for so long. It startled me to realize she'd been sleeping in it alone for even longer. She came back out with my father's book of poetry.

I opened it at random and read aloud.

Maybe, just maybe he'll come to love me,
Like the kind of love that takes you away.
The kind that sweeps you off your feet.
Or maybe he won't and I'll just be his doll.
Sitting pretty and collecting dust in a corner.
I don't believe in a
Jesus
Buddha

Kami
God.
But if you are up there,
Then I pray,
With all my heart,
For you to send
Some love my way.

"I still don't care for it," my mother said. "Did you ever find out where it came from?"

"A friend – a man I was dating – researched it. He said it belonged to a EuroD girl who was in an arranged marriage. Her teacher – Dad's friend Davet – tried to counsel her. She ended up killing herself, and he lost his job for getting involved."

My mother winced. "Maybe that's why your father kept reading it. He was trying to feel what you were feeling."

I flipped to the back of the book where the picture was stored. Eleta. She'd only been sixteen when she ended her life.

"I'm sorry we didn't give you a choice."

"And I'm sorry I didn't understand why you couldn't."

The muscles of her throat worked underneath her uniform's collar. "I love you," she finally said.

"I love you."

There were tears, and, after that, I let her cook me something that tasted like my childhood. I told her about life on the *Hajj* and the friends I had made there. She told me about life in Versailles City. The last decade had been really hard on anyone who didn't live in *La Mur*. Shortages, riots, bombings...

"Come back to the ship with me," I said. "I'll buy you a share and you can come on as crew."

"Ha, what would I do on a Trader ship?"

"I happen to know the captain needs an executive assistant. I could put in a good word." I took her hand. "It would be really nice to have my family with me."

Over the next few days, I helped her pack. She protested when I hired movers to take her things to the elevator, but I showed her my account balance. Then, she insisted on bringing my father's chair along and stopping for lunch on the way. While we waited for a car up, I told her about Rakin and the *Hadfield*. My team – minus Mateo who we'd dumped nearly naked on Nov Tero – had broken the squeezer down into spare parts. Then I got busy learning the ins and outs of the *Hajj* with Adem as my tutor. If I wasn't as competent as he was yet, I was on my way.

Adem was the fifteenth person to debark after the elevator car touched down.

"You remember my mother," I said. "She's joining the crew."

The bow he offered her swung the guitar case on his back dangerously close to her nose.

"Is that the Martin?"

He reached back to put his hand on it. "I left the terrible one with Lucy."

"How much of the *Hadfield* data did you take with you?"

He grinned. "Only the safe stuff."

"The captain's not going to be happy about that."

"She'll get over it. You know how families are. They forgive each other a lot."

ADEM

Versailles City, Apr 1, 3260

The guards kept the door and walkway clear, but outside the walls of the elevator depot was a wash of color and sound. Scrawny children chased each other in circles and ducked into dilapidated shacks that leaned here and there and upon each other for stability. Old men and women sat under crude canopies to drink tea and complain about the EuroD and the younger generations. The air was pungent with smoke and spices.

I found a spot along the depot wall to park my closet and used it as a seat. It didn't take long for the children to notice and present their bowls and outstretched hands to me. My pockets were full of coins of the smallest denomination, and I traded them for names and stories.

My reader buzzed with a message from Hisako, who was already above the clouds and headed back to the *Hajj* with her mother. She sent me the name of a EuroD man she used to know and said he had a history of good works in *La Merde*. She also put me in touch with the lead singer of the Sandcats in case I wanted to pay my respects or crash a show.

An hour passed. Out of coins, I offered songs. My young audience kept time with me, banging on their bowls, clapping their hands, and slapping their thighs. I taught them a few of the simpler tunes, and we sang together. My fingers and throat were getting sore by the time the battered cargo van pulled up.

I waved to it. "Is that the best you could find?"

Raul leaned out of the window. "You told me not to spend too much."

I lugged my closet to the van. The money Lucy gave me for my shares had to last until the *Hajj* returned and transferred my share of the profits from the run.

Raul was taller and was attempting a mustache but otherwise looked much like he did when I gave him my best reader and told him to learn something useful. He put the van in gear, weaving it skillfully among the pedestrians and carts.

"Did you get the warehouse space?" I said.

"Right near the junkyard. Independent power source and a good space for a workshop." He grinned. "Even a dry place to sleep if you're not picky."

I wanted to say that I wasn't, but I had nothing to base it on. I'd spent my life on a starship, flying above and out of reach of it all. The next few weeks were going to be interesting. "What about a crew?"

"Twelve people. Basic engineering skills. Starting full-time next week."

"Good work." I stretched my back against the patched seat. "I have a pod of parts and tools coming down the elevator tomorrow. We need to come back and pick it up."

"I'll be doing a job for my uncle. But look." He showed me that he had modified the truck so it could be operated by someone with one arm. "She can take you. Her name is Rosita now."

I wiped the dust off the inside of the windshield so I could see out and tried to find a comfortable position on the bench seat. I had an appointment at New Sorbonne University, but it was still hours away.

"They say war is coming soon," Raul said. "What will we do then?"

"Try to stay out of it. I didn't come here to fight." *In the name of Allah, the merciful, the compassionate...*

"What was that?" Raul said.

I hadn't realized I'd said the last part aloud. "Just something my great-grandmother used to say. Are you hungry? Let's find something to eat then we can take a look at this warehouse you found. We have a lot of work to do."

ACKNOWLEDGMENTS

I am grateful to the Rob Greene of 2015 for his work on this book. He set the alarm for 4:30am so he could write before going to work and spent day after beautiful day indoors on the project. I am also grateful for the forty year-old Olympia SM9 typewriter Past Rob used to bang out the first draft. Thanks to both of them for not breaking down.

Many of the characters in *The Light Years* were inspired, in spirit, by students I worked with at Nashua High School South in Nashua, NH, USA. I taught for more than a decade there, working with trans kids, short kids, gay kids, gender-fluid kids, brown kids, bi kids, white kids, smart kids, cis kids, funny kids, anime-loving kids, feckless kids, bookish kids, weird kids, sporty kids, community-minded kids... beautiful, brilliant kids. They had more than forty different languages among them and came from all walks of life and all over the world. These kids filled my head and leaked into the universe I was imagining. I cannot picture a future that does not have them in it. Two of them, Samantha Janosik and Emily Kim, wrote the poems for this book. Thanks, guys.

The Light Years grew out of a short story called "Love in the Time of Light Speed," and I offer thanks to Scott T. Barnes and Susan Shell Winston of *NewMyths* for buying it for their quarterly and later republishing it in *Passages: The Best of NewMyths Anthology*. The good folks at *NewMyths*, along with many other dedicated publishers, are keeping the short story form alive.

My thanks to the good people at Angry Robot, especially Etan Ilfeld, who sent me a near-Christmas message asking if *The Light Years* was still available; Gemma Creffield, who held my hand every step of the way; Kwaku Osei-Afrifa, who read the thing when it was ugly and helped me make it better; copyeditor Amanda Rutter; Head Robot Eleanor Teasdale, and Francesca Corsini who designed the cover.

This is where I acknowledge and thank *you*, the Reader. This book would exist without you, but it would be sad and unread.

It takes more people to make a writer than it does to make a book. My mother and father, Marion and John Greene, through referrals, endless repetitions of *The Poky Little Puppy,* and rides to the library made reading as fundamental to me as oxygen. I have been gifted with grand mentors – Merle Drown, Katherine Towler, Craig Childs, Elaine Isaak, and James Patrick Kelly, to name a few – and I've shared the road with the best possible fellow travelers: Robin Small, John Murphy, Iain Young and E.C. Ambrose, all of the Bigfoot Appreciation Society.

Fortunately, there are many synonyms for the word "thanks," and I can offer my appreciation to my beta readers Dan Brian and Ala Yamout, as well as to the New Hampshire Writers' Project, Omar Saif Ghobash for his book *Letters to a Young Muslim,* and to OmniCalculator.com.

Lastly, to Brenda Noiseux, who has built a life with me that has room for our creativity to flourish and tangle together like puppies: I love you, and I thank you. We should get married.

(If I have forgotten to thank you, I am sorry. My thanks to you, whoever you may be.)

CHAPTER 1

Loitering was an art form.

Especially when one was loitering with purpose. Simon Kovalic's gray eyes cast over the shelves with just the right mix of interest and vacancy. Not so bored that somebody would want to engage him in conversation, and not so interested that he missed what was going on around him.

He took in the antique shop in a glance, eyeing the few other customers on this frigid false night. Regulars, most of them, he guessed, with a sprinkling of tourists from elsewhere in the Illyrican Empire. Though why anybody would voluntarily choose to visit Sevastapol he had little idea; it wasn't as if *he* would be here if it weren't for the job. But he went where the Commonwealth told him to go, even if it meant going deep into enemy territory to a moon where even the nice parts didn't get far above freezing for much of the year.

Still, humanity – or the Illyrican portion of it, at least – had decided this rock was worth colonizing. Mineral deposits were one reason, but when it came right down to it Kovalic was pretty sure that they'd done it just because they *could*. Even in their pre-Imperial days, the Illyricans had felt they'd had something to prove, and what better way to do so than to tame a wild planetoid to their whims. It didn't really matter that it was a barren, snowy rock; it had a breathable atmosphere and temperatures that were within the habitable range – if only barely.

Through the thick, insulated windows Kovalic could see the snow hurling down outside. Blizzards were all too common on Sevastapol, and they were brutal and unforgiving; there were more deaths from exposure than almost anything else. Weather-related accidents were a close second.

Inside, however, it was perfectly comfortable; tapped geothermal pockets provided efficient heating for much of the populace. Kovalic had unwound his scarf and unzipped the parka he was wearing, stowing his balaclava and gloves in one of the coat's voluminous pockets. He raised his arm, the motion splashing a colorful display across the fabric which included the local time. Orbiting a gas giant gave Sevastapol an irregular day/night pattern; they were in false night, the sun itself down, but the light never quite extinguished as it reflected off the huge mottled planet that dominated the sky.

"'Scuse me," said a gruff voice, as a compact figure brushed past him.

"Not at all," said Kovalic.

The shorter man continued on, browsing a shelf of antiquated books, most with faded printed covers, others covered in moldering leather. He didn't seem to be reading them, though – mostly just staring glumly at the shelves.

"Anything?" murmured Kovalic.

"Not a thing, boss," said Tapper. "Quiet as my Aunt Mary's funeral."

"Wasn't that the aunt who wasn't actually dead?"

"Yeah, but she didn't want anybody knowing."

"Right. Well, stay sharp. It's almost showtime."

"I was born sharp."

Kovalic coughed to cover his smile. The general consensus was that Tapper was in his sixties, but nobody was sure exactly how old he was – even Kovalic, and they went back twenty years. But, despite the hair that had long gone steel gray and a face like a worn leather boot, Kovalic would have put him up against any operative half his age.

"Any of these good?" Tapper asked, nodding at the books.

"From a reading perspective or a collector's?"

Tapper shrugged. "Your pick."

Kovalic scanned the titles. "Definitely some classics among them, but I don't collect them. Ask Page."

"I don't get it," said Tapper, shaking his head. "These things just take up space. You can download any text you want. Why would you want to clutter up your home with these musty old things?"

Kovalic ran his fingers over the spine of one of the books. There was something tangible about it, he supposed: a connection you got with a physical book from turning its pages, that you didn't get from reading the same text on a screen. The idea that, for hundreds of years, the same volume had passed through the hands of countless others, linking all of them together in one continuous thread. Not that he had any intention of starting his own collection: they were a serious pain in the ass to move.

A sedate chime tinkled from the door at the front of the shop. He checked his sleeve again; it was just about time.

He nodded to Tapper. "Go mingle."

"Aye aye," said the shorter man, drifting off towards another corner of the shop.

Kovalic returned to perusing the shelves, taking his time before casually turning around to survey the display behind him. That gave him a chance to study the front of the shop and its occupants. Besides the shopkeeper – a tall, thin man, with tufts of gray hair that looked like they'd been glued on – there were a few other men and women scanning the shelves with the hungry looks of collectors searching for a find, and a couple who were poking about in the furniture section of the shop, wearing bright new parkas and exclaiming about each new item. Those would be the tourists.

Then there was the new arrival.

Bundled up as the figure was, about all Kovalic could tell was that it was a man – a short, stout man with a ruddy nose protruding over a subdued plaid scarf. Rather than a parka, he wore a sleek wool overcoat; more elegant than functional in the brisk Sevastapol weather. That made him a man concerned with appearances, especially when combined with the wide-brimmed felt hat pulled down tightly on his head. As disguises went, it was amateurish at best, unnecessarily conspicuous at worst.

The man walked past the shopkeeper, who was too busy reading from a thin volume held at arm's length to notice. He made his way stiffly towards the back of the shop in a manner so painfully casual that it practically shouted LOOK AT ME, I'M STROLLING, NOTHING TO SEE HERE.

Kovalic tried to avoid rubbing his forehead, and stared instead at the wall of books. He'd known going in that their contact wasn't trained for this sort of thing, but the general, Kovalic's boss, had deemed it an acceptable risk, given the man's stature and the value of the information on offer. Then again, the general didn't have to sit here and watch the worst tradecraft this side of an espionage vid.

As the man got closer, Kovalic's eyes narrowed. Something was off. The way the man was moving was *wrong*; his steps were wavering, unsure. Like he'd been injured. As if on cue, he clutched the side of the bookcase nearest Kovalic, his gloved hand gripping the wood as if his life depended on it.

Hefting the book in his hand, Kovalic opened his mouth to speak his part of the sign/countersign when he was interrupted by a mumble from the man in the hat.

"It was the... worst of times..." The voice was strained, hoarse, as if each word were being dragged out of it. The man was leaning heavily against the bookshelf. All the hair on Kovalic's neck stood to attention.

Kovalic reached over and tugged the scarf down, recognizing the face that he'd seen in the dossier: wrinkled, pale, and jowly. But the man's complexion was flushed, like he'd spent too long in the cold. Sweat beaded on his forehead, and his eyes had gone glassy. They met Kovalic's briefly, but there was no recognition there – they were empty and unfocused. The man swayed briefly, then started to crumple. Kovalic stepped over quickly, easing him gently to the floor.

"Shit." He pressed his fingers to the man's neck. There was a pulse, but it was thready and irregular.

Tapper, having seen something was off, made his way back over to his boss.

"What the hell happened?" he asked, his eyes flitting between Kovalic and the man on the floor.

Kovalic shook his head. "It's Bleiden, all right, but he's sick or something." His gut clenched. He supposed that it could have just been bad luck: maybe he'd gotten the flu that was going around. Maybe he'd eaten some bad shellfish. Weird coincidences happened all the time.

Then again, Kovalic had found himself rather attached to his life over the years, and part of what had kept him alive had been sweating the small stuff. He glanced up at Tapper. "See if this place has a first aid kit."

Tapper nodded and headed towards the front of the shop. A few of the other customers were now eyeing them curiously, though none had made a move to intervene.

His eyes alit upon a tall, dark-haired man who was watching the scene with studied disinterest. Snapping his fingers, Kovalic got his attention. "You. Gimme a hand."

The man looked almost surprised to be addressed, then reluctantly made his way over and crouched down by them.

"How's your field medicine training, lieutenant?" Kovalic murmured.

The man's expression morphed from confused to sharp so fast it was a wonder it didn't give Kovalic whiplash.

"Rusty at best, sir," said Aaron Page. "Is he wounded?"

Kovalic patted the man down, checking for any obvious sign of injury, but, as he'd suspected, there was nothing. "I'm thinking poison."

Page's eyebrows went up at the conjecture. "But that would mean..."

"...that he was compromised. And that they knew we were coming."

Tapper chose that moment to reappear with two things: a small dingy looking medkit that might have been new when the sergeant was young, and a troubled expression. "Uh, boss? We got company." He jerked his thumb back at the windows.

Of course – he should have known there'd be another shoe.

"Uniforms?"

"Armed response troops, with a few plainclothes running the show."

Kovalic sucked in a breath through his teeth. "That'll be Eyes. Well, shit." He'd hoped they'd managed to fly under the radar of the Imperial Intelligence Services, but with his luck he clearly shouldn't be buying lottery tickets anytime soon.

Tapper gestured at the shop. "Boss, this place is a kill zone. We gotta move."

Page had taken the medkit from Tapper and unzipped it, and was now rifling through the contents. "Without knowing what they dosed him with, I'm not sure which antidote to administer."

Kovalic rubbed his forehead. Saving Bleiden would be ideal, but at the moment even getting themselves out of here was starting to look like a tall order. "Lieutenant, talk to me about options, and make it quick. Sergeant, see if there's a back door." He nodded towards the rear of the shop, where a path snaked between two bookshelves. IIS wouldn't be dumb enough to leave an exit uncovered, but if there was any chance of getting his team out of here, Kovalic needed to know the lay of the land.

Tapper disappeared towards the rear of the shop while Page pulled out a vial and an injector. "It's mostly bandages and ointments, but there is a dose of epinephrine that's only a few months past its expiration date. If whatever they gave him triggered anaphylactic shock, that might help."

Well, if it didn't, he'd probably be dead anyway. Kovalic nodded to Page, who locked the vial in place and, without much in the way of ceremony, stabbed it into the man's thigh. There was a *click* and the man jerked.

Kovalic looked over at Page. "How do we know if it wor–"

The man gasped and convulsed, his eyes springing open as he tried to sit up.

Grabbing him by the shoulders, Kovalic held him steady. "Easy there."

The man's gaze swung wildly, seizing upon Kovalic. "Are you… Conductor?" he wheezed.

Protocol had gone out of the window by this point, so Kovalic just nodded. The man's hand came up and gripped Kovalic's arm tightly. His voice was strained again, and he fought to get each word past clenched teeth. "Eyes... watching me." His grip curled Kovalic's parka sleeve, insistent, and the colors of the display flickered and warped. "Important... meeting. Bayern. Three... days. Per–" Suddenly, his eyes rolled back into his head and he started convulsing again. White foam leaked from the edges of his mouth as his face twisted into a pained rictus. After a moment, he went limp.

Kovalic put a finger against his neck, but this time there wasn't so much as a faint pulse. Gesturing to Page, they gently laid the man down on the floor. Kovalic closed the blank eyes and let out a long breath, hand over his mouth.

Tapper caught Kovalic's eye from the back of the shop and jerked his head. There was an exit, then. He also raised five fingers and pointed them towards the rear. Five men watching it, probably waiting for the order to breach. Kovalic waved him over.

"Shit," said Tapper, glancing down at the body. "He didn't make it?"

Kovalic shook his head. "But he gave us something – we just need to make sure it doesn't go to waste."

"What's the plan?"

"I'm thinking we need to give the abort signal," said Kovalic, raising his sleeve and tapping an icon on the display. A burst of static exploded directly into his earbud, eliciting a curse.

"Too late," he said, tapping it off. "They've already set up a jamming field."

Tapper shook his head. "Not good. Standard portable jammer has an effective radius of about twenty-five meters."

Kovalic peered at the wall behind them, measuring in his head. "That easily covers the whole shop. And getting out of its range is going to mean fighting our way through whoever's out there."

"So, maybe we don't go through," said Tapper, pointing a finger at the ceiling. "Maybe we go up?"

Kovalic looked up. The shop occupied the ground floor, but the building was at least four or five stories tall. Not quite high enough to get them all the way out of the jamming field, but it didn't need to be – there ought to be a comm array on the roof that they could hijack to boost the signal. He didn't like the idea of being trapped on the roof, but it was better than walking out of here and into the Illyricans' hands. He glanced at his sleeve; it had been five minutes since Bleiden had come in, and Eyes surely had the place surrounded by this point. They had to move now.

"Did you find a set of stairs back there?"

"Not quite. But I think I've got something."

Kovalic turned to Page. "Keep an eye on the situation here. Let me know if it looks like they're about to breach." The lieutenant acknowledged with a tip of his head. Kovalic followed Tapper to the rear of the shop, which turned out to be a small storeroom with a side door that looked like it hadn't been used since the founding of the Illyrican Empire.

"Jesus, would it kill them to send in a building inspection team every once in a while?" said Tapper, kicking at a soggy cardboard box filled with decaying books. Slivers of paper launched into the air, fluttering to the ground like dying moths.

"We'll have to come back and enforce the fire code some other time. Talk to me about this exit."

"Right," said Tapper. "That door lets into a side alley, which feeds into the street out front, but there's also roof access via a fire escape – I caught it on my recce earlier. They're using standard breach tactics, stacking up right here." He nodded to the wall to the left of the door. A workbench sat against the brickwork there; they each took an end and managed to shift it away from the wall, disturbing a cloud of what was undoubtedly valuable antique dust.

Wiping his hands, Kovalic rifled through his pockets, but they were empty aside from his backup comm unit. Weapons were a liability more often than a benefit in these types of missions, though he was wishing he'd reconsidered that stance right about now.

Tapper, meanwhile, had produced a fist-sized tube from his satchel and had set about drawing a rectangular outline in some sort of white substance onto the brick wall.

Kovalic blinked. "Do I even want to know where you got that?"

The older man chuckled. "You know me, boss. Always prepared. I know a guy around these parts who owed me a favor, and he just *happened* to have a spare tube of detpaste going to waste. Imagine that."

Kovalic opened his mouth, then snapped it shut. Some people collected books. Others collected high explosives. Who was he to judge?

"Carry on."

Finished with the outline, Tapper peeled an adhesive tab from the rear end of the tube, slapped it on his sleeve, and gave Kovalic a thumbs up.

Kovalic nodded and ducked back into the front room. At some point, the shop's other patrons had begun to catch on to the fact that something was amiss – except for the shopkeeper, who had remained engrossed in the text he was studying and who, Kovalic was becoming increasingly convinced, was hard of hearing.

Instead of browsing the wares, the rest of the customers were eyeing Page, who had taken up a spot near the door, but clear of the windows just in case IIS had deployed sharpshooters. Though he was leaning casually against the wall and staring off into the middle distance, that seemed to have just made the rest of the shop's patrons even more nervous. They'd huddled together, watching him, and every time one of them so much as shifted their weight, Page's eyes would snap to them and he'd give a curt shake of the head.

Kovalic cleared his throat and addressed the room. "Ladies and gentlemen, may I have your attention?"

Half a dozen gazes shifted to him, so he put on his best calming smile.

"This is an IIS security action. I apologize for the inconvenience, and we'll have you on your way in just a moment. In the meantime, if you could just seat yourselves against the far wall?"

Quite a few of them blanched at that announcement – nobody really *liked* the Imperial Intelligence Services, but that didn't extend to questioning or disobeying them. That was way too much heat for the average law-abiding citizen. Although none raised an argument as they shuffled over to the indicated wall.

Tapper materialized at his shoulder. "We're ready to go."

"Good," said Page, joining them. "Because they're coming in."

"In that case, exit, stage right." Kovalic gave a last look over his shoulder at Bleiden's body, lying limp against one of the bookshelves, and his lips thinned. But there was no time to linger on regrets – they had bigger problems. He looked up and pointed a finger at Tapper. The sergeant touched a blinking icon on his sleeve and there was a deep bass *thump* that rattled the antiques on their shelves.

Yanking open the door to the back room, they darted in. Particles of dust were floating everywhere, but, with the exception of the giant gaping hole in the wall, it was hard to say whether the back room was actually in worse shape than before. Wind and snow whistled in from the makeshift door.

The three men clambered over the rubble that lay in the threshold of the new door, finding themselves in a narrow alley between two tall buildings. In addition to the debris from the explosion, there were five armed response troops scattered about: two of them were down and not moving, apparently flattened by the explosion, while one was staggering to his feet. The last two had their hands clapped over their ears and were shaking their heads slowly. Carbines hung from slings over their shoulders, and pistols were holstered at their waist alongside a standard issue pair of grenades. Their heads were swathed in helmets, balaclavas, and goggles.

Kovalic pointed Tapper towards the one who was trying to get up. The sergeant jogged towards him, then dealt him a swift kick to the head that knocked him back to the ground. Page had already closed the distance to one of the two standing members of the team, delivering a knee to the gut that doubled the trooper over, followed by a sharp elbow to the back of the neck.

The last was standing against the opposite alley wall; he'd started to regain his balance, and when he saw Kovalic coming towards him he fumbled for his carbine. But he was clearly still reeling from the explosion's concussion, and as Kovalic's hand came around – still clutching the hardcover book he'd been perusing earlier – it clipped him just under the chin, slamming his helmeted head back into the brick wall with a satisfying *thunk*. Not enough to knock him out, but it would at least ring his bell. Kovalic gave him a kick to the ribs, just to make sure he'd stay down.

Tapper had already liberated the weapons of the trooper he'd downed, slinging the carbine over one shoulder. He'd also grabbed a comm unit, and was starting to collect the grenades from the other troops as well. Page had likewise stripped another fallen trooper's equipment, checking the magazine on the weapon before locking it back into place.

"They'll localize the explosion any second," said Tapper. "We'd better make ourselves scarce."

Kovalic looked around: the alley dead-ended here, but, as Tapper had said, there was a metal fire escape on the side of the building – so at least the fire code hadn't been wholly ignored. The last flight was retracted, but with a short jump Kovalic pulled it down, clanging loudly to the ground.

"Go," he said, gesturing at Page and Tapper. The two didn't need any further encouragement as they scrambled up the ladder, Kovalic following close behind.

It was five stories to the top, navigating stairways that switched back and forth upon themselves as though they were sailing ships taking advantage of prevailing winds. Snowflakes bit at Kovalic's face, which had already started to numb from the cold. Reaching the top, he swung himself over the small lip that ran around the edge of the roof.

The roof itself contained an extensive collection of venting pipes, an emergency exit, and – Kovalic let out a sigh of relief – a comm array. Page was already ripping the cover off its junction box. As Kovalic joined them, Tapper took up position at the top of the fire escape, waiting for their pursuers.

Kovalic hoped to be long gone by the time they showed up.

"Stay low," he muttered to Tapper. "Eyes probably has snipers on the surrounding rooftops. No reason to make it easy on them." The curtain of snow around them made it hard to even see the adjacent buildings, but in a sniper's thermal scope they'd stand out like a parade float.

Tapper gave him a dry look. "Not my first dance, boss."

"Fair point."

"Just go get us our ride home."

With a nod, Kovalic went to join Page at the comm array. The younger man had a multitool clenched between his teeth as he twisted a pair of wires together; he looked up when Kovalic arrived, and took the tool out of his mouth long enough to say, "Two minutes."

Running a hand through his snow-covered hair, Kovalic glanced over his shoulder at the fire escape. Two minutes might be pushing it, depending on how fast the rest of the shock troops figured out where they'd gone. That meant the three of them would have to hold the roof while waiting for pickup, which was made easier by the fact that they had the high ground, and much, much harder by the fact that they were severely outnumbered.

"Do what you can."

Page didn't bother to respond, just delved back into the mess of wiring. Kovalic returned to Tapper, who was at the top of the fire escape, sitting with his back against the low wall.

The older man gave him a searching look as he sat down. "What do you think, cap? We're in it this time, for sure."

"Come on," said Kovalic, nudging the sergeant. "We've been in tougher spots before."

Tapper pursed his lips. "I can think of maybe one," he admitted. "But I wouldn't exactly put it in the win column."

"Hey, any fight you can walk away from."

The sergeant gave a noncommittal grunt and checked his purloined weapon again.

Sighing, Kovalic looked up at the sky; between the city lights, the blizzard, and the false night, the sky had turned gray with tinges of pink. On a clearer evening you'd have a nice view of Yalta, the gas giant that Sevastapol orbited – its rings were spectacular. Certainly a hell of a lot pleasanter than a snowstorm.

"Boss." Tapper's hiss broke his train of thought. The sergeant caught his eye, then nodded towards the fire escape. "They're in the alley."

Kovalic looked across the roof at Page. "How's it going?" he called softly.

Without turning around, Page held up one hand with a single finger extended, then returned to his work.

"We're going to have to buy him some more time," said Kovalic, grimacing.

"I was hoping you'd say that," said Tapper. He hefted two of the grenades that he'd taken from the downed response officer below, then pulled the pins on both and lobbed them casually over the wall. Distantly, Kovalic heard them clink to the ground, followed by an exclamation of surprise that was cut short by a pair of explosions that echoed back up to them.

Leaving Tapper to watch the fire escape, Kovalic crossed over to Page, keeping his head low. "Page?"

The younger man pulled a circuit board from one slot, slid it into another, then slammed the junction box closed and handed Kovalic his own sleeve, which he'd peeled off and attached to the box by a pair of jury-rigged wires. The display rippled and blinked but showed a solid signal.

"Good work, lieutenant," said Kovalic. He punched in a code and opened the channel, patching it to his earbud. "Skyhook, this is Conductor. Copy?"

A buzz of static flooded the channel, but a moment later a somewhat broken-up voice cut through. "Copy, Conductor. Three by three."

"Roger. This is an abort. Repeat: abort. Immediate extraction required at source coordinates."

"Confirm abort."

"Sigma nine seven five."

"Confirmed. Skyhook en route, ETA three minutes."

"Best news I've heard all day. Heads up, the EZ is hot."

"Acknowledged, captain. See you in a jiffy." The comm beeped as the link was disconnected.

Kovalic looked up at his two teammates, but both of them had heard the conversation. "Three minutes to hold?"

Page raised his eyebrows. "Not going to be easy."

"When is it ever?" Tapper said.

"Hey," said Kovalic, with a shrug. "It could be wor–"

A shot pinged off the brickwork just behind him, sending shards flying in every direction.

"Down!" All three men hit the deck.

Kovalic rolled over to look at Page.

"High-caliber sniper rifle," the lieutenant said, cool as a frosty beverage on a summer day. "Impact point suggests it came from over there." He nodded in the direction of the next building over. There was a hiss and a sizzle, and Kovalic saw a shower of sparks cascade from the junction box, which had apparently caught part of the sniper round. Well, they wouldn't be making any more calls.

"We're going to need suppressing fire when Skyhook gets here," said Tapper.

"Congratulations. You've just volunteered."

"And I wondered how I always end up with the best jobs."

Kovalic looked over at the fire escape. Tapper's grenades had evidently thrown them into a bit of a disarray below, given that nobody had tried to come up and over yet. Still, they couldn't count the rest of the armed response troops out of the fight. The net was being drawn fast.

Which was fine, as long as they weren't in it when it closed. Bleiden's intelligence might have been scant, but it was going to live or die with them.

"Two minutes. Page, hold off the sniper. Tapper, on three, suppressing fire into the alley."

"Copy that," said Tapper.

Sucking in a lungful of air, Kovalic steadied himself. "One… two… *three*."

Page lifted his weapon, and sent a series of bursts in the direction the shot had come from. Simultaneously, Tapper and Kovalic popped over the low wall and fired down into the alley, the shots singing against the bricks and metalwork. A few muzzle flashes signaled return shots, but at this range and angle they were little more than blind fire.

After a few seconds, all three men slid down with their backs against the wall again.

"How long on the clock?" Tapper asked.

"Minute and a half," said Kovalic. "We should be able to see him." He scanned the sky in the direction that he was pretty sure was south, but the storm made it hard to see more than a few meters off the roof. The snowflakes kept flying into his eyes, refracting what little illumination there was from the streetlights below and the one flickering star above.

Star?

"Heads up! One o'clock high!"

Tapper and Page's heads both swiveled to follow Kovalic's glance.

"You sure that's him?" the sergeant asked.

"If it isn't, then we are in a hell of a lot more trouble."

As the light came closer it resolved into a pair of points –
two headlights – blinking rapidly on and off, in a very specific
pattern. The whooshing noise of the engines was audible now,
reaching them at a delay, given the craft's speed.

"That's him," said Kovalic. "Sergeant, the signaling laser if
you please."

Tapper fumbled in his bag, then pulled out a small device
about the size of a pen, and flicked it on and off rapidly, in the
same pattern that the ship had blinked its lights. The headlights
blinked again in confirmation.

"Suppressing fire again," said Kovalic, circling a finger in the
air. "Let's keep the area clear for him. One… two–"

He never reached three, as a brilliant column of light
descended from the heavens, piercing through the gray veil
of snow and striking the incoming ship dead center. A fireball
ignited in the sky, sizzling through the snowstorm. A moment
later the sound of the explosion and the accompanying
shockwave hit, blowing back Kovalic's hair even at this
distance.

And then, in its wake, a sound of emptiness so loud it almost
threatened to deafen him.

"Holy shit," breathed Tapper. "I thought the fake
transponder–"

Kovalic swallowed, his mouth suddenly parched. "They must
have found out from Bleiden." Though how *he* knew, Kovalic
couldn't imagine.

From below came indistinct shouts and the rattle of feet on
metal.

"Boss," whispered Tapper, "they're coming. We need to go."

Go? Go where? Their escape route had just been blown out of
the sky. If IIS had identified the ship before destroying it, they'd

have all the IDs his team had used to get on planet. Which meant they needed new ones – and that meant time. And a place to hole up.

He took a deep breath. Roll with it, he reminded himself. First things first: getting off the roof.

"Page," he said, catching the lieutenant's eye. "How far to the next roof?" He nodded in the direction opposite from where the sniper had taken his shot.

The younger man shrugged. "Three meters, but it's down. Doable." More challenging, it meant jumping the alley where the troopers – and their many weapons – were currently hanging out.

Kovalic nodded at him. "You first. Tapper and I will cover for you."

Page didn't question the order, just nodded and got to his feet. Crouching, he got some distance from the edge of the roof and then looked at Kovalic expectantly.

With a nod, Kovalic raised one finger. Then a second. Then a third. At the third finger, Page took off, sprinting for the edge of the roof. As his foot planted on the low wall, Tapper and Kovalic swung their guns over the side, and fired off a few bursts towards the alley.

There was at least one *thwack* as a round struck home on body armor, followed by a grunt and a clatter as the trooper hit the deck. Out of the corner of his eye, Kovalic saw Page land and roll on the opposite roof and then spring up again, flashing them a thumbs up.

"You next, old man," said Kovalic.

Tapper looked like he wanted to argue, but years of taking orders won out and he just gave a silent nod, then followed Page's example. This time there were plenty of rounds flying upwards, but with both Kovalic and Page providing cover fire from opposite sides of the gap nobody had time to draw a bead on Tapper. The sergeant didn't stick the landing quite as gracefully as his compatriot, but Page helped him to his feet and the two waited for their commanding officer.

Kovalic rolled his neck, and then tightened the cinch on the gun's strap. He crept towards the same place Page and Tapper had started their run, and took a deep breath. Then, counting silently to himself, he pushed off and sprinted all out to the edge.

The scariest part of making a jump was that moment of commitment: planting a foot and pushing off, floating over the void. As long as you didn't hesitate, you'd be fine. You just had to trust that you'd make it. It had to be automatic, instinctive.

Kovalic didn't think twice as his foot went down and his leg muscle tensed, sending him up and off the edge of the roof, arcing over the alley. He saw the roof of the neighboring building in front of him, and relief washed over him as he realized he'd make it with room to spare.

And then the biggest bee in the history of the universe bit him right in the shoulder, sending surprise and, shortly thereafter, stabbing pain through his whole torso. A split-second later he dimly registered the crack of a rifle report. Then he was just falling.

Introducing The Aleph Extraction
Available May 2020